DARK ROOM

STRIPES PUBLISHING LIMITED
An imprint of the Little Tiger Group
1 Coda Studios, 189 Munster Road,
London SW6 6AW

www.littletiger.co.uk

A paperback original
First published in Great Britain in 2015
Text copyright © Tom Becker, 2015
Cover copyright © Stripes Publishing Limited, 2015
Photographic images courtesy of www.shutterstock.com

ISBN: 978-1-84715-457-6

The right of Tom Becker to be identified as the author
of this work has been asserted by him in accordance with
the Copyright, Designs and Patents Act, 1988.

Printed and bound in the UK.

10 9 8 7 6 5 4 3

DARK ROOM

TOM BECKER

RED EYE

Prologue

Saffron Hills, South Carolina – 1995

Walter West was placing the final picture into his new photograph album when he heard the delicate chime of the doorbell. Frowning at the interruption, he checked that the photograph was aligned perfectly before closing the album. He walked up the steps out of his basement studio, blinking in the light as he emerged into a grand hallway lined with large windows. Opening the front door, Walter saw a girl standing on the step outside.

"Hi," she said. "We're in biology class together, I'm—"

"I know who you are," he said with a grin. "Please, come in."

The girl flashed a quick, uncertain smile before creeping through the doorway. She was pretty: dark eyes and high cheekbones, her face framed with shoulder-length brown hair. Reaching into her schoolbag, she pulled out a sheaf of papers and handed them over to him.

"Um, I think our assignments got mixed up," she said, pointing to the handwritten name at the top of the page. "Unless my parents changed my name to Walter and didn't tell me about it."

"Hey, thanks for dropping this over. I'm going to need all the time I can get." Walter looked up from the assignment, checking the drive through the doorway. No sign of a car. "Did you *walk* all the way up here?"

"On my own two feet," the girl replied brightly.

"Wow."

It was a long walk from school to Walter's house, and an even longer walk down from the hills to the creek, where he knew the girl lived. None of his friends would dream of trying it, but then all of his friends had a car. There was an invisible line running through the heart of Saffron Hills separating the rich from the poor, and folks on either side didn't tend to cross it unless they had to.

He closed the door behind the girl. "I'll see if I've got your assignment," he told her. "I can give you a ride home after, if you want."

She followed him along the hallway, openly

admiring the oil paintings on the walls and the crystal chandelier hanging down from the ceiling.

"You have a beautiful home," she told him.

"Yeah, it's not so bad," Walter said easily. "Just be grateful my dad isn't here, otherwise you'd get the full Tall Pines tour. I swear he knows the exact date when every single piece of furniture in this house was made, and he's not afraid of telling people."

"It's so *quiet*... Are you on your own?"

Walter nodded.

"Where is everyone?"

"Let me see..." He ticked off his fingers. "Mom's visiting our aunt Gracie in Tennessee, Dad's in Malaysia working on some big skyscraper project, and my sister is out riding and won't be back for hours."

"What about the maids and the butler?" she teased.

He laughed. "Believe it or not, we clean our own rooms here."

"Doesn't it get a bit creepy, being in this big old place all on your own?"

"You get used to it," Walter replied. "There used to be stories about a ghost that floated around here in the middle of the night – apparently some lady suffocated her kids in their beds a hundred years ago. But then my dad got a priest to come over and perform an exorcism, and after that everything was OK."

The girl stared at him. "You're kidding, right?"

"Yes."

"Please don't do that. I was *this* close to peeing myself."

Walter laughed again. Something about her openness was refreshing. Girls usually liked Walter. He was smart and good-looking and polite, and his family was the most influential in Saffron Hills. But sometimes he suspected that the girls liked the idea of going out with 'Walter West' more than they actually liked *him*. They didn't really know him – what he liked and disliked, what he wanted to do with his life. His male friends didn't care either, they were too busy making lame jokes and insulting one another. His family were hardly ever in the same room at the same time. When Walter thought about it, no one really knew him at all.

They shared a polite, awkward silence as they walked through Tall Pines, the girl's sandals slapping against the hardwood floor.

"Don't think me rude, but I can't stay long," she said. "My mom doesn't want me out on my own after dark. Everyone's kinda jumpy at the moment. Ever since Crystal went missing, you know?"

He did. It had been a week now since the local beauty queen, the newly crowned Miss Saffron, had vanished on her way home from school. Walter had joined the volunteers combing the local woods, a solemn line picking its way carefully through the undergrowth. He hadn't seen Crystal, though. Nobody had.

The girl tugged at a loose thread on her schoolbag. "Do you think she's dead?"

Walter shrugged. "I don't know. I mean, I hope not, but it's been a week and no one's seen her. And that family of hers…"

He didn't say any more. He didn't have to. Everyone in Saffron Hills knew that Crystal's family were bad news. Trailer trash, they were called at the country club and at dinner parties in the hills – and other, even less pleasant, names.

The girl shook her head. "It's so sad," she murmured. "Crystal was a sweet girl."

"You were friends?"

"Kinda – when her creepy brother wasn't hanging around. We'd stop and say 'hi', you know."

Walter led her into the dining room – more of a hall than a room, really – dominated by a vast mirror that stretched the length of the wall and a mahogany dining table.

"Look at this thing!" the girl giggled, running her hand across the polished wood. "You could get twenty people around here."

"Closer to thirty, actually," corrected Walter. "It doesn't make Mom's dinner parties any more fun, though."

The girl smiled. "You should come round to our place some time," she said. "Have mac and cheese in front of the TV."

"I'd like that."

She shot him a defensive look, unsure whether he was making fun of her or not. Something about the way the girl was looking around the house made Walter feel unexpectedly embarrassed. All of a sudden, his home felt over-the-top and ostentatious. He felt like he should apologize – though for what, he wasn't sure. The girl stopped by a large framed photograph. It was a family portrait, taken a couple of years earlier: Mom and Dad sitting together on a couch, their hands clasped, whilst Walter and his sister stood dutiful guard either side of them.

"The West family, in all their glory," he said dryly. "Terrible, isn't it?"

"It's sweet!" she replied. "Don't you like photographs?"

"Actually, I do – when I'm not in them." Walter paused. "In fact I have my own studio here in the house. Would you like to see it?"

"Sure," she said politely.

He led her out of the dining room and along a corridor, moving quickly now. Stopping at a door beneath the main staircase, he pushed it open to reveal a set of narrow steps leading down into the basement. When he gestured eagerly at the girl to go down them, she hesitated.

"No light?"

"The bulb on the stairs needs changing," he said apologetically. "Keep hold of the handrail and you'll be fine."

A little reluctantly, she started down the stairs. Walter closed the door behind him, plunging them into darkness. Sensing the girl's nervousness as she edged towards the basement, he began to chatter in what he hoped was a reassuring way.

"It kinda sucks that I have to come down here," he said. "I told Mom and Dad that I needed a better room but they told me this was the only space they had. I said, OK, let's move my sister down here and I can use her bedroom, but I got outvoted."

The girl didn't laugh, too busy concentrating on navigating the steps through the gloom. When they reached the basement floor Walter slipped past her, feeling his way over to the wall.

"Wait, let me get the light."

His fingers closed upon the switch, and he flicked it on. Bright, safe light poured into the basement. The girl found herself staring into a dusty, full-length mirror leaning against the wall – she jumped, startled by her own reflection.

"You OK?" asked Walter.

She laughed nervously. "Sorry. I scared myself there."

The girl looked around. The basement had been converted into a makeshift studio, centered around a modelling space surrounded by flashlights on stands and a white screen backdrop. Expensive cameras perched on tripods, lenses glinting in the light. Framed photographs covered the walls.

"Phew!" she said, placing a hand over her heart. "For a minute there I was expecting some kind of dungeon."

"I clean up the bloodied corpses before the guests come round," Walter replied, deadpan. "Mom insists."

The girl smiled, starting to relax a little. She went over to the far wall to examine the photographs. They were a series of landscape shots of the woods around Saffron Hills. Dawn sunlight shimmered through the pine trees.

"These are *beautiful*," she said.

"Thank you," said Walter. "The hard part is getting up early enough to catch the light."

"You should become a professional. People would pay good money for these."

"Maybe. I don't know how many more tasteful landscapes the world needs."

As the girl peered closer at the photographs, an idea occurred to Walter. Quietly he picked up a camera and focused it on her. He waited until he had framed her face — unguarded, absorbed, biting on her lip in a slightly pensive way — and then he took her picture.

"Hey, quit it!" she laughed.

"Come on, just a couple of photos for my portfolio!" He fired off another before the girl could protest. "You look great!"

She laughed — flattered, but trying not to show it. Walter meant what he said. She really was very pretty, in a naive and utterly natural way. Like a startled deer in the woods.

"I've just finished my latest album," he told her, his heart beginning to beat a little faster as he trained the camera on her face. "Take a look, I think you'll like them."

"This one, you mean?" she replied, going over to the desk and pointing at the embossed album.

Walter waited until he had the shot. "Perfect," he said quietly.

The girl opened the album.

Crystal's ruined face stared back at her. The beauty queen's blue eyes had been dulled, her long blond hair matted with blood and the top of her skull crushed almost beyond recognition.

The girl screamed.

As she reeled away from the photo album, her hands over her face, Walter's finger clicked rapidly on the shutter button, firing away like it was the trigger of a gun. His pulse was racing, his heart thundering in his chest. He was so excited he could barely breathe. Sternly he forced himself to concentrate, to focus on capturing the screaming girl.

"What have you done?" she gasped.

"I told you I was bored of landscapes," Walter said.

She stared at him in disbelief. "Y-you killed her?"

He hadn't planned to – Walter hadn't killed anyone before, hadn't even realized what he was capable of. He had invited Crystal round on a whim, figuring that some shots of Miss Saffron might look good in his portfolio. She had been so *eager* – so pathetically pleased just to be in his house. She couldn't stop talking and giggling and flirting, messing up the shots he was trying to take of her. As he had trained his camera upon Crystal's beautiful face, Walter had felt overwhelmed by sudden anger.

The first blow, with the lighting stand, had taken him almost by surprise. But later on, in the dazed aftermath, it seemed to make perfect sense.

No one knew what Walter West was like, not really. They didn't know what he liked, what he disliked. What he wanted to do with his life.

Sobbing hysterically, the girl realized too late that she had to run: Walter had already moved across the basement to cut off the stairs. Placing his camera down on an old bureau he opened the drawer, pulling out a hunting knife he had dug out from a box of his grandfather's possessions in the attic. It wouldn't be missed. That was the thing about being rich: if you were smart, you could get your hands on anything you wanted.

At the sight of the gleaming blade, the girl moaned with fear. Walter was starting to enjoy this.

"Why me?" she sobbed. "What did I do?"

"You came to visit me," he said simply. "Turned up on my doorstep like a little glimpse of heaven. I like pretty things, and you're just as pretty as Crystal was. But by the time I had finished with her she was something else — her skin had turned this delicate shade of blue, she looked like a watery angel.

Wouldn't you like to be an angel too?"

"P-please let me go," the girl whispered.

"I'm afraid that's not an option."

"I won't tell anyone, I swear. Not a soul."

Walter sucked in through his teeth. "Right now, I think you'd say just about anything to try to escape this house alive," he told her. "I understand why, it's perfectly natural. But once you get home you might change your mind and start running your mouth off to people, and then there's no telling what you might say. No, I think you need to stay here."

She screamed, but even if they hadn't been underground there was no one within a square mile who could hear her. Walter had been telling the truth: the rest of his family were all out, and the maids and the kitchen staff – whom he *had* lied about – had the day off. It was almost as if someone was making him kill again. He would do just as he had done with Crystal, using the roll of plastic sheeting in the corner of the room to wrap up the girl's body before photographing her. Then Walter would wait until the middle of the night and take her to the creek, where he would weigh her corpse down with chains and tyres and let the murky water claim it.

"Don't look so sad," he told the girl. "You're going to have an album all of your own, just like Crystal. My pair of beautiful angels – one light, one dark."

"You sick freak!"

Her eyes flashed with anger, and she snatched up a lighting stand. There was some fight in her, after all.

Perfect.

She jabbed the stand at him as he advanced towards her, trying to keep him at arm's length. He didn't hurry. They had all day. No one was going to come and rescue her. With his free hand Walter picked up his camera from the bureau and zoomed in on her trembling face.

"C'mon," he said cajolingly. "Smile for the camera."

Chapter One

When Darla O'Neill was a little girl her dreams had been like fairy tales – bright cartoon fantasies of brave princes and beautiful princesses. But life had soon taught Darla that most stories didn't have happy endings – especially not her own. By the age of seven she had stopped dreaming about golden carriages and lavish palace balls. Now, aged sixteen, she didn't dream of anything at all.

She was lying awake, the springs of the trailer's foldout bed digging into her back, listening to the summer rain thud down on the roof and her daddy's buzz-saw snores. From her bed Darla could see Hopper's silhouette slumped across the couch, an arm trailing down on the floor by a half-empty beer bottle. He had come back from the bar late, dropping his keys as he staggered in through the door. Darla had closed her eyes and pretended to be asleep, waiting for Hopper to pass out. It hadn't taken long. It never did.

Even with the rain and the windows open, the trailer was hot and airless. Darla lay on top of the sheets in an oversize T-shirt, sweat glistening on her bare arms and legs. Nights were easier in the winter, even when the snows came and turned the trailers into frozen shells. Darla could burrow under the blankets and create a warm little nest for herself. But there was no escaping the late August heat in South Carolina. Somewhere above her head, she heard a mosquito whine. Water dripped sullenly through a leak in the roof, landing on the jumble of plates and dishes piled up in the sink.

There was a loud bang on the trailer door. Darla jumped.

"Hopper!" a man's voice yelled. "Where are you?"

Hopper mumbled something in his sleep and turned over. A fist banged on the door again, louder this time. Darla slid under the blankets.

"I know you're in there, Hopper! Get your ass outta that trailer now!"

Hopper sat up with a groan, rubbing his face. It always took him time to come to, especially when he had been drinking. He swore as he stumbled to his feet, knocking over the beer bottle. Outside the man continued to hammer on the door. Through the net drape Darla saw lights flickering on in the neighbouring trailers.

"OK, OK!" Hopper shouted through the door. "Gimme a minute, will you?"

He was fully awake now, moving quickly and quietly through the shadows. Opening a cupboard, he pulled down a cookie jar and prised it open, transferring a wad of dollar bills into his jeans' back pocket. There was always a hiding place for the money, wherever they stayed, always different each time. Hopper never told Darla where — as though she was the one who couldn't be trusted, not him. He slipped a pair of shoes over his bare feet and put on his favourite leather jacket. Then he crept over to Darla's bedside.

"You awake, darlin'?"

Darlin' Darla. Hopper's little girl. Darla didn't move.

"It's time to go, darlin'," Hopper whispered, his breath stale with sleep and liquor. "You need to grab your things."

21

Wordlessly Darla rolled out of bed, slid on a pair of jeans and slipped her feet into a pair of old trainers. Reaching under the bed, she pulled out a sports bag crammed with her things. Everything she owned in the world, her whole life, could be squeezed into a single bag. It was always packed – years of living with her father had taught Darla to be ready to leave at a moment's notice.

A chink of light appeared in the darkness: Hopper opened the fridge and grabbed a fresh beer bottle. He twisted off the cap and took a swig, glancing at Darla to check she was ready before unlocking the trailer door.

The rain was coming down in hard, straight lines, splattering the muddy ground between the rows of trailers. A fat man in khaki fatigues and a cap was hunched in the rain, his gut lurching over his belt.

"'Bout time," he growled. "I'm gettin' soaked out here."

Hopper sighed. "I was sleeping, Marvin. What do you want?"

"My grampa told me about the money you talked outta him. I'm here to take it back."

"Take it back?" Hopper's tone was one of smooth

surprise. When it came to talking his way out of things, he'd had a lot of practice. "Why would he want to do that? I told your grampa he'd see a handsome return on his investment. But these things take time, Marvin!"

"Don't care about fancy talk," Marvin said obstinately. "I just want the money."

"I don't have it!" laughed Hopper. "It's tied up in stocks and shares. How else do you think we were going to make a profit? Now, if your grampa can just wait a few days—"

Marvin lifted up his khaki jacket, revealing a pistol tucked into his belt.

"You're gonna give me that money," he said darkly, "or we gonna have ourselves a *serious* problem."

Darla shrank back into the shadows.

"Whoa there!" Hopper said quickly, holding up his hands. "OK, OK, I'll get your money." He took another swig from his beer bottle. "Why don't you come in out of the rain and we'll sort it out, hey? Want a drink?"

Marvin shrugged. "OK."

Hopper grinned, and threw his beer in the man's

face. As Marvin spluttered and staggered backwards, Hopper dropped his shoulder and charged into him, knocking him to the ground.

"Run, Darla!" he cried.

She did as she was told, her feet splashing through muddy pools as she sprinted up the narrow cut between their trailer and its neighbour. Hopper headed straight on, arms pumping as he hared through the darkness. Suddenly the night was alive with angry shouts, barking dogs and blaring TV sets. At the end of the cut Darla darted left, making for the entrance to the park. From somewhere among the trailers she heard the sharp crack of a pistol shot. Terrified, Darla looked behind her, only to slip on the soggy ground and fall face-first in the mud. A Doberman on a rusted chain snarled and lunged at her, jaws snapping in the air. But Darla was already scrambling to her feet, picking up her sports bag and racing away.

When she reached the entrance to the trailer park, Darla spotted Hopper climbing into the front seat of their battered Buick. He always left the car in the same spot, no matter how much he had drunk. They had a habit of leaving town in a hurry, usually with someone hot on their heels.

Darla ran over to the car and almost fell into the passenger seat, slamming the door shut behind her.

"You OK, honey?" asked Hopper.

Darla didn't have the breath to reply. She nodded.

Hopper turned on the engine and flicked on the headlights, trapping Marvin in the glare as he came charging through the rain. The fat man's cap had fallen off and his face was bright red with fury. As Hopper hastily threw the Buick into reverse, Marvin took aim with his pistol. Darla cried out, ducking down and throwing her hands over her head. There was a loud bang as the car hastily backed away from the trailer park, a bullet winging the bodywork. The Buick swung round with a screech of tyres and flew away down the road. Marvin's threats echoed in the night, his bulky silhouette melting into the darkness.

"Well now," chuckled Hopper. "That was pretty damn close!"

Darla stared at him coldly. Hopper's smile faded. As the Buick rattled down a deserted country road he shook his head and slapped his face a couple of times, trying to sober up. He turned on the radio, hopping from station to station in search of his favourite country music songs. Darla's panicky breaths began to slow, and her heart stopped pounding against her ribcage. She had seen it all before. Another midnight flight, another strange town in the morning. It was barely worth learning each new place's name.

They drove for hours without encountering a single car, just the Buick and an endless stretch of road. Eventually the needle on the fuel gauge dropped dangerously low, and Hopper was forced to pull over at a gas station in the middle of nowhere. A revolving sign rattled in the wind on the edge of the empty forecourt. Through the window of the gas station, Darla saw an old man dozing behind the counter. Hopper gave her a nudge, pointing at the restroom sign over the right-hand side of the building.

"How about you go freshen up while I fill the tank?"

Darla shook her head. "I'm OK."

"You're covered in mud!" exclaimed Hopper. "What do you think people are gonna say if they see you walking around looking like the Swamp Thing? You want a state trooper thinking I'm neglecting you, asking us all kinds of questions? Go on now, darlin', clean yourself up."

Darla stared at Hopper. Even with tousled hair and beer breath he was still a good-looking man, although she knew it wouldn't be long before the drink took his looks the way it had taken everything else. She wanted to hate him so much. But the truth was her hopeless, drunken daddy was all she had in the world. Without Hopper, she would be totally alone.

Reluctantly Darla opened the car door and climbed out of the Buick. It was raining hard as she hurried over to the restroom, and she was relieved to find the door unlocked. Inside it was pitch black, the air sour with the stink of urine. After a few seconds scrabbling about on the wall, Darla's fingers found the light switch. The strip light buzzed like an angry hornet above her head, casting a harsh light over the restroom. The floor was covered in paper towels and crude graffiti was scrawled over the walls and the cubicle door. A jagged crack ran the length of the mirror above the basin.

"Great," Darla muttered.

She went over to the basin and turned on the faucet. It coughed painfully, spitting out a thin stream of water. Darla squeezed some liquid soap out of the dispenser and quickly washed the mud off her hands, aware that Hopper would give her hell if she kept him waiting too long. She splashed her face with warm water, the basin turning brown as mud gurgled down the plughole. Her clothes were damp but there was no way Darla was going to go back to the Buick to get changed. She didn't want to spend a second longer in this place than she had to.

As Darla stared at herself in the mirror, the strip light flickered and the walls of the restroom seemed to shiver. Suddenly Darla had the unsettling sensation of looking at the world through someone else's eyes, of her chest rising and falling with ragged breaths that weren't her own. The restroom had vanished; instead she was hunched over a desk inside a small, windowless room lit by a single red bulb that lent a bloody hue to the shadows. Photographs hung pegged from strings crisscrossing the room like cobweb strands, and floated inside processing trays arranged side-by-side on a long table.

A pair of gloved hands reached out and opened a photograph album on the desk in front of her, turning it to a fresh page. As Darla looked at it through unfamiliar eyes she felt her breaths come faster – a combination of her own growing unease and another's excitement. She glanced up again at the pegged photographs. They were all terrified faces – bulging eyes and gaping mouths, hands flung up in front of the lens in futile defensive gestures.

Darla screamed.

The dark room and its photographs vanished, and her senses were her own again. Sick with dizziness, Darla had to clutch hold of the basin to keep herself from falling over. She turned and stumbled out of the restroom into the rain. Hopper had emerged from the gas station at the same time – at the sight of her pale face, he gave her a quizzical glance.

"Everything all right, darlin'?"

Darla took a deep, steadying breath and nodded. "I'm fine," she said. "Let's get out of here."

They climbed back into the Buick and Hopper gunned the engine into life. The last sound Darla heard before the night swallowed them up was the restroom door, banging mockingly in the wind.

Chapter Two

Around dawn they pulled into the lot outside Harley's Diner, a small, tired-looking building just off the highway. A bell tinkled above their heads as Hopper pushed through the door. The only other customer was sitting at the counter — a heavy-set trucker in a plaid shirt poring over a newspaper. A bored-looking waitress wearing bright red lipstick gazed at the television in the corner of the diner. Pans clattered loudly in the kitchen. The air was thick with the smell of grease and exhaust fumes.

Hopper went straight to a booth by the window and ordered coffee and a plate of bacon and eggs over easy for Darla — she wasn't hungry, but he hadn't bothered asking. She had barely spoken two words since the gas station, still haunted by what had happened in the restroom. Darla wanted to dismiss it as nothing, a strange mental blip, but the dark room and its eerie photographs had felt so *real*.

Even hours later, it was hard to shake the sensation of being in someone else's skin. Hopper was too preoccupied to notice Darla's silence, but even if he had she wouldn't have told him what had happened. Darla had learned to keep her problems to herself.

The young waitress appeared with their order, smiling at Hopper as she put down the plate in front of Darla. Hopper murmured a thank you and flashed the waitress a grin. Darla stared down at her food. The eggs were grey and filmy, the bacon almost burnt. She pushed the plate away and poured sugar into her coffee, cradling her hands around the warm mug.

"Food's getting cold," said Hopper, nodding at her plate.

"I don't want anything," Darla said.

"You got to eat, darlin'."

"*You* ain't eating."

"I ain't hungry."

"Neither am I!"

"Dammit, Darla!"

As Hopper stared at her, exasperated, Darla picked up a piece of bacon, snapped it in two and shoved a piece in her mouth.

"There," she said. "Happy now?"

"Ecstatic, darlin'," Hopper replied dryly. "Fit to burst."

He took another sip of coffee, and went back to staring out of the window. In a dark bar Hopper could easily pass for late twenties, but the drab dawn light seemed to linger on the grey flecks in his hair and the lines around his eyes. Darla hated it when he tried to act like a concerned father. If Hopper *really* cared about her he'd quit drinking and get a proper job. Maybe then they wouldn't end up being chased around trailer parks by angry men with guns.

Hopper's expression softened, sensing Darla's mood.

"Look," he said, taking hold of her hand. "I know you're angry about what happened back there. At the trailer park, I mean. And I'm sorry about that. Obviously there was a misunderstanding with Marvin's granddaddy and—"

"A *misunderstanding*?" Darla laughed incredulously. "Is that what we're calling it now?"

"Don't start on me, Darla," Hopper said irritably. "Not now."

Truth was, Darla wasn't sure what to call what Hopper did. There weren't many jobs he hadn't tried his hand at – carpenter and crayfisherman, ranch hand and salesman, even (briefly) a private detective. When he was younger he'd played guitar in country bands around the South, with a couple of famous names, too, if you believed him. But he never lasted long at anything, even when Darla's mom Sidney had still been alive. He'd get too hungover and miss his shifts, or worse he'd turn up drunk. After Sidney's death the drinking had got even worse, and the jobs dried up completely. Hopper became evasive when Darla asked where the money was coming from. But she knew the answer without him saying a word: conning and shamming, grafting and hawking, selling and stealing – anything for a dollar.

"Taking money from Marvin is one thing," said Darla, "but his *granddaddy*? You're stealing from an old man!"

"Keep your voice down," Hopper said quickly. "I wasn't stealing, never did anything of the sort. I offered him an investment opportunity and he took it. There weren't any guarantees."

"Of course there weren't! The only one who ever

makes any money from your schemes is you!"

"They don't know that! For a few dollars, a pocketful of change, ordinary people – people like you and me and Marvin's granddaddy, who ain't never had a break and ain't never going to get one – can think that it's their turn to get lucky, that they're going to be rich. I'm selling dreams, Darla. Ain't no one can put a price on that, on *hope*."

Hopper leaned forwards as he spoke, his voice low, his eyes wide with sincerity. He could have been a preacher, Darla thought sourly.

"Nice speech," she said. "But I heard it already, and I ain't got no money to give you."

Defeated, Hopper let go of her hand. He slid her plate in front of him and began to eat the bacon and eggs – not because he was hungry, Darla knew, but because he'd paid for the food and wasn't about to let it go to waste. When the trucker got up from his stool and waddled out of the diner, Hopper retrieved his discarded newspaper. At the sight of the name above the headline, the Saffron Hills Bugle, he started.

"What is it?" asked Darla.

For a time Hopper said nothing. "That's the

problem with driving blind," he said softly. "There's no telling where you might end up."

"What's wrong with Saffron Hills?" Darla let out a groan. "Don't tell me — you had one of your *misunderstandings*, and you're not welcome here no more either."

Hopper shook his head. "It ain't that," he said. "I haven't been in these parts for a very long time, believe me. Never thought I'd return, either."

As far back as she could remember, Darla had been on the move, following her parents on a restless, meandering path across the southern states of America — from Arizona and New Mexico to Louisiana and Georgia, and now South Carolina. In all that time, she had never seen her daddy react this way. She was curious why, but she knew there was no point in asking him. Instead she watched Hopper flick through the small ads, his brow creased in concentration.

Turning the page, he let out a soft whistle. "Would you look at that?"

Peering over his arm, Darla saw a large advert for a man calling himself the 'Realtor King of Saffron Hills'. His name was Luis Gonzalez — a short, bald man with a dazzling smile. He was standing on the front lawn of a beautiful white mansion, his arms spread wide in a welcoming gesture.

"Who's that?" asked Darla.

"An old friend," Hopper replied. "Looks like someone's gone up in the world."

He didn't say any more, which was fine by Darla. She wasn't in the mood for any more mysteries that morning. Finishing her coffee, she got up to use the restroom, her pulse quickening as she pushed open the door. But it was just a normal restroom – there were no flickering lights or shivering walls, or eerie visions hiding in the mirror for her. She came back into the diner to find Hopper settling up the check, the waitress leaning against the booth by his shoulder.

"You passing through or sticking around?" she asked him.

"That depends," drawled Hopper. "All the girls round here as pretty as you?"

The waitress giggled, pushing a lock of hair behind her ear. She shook her head.

"Nope, I wouldn't think so," said Hopper. "Word woulda gotten around."

Darla marched up to the booth, pushing past the waitress and standing directly in-between the two of them.

"Ready, *Daddy*?"

"Of course, darlin'," said Hopper. He got to his feet. "You have a good day, now," he told the waitress.

"You too," she smiled.

Darla stalked out of the diner, not looking behind her to see whether Hopper had followed. The rain had stopped but the ground was still strewn with puddles, the air warm and thick as syrup.

"Hey, wait up!"

Hopper jogged after Darla, the newspaper folded up under his arm. "You taking up track this year?" he laughed. "I'm struggling to keep up here!"

Darla whirled round. "You are *unbelievable*!" she said through clenched teeth.

Hopper blinked. "What did I do?"

"Back there, with that giggling Barbie doll – I leave you for thirty seconds and you're hitting on the waitress!"

Hopper looked wounded. "It wasn't nothin' like that, Darla. I was only being sociable. Everyone likes a compliment."

The most irritating thing was, Darla believed him. Hopper didn't mean to sweet-talk that waitress, just like he never meant to upset Darla or put her in danger. But that was what he did, all of the time. Grudgingly she let him open the passenger door of the Buick for her, and climbed inside. Hopper tossed the newspaper on to the backseat and started up the engine.

"So what now?" asked Darla.

"We go and pay the Realtor King a visit," Hopper replied, guiding the Buick back out on to the highway before making a right at the next intersection. "Marnie said Saffron Hills isn't ten minutes along this here way."

"Marnie?"

Hopper shifted uncomfortably in his seat. "The waitress."

"Oh," said Darla. "That was her name."

"Darla…"

"What? I didn't say anything!"

Hopper turned and looked at her. "I swear, darlin', that if you don't give me a break we're going to have some serious words. I'm a patient man but there's only so much I can—"

"Look out!" screamed Darla.

She heard the angry roar of an engine, and a shadow fell across the Buick's windshield. A red pick-up truck was hurtling along the narrow road in the other direction – headed straight for them. Hopper swore and yanked on the steering wheel, sending the Buick veering out of the way. Darla clung to her seat as the car rattled through the scrubland by the roadside, scraping against bushes and tree branches. As the pick-up hurtled past, through the driver's window Darla caught a glimpse of a scrawny man hunched over the wheel.

Battling the Buick, Hopper somehow managed to steer the car back on to the road, coming to a halt in a squeal of brakes.

"Asshole!" he yelled at the disappearing truck. He turned to Darla. "You OK?"

Darla nodded.

"What was that guy doing?" Hopper said incredulously. "He coulda killed us!"

He punched the steering wheel, and for a moment Darla thought he was going to turn the car around and chase after the pick-up. But then, to her relief,

Hopper let out a deep breath and restarted the engine, guiding the Buick in the opposite direction – towards Saffron Hills.

Chapter Three

The road wound up a steep hillside before disappearing into a forest of pine trees, their slender trunks like black matchsticks. Darla felt surrounded by a gnarled army standing silently to attention. The sun might have disappeared overhead but it was still baking hot inside the car. Winding down her window, Darla was assailed by a barrage of cricket chirrups. Hopper seemed uneasy, gnawing on his lip as he drove through the trees. Probably still going over their near miss in his mind, she guessed.

They emerged from the wood without warning, returning into brilliant sunlight. Darla gasped. The trees had been cut back, revealing a breathtaking landscape of rolling green hills. Huge mansions sat behind forbidding iron railings, sprinklers squirting jets of water over the lawns. Sleek sports cars rested in the driveways, polished chrome gleaming in the sunshine. Through her open window Darla heard a loud splash and a peal of laughter; she turned in her seat, and saw the blue glimmer of a swimming pool. Outside the house next door, bare-chested teenage boys tussled beneath a basketball hoop fixed to the garage, whooping as one of them sank a shot from the back of the court. Darla tried to imagine what it was like living in one of these houses, and gave up. It was as though the iron railings marked the edge of another world.

"Welcome to Saffron Hills," said Hopper.

"It's *amazing*," she said.

"It has a certain charm," Hopper admitted grudgingly. "In a flashy sort of way. These here houses were built by a local developer called Allan West back in the day; managed to attract some of the wealthiest people in South Carolina – Georgia and Tennessee too. Bankers and businessmen, lawyers, former senators. That's the thing about money: it tends to attract more money."

"That why we're broke?"

"Among other reasons."

As the Buick followed the winding road through the hills, Darla became aware of a dark-coloured car with muted flashing lights following behind them. Hopper glanced up into the rearview mirror.

"Now there's a surprise," he muttered sourly. "Haven't been here five minutes, and already the rent-a-cops are on our tail."

Darla frowned. "Rent-a-cops?"

"Local security," Hopper explained. "People round here prefer to have police they can trust. After all, you never know whose son might be found passed out drunk in the gutter, or caught speeding with a joint in his pocket."

He pressed down on the accelerator, urging the Buick towards the intersection at the bottom of the hill. The mansions haughtily withdrew from view, disappearing back behind their high walls and railings. When the Buick reached the intersection and turned on to the main strip the car behind them pulled up, the security guards content to watch them drive away.

Luis Gonzalez, the self-styled 'Realtor King of Saffron Hills', worked out of a bright glass-fronted office in the middle of the main strip. Hopper parked the Buick outside and stepped briskly across the sun-drenched sidewalk into the office. Darla followed behind, her skin prickling pleasantly under the cool breath of the air conditioning. A middle-aged man in a smart suit was working at a desk. He stood up as they entered the office and gave them a broad smile.

"Good morning, sir. How may I help...?" His smile melted as Hopper approached. "What are you doing here?"

"Aw, come on now, Luis!" Hopper said warmly, clapping him on the back. "Is that any way to greet an old buddy? How long has it been — ten, twelve years?"

Luis said nothing. Hopper glanced around the plush office, and let out an admiring whistle. "Life sure has picked up for you since New Mexico," he said. "You've landed on your feet."

"I earned every cent," Luis replied stiffly. "A man can change, Hopper."

"No doubt, no doubt." Hopper nodded. "You were in a different business back then, as I recall."

"I don't know anything about that," Luis said quickly.

"It was a business kinda like this one, wasn't it?" said Hopper. "You did spend a lot of time going around other people's houses – only they didn't know about it."

Luis's eyes flicked over towards Darla. Her family had left New Mexico when she was very young – she wondered whether he knew who she was.

"How did you find me?" the realtor asked.

"Saw your picture in the paper," replied Hopper. "Gotta say, you were the last person I expected to see here."

Luis shrugged. "After you left New Mexico I decided to start over. I remember your Sidney saying how rich people were in Saffron Hills, so I thought—"

"I get the picture," said Hopper. Darla glanced at her daddy, but he refused to meet her eye.

"So what do you want?" asked Luis.

Hopper raised his eyebrows in mock surprise.

"Why, we're looking for a place to stay, of course! This *is* a realtor's office, right?"

Luis held up his hands. "I'd like to help you, Hopper, but I don't think I can. Saffron Hills is a very exclusive market – some of our properties run into millions of dollars."

Hopper shook his head. "That would be beyond

our budget, which is modest, not to say almost non-existent. My darlin' girl here was crying and fretting and worrying that we wouldn't be able to find a place to stay but I said to her, 'Darla – don't you worry now, girl. My good friend Luis will be able to help us out. He is, after all, the Realtor King of Saffron Hills.'"

Darla shifted uneasily. It was bad enough having to watch her father put the screws on someone without being dragged into it too. It made her feel like an accomplice.

"I'm sorry, I can't help you," Luis said firmly. "You'll have to leave."

Hopper picked up a photograph of a pretty blond-haired woman from Luis's desk and studied it.

"She's *real* nice," he said. "Classy, too. Your wife?"

Luis nodded. "Celeste."

"We should meet up some time, swap old stories. Does Celeste know about New Mexico? I bet I could tell her some tales that would make her look at you in a whole new light."

Luis slumped down behind his desk.

"What do you want from me?" he said helplessly. "I can't just *give* you a house, Hopper."

"I'm not asking for one. Just somewhere we can lay our heads for a few nights."

The realtor let out a long sigh. "There's a vacant house down by the creek," he said finally. "The old lady who owned it died a few months back and didn't have any family to claim it. I guess it'd be OK for you to stay there for a few days."

"Perfect!" said Hopper, clapping his hands together. "We'll take it!"

As the Buick followed Luis's silver Mercedes along the strip, Darla caught snapshots of Saffron Hills through the window: a busy mall, a tall church spire, the performing arts centre, a row of convenience stores. Gradually the countryside wrestled back the land, the stores giving way to wild fields bordered with trees of sugarberry, sourwood and sassafras. There were no iron gates and grand estates here, just the occasional shack huddling behind a wire fence.

Hopper glanced over at the passenger seat, and saw his daughter glaring back at him.

"Don't look at me like that, Darla."

She folded her arms.

"What?" said Hopper. "I found us a place to stay, didn't I?"

"Only by blackmailing that poor man! I thought he was your friend!"

"If you've got another way of finding a place to stay without rent money, by all means go ahead, darlin'," Hopper said defensively. "I'm doing the best I can here."

"Why did he mention Mom? What's she got to do with Saffron Hills?"

"You pay no attention to what he says now, Darla. Luis might look all dressed-up and respectable but he's a liar and a thief." Hopper flashed her a smile. "How else d'you think I know him?"

Ahead of them the silver Mercedes turned off at the intersection and went rattling down a narrow country lane. A creek ran beside the way, black willow trees trailing their delicate fingers through the water. The Mercedes stopped outside a rundown two-storey house and Luis climbed out. He fidgeted nervously with a bunch of keys as the Buick pulled up behind him. Hopper got out, shielding his eyes against the sun as he examined the house.

"Gas and electricity are paid up till the end of

next month," Luis told him, mopping his glistening brow with a white handkerchief. "But the property has seen better days, there's no denying it. We haven't had one person come to view it. People round here prefer to stay up in the hills rather than come down to the creek."

"It'll do just fine, Luis," Hopper said. "I appreciate it most sincerely."

The realtor glanced across at the Buick, noting the fresh dent Marvin's pistol had left in the bodywork. "What kind of heat have you got on you?"

"Nothing I can't handle," Hopper replied easily. "There's nothing to worry about, I swear."

He held out his hands for the house keys and Luis handed them over – after a brief pause.

"Say, there's one more thing you might be able to help me with," Hopper said. "I bumped into someone on my way into town, and wondered whether you knew him. Tall, ratty-looking fella, driving a red pick-up like a bat outta hell."

Luis nodded knowingly. "Sounds to me like Leeroy Mills," he said. "A redneck who lives in a trailer a ways on down the creek. I'd steer clear if I were you."

"Duly noted," said Hopper. "Don't want the good people of Saffron Hills thinking we're mixing with the wrong crowd, do we?"

He held out his hand for Luis to shake but the realtor was already hurrying back to his Mercedes. Luis revved the engine into life, and the car bounced away down the lane in a cloud of dust.

Hopper held open the front gate for Darla and handed her the keys.

"After you," he said.

Darla went up the verandah steps and unlocked the front door. The air inside the gloomy house was musty and stifling. White sheets were draped over the furniture. In the living room she pulled back the drapes from the window and forced open the rusty catch, letting a welcome breeze sweep inside the room. She looked out through the window over a tangle of waist-high grass and overgrown shrubs. The yard sloped down towards the creek at the bottom. A rope swing dangled from the limb of a sturdy cypress tree.

"What d'you think?" asked Hopper.

"It's beautiful," Darla said quietly.

She went back out to the car and fetched her

sports bag from the trunk, carrying it upstairs. Faced with a choice between two bedrooms, she took the smaller one with the view over the yard. Her own room. Darla couldn't remember the last time she'd had a space to call her own. She smiled as she closed the door behind her, putting her bag down on her bed and going to the window to stare out over the creek. When she turned back, Darla found herself confronted by a large, ornate mirror on the dresser. Her reflection brought back unwanted memories of the gas station restroom – she shook her head, pushing the image from her mind. It was bad enough she was seeing things, without driving herself crazy over it.

When they had unpacked and removed the sheets from the furniture, Hopper drove out in search of food, returning with some bags of groceries and two large pepperoni pizzas. They ate in front of the TV, balancing the pizza boxes on their laps. Darla looked up from her slice to find her daddy looking at her thoughtfully.

"What?" she said. "Have I got cheese round my mouth?"

Hopper smiled. "Nothing like that," he said.

"I was just thinking… I don't know, maybe Saffron Hills will be good for us. Give us a chance to start again – turn over a new leaf."

Darla grunted non-committedly. She had heard it all before. There had been plenty of fresh starts over the last couple of years; enough new leaves turned over to fill a forest. It never lasted. 'A man can change', Luis had told Hopper. Darla wasn't convinced.

Sure enough, later that evening, after they had finished watching TV and Darla had gone to bed, she heard the telltale creak of the screen door on the porch and the Buick's guilty cough as the engine started. Hopper had crept out to find a bar. Darla rolled over in her bed, and drifted off into a dark, dreamless sleep.

Chapter Four

Darla must have been exhausted, because it was almost noon before she opened her eyes and got out of bed. She wrapped a thin dressing gown over her T-shirt and padded through the house towards the kitchen. The door to Hopper's bedroom was ajar, his snores echoing out into the corridor. His car keys were downstairs on the kitchen table, beside a quart of whiskey and a pack of matches from a bar called Shooters. Darla shook her head. So much for new leaves. She emptied the quart down the sink, wrinkling her nose at the smell of strong liquor, and threw the bottle into the trash. Chances were Hopper wouldn't remember he had bought it anyway.

Opening the fridge, Darla drank orange juice straight from the carton, a yellow dribble running down her chin. She wiped her mouth and looked around her. Things had happened so quickly since they had fled the trailer park she felt as though she hadn't had time to take a breath. Twenty-four hours ago she had been running through the rain with gunshots going off above her head, and now she was standing in the kitchen of her new home – for the time being, anyway. Were they really going to be allowed to stay there? How long could Hopper go without screwing everything up?

Darla shrugged. No point playing guessing games with herself. She went into the bathroom where she brushed her teeth and took a long shower, revelling in the hot blast of the water as it poured down around her. Afterwards Darla wrapped a towel around her body and carefully wiped condensation from the bathroom mirror. Her pale, thin face stared back at her, freckles clustered around her nose and cheeks, and her wet hair sticking to her ears like seaweed. Darla knew she was never going to be pretty – and maybe that would have been OK, if it hadn't been for the fact her mom had been so beautiful. With her long blond hair, flawless skin and soft, sorrowful eyes, Sidney O'Neill had attracted admiring glances wherever she went. Somehow Darla felt that she was letting her mom down, being so plain. Looking in the mirror had become a small, daily punishment.

Drying herself off, Darla changed into a yellow tank top and denim shorts and slipped on a pair of battered sandals. It would be hours before Hopper got up and anyway, she wasn't in the mood for hungover excuses. He could fix his own coffee.

She pushed open the screen door and walked down the yard path into the lane. Crickets chirruped in the long grass by the tarmac. Telephone poles stretched up into the sky. It was still hot but the first scent of fall was in the air, a distant smell of burning wood on the breeze. Save for the parked Buick, the road was empty. The houses here were all vacant, ramshackle shells covered in peeling paint. Luis had said that people in Saffron Hills tended not to come down this way. He had also said – before Hopper had hurriedly cut him off – that he had come here because Sidney O'Neill had told him about it. Darla wondered how her mom had known about this wealthy, secretive little town.

The creek wound sharply to the left, abruptly cutting off the lane. The water was still and black, a dark liquid scar running through the earth. Darla stood on the bank and stared into the creek, her thoughts as murky as the sullen water.

It seemed that with each passing day Darla's memories of her mom grew fainter, like a fading photograph. Sidney had been just eighteen when Hopper first saw her, standing in the front row of a gig in a club in Charleston – "pretty as a picture," he had remarked wistfully. They had tumbled into a whirlwind romance, marrying before the month was out. Darla could never understand what her mom had seen in Hopper; had she been foolish enough to fall for his glib lines? She remembered her mom as a quiet, withdrawn figure, somehow never fully present even when she was in the same room. With her daughter in one hand and a suitcase in the other, Sidney had followed her husband across the south, from one failed scheme to another. She hadn't argued, hadn't complained, not even when Hopper came home stinking of beer and women's perfume, or when he crashed the car drunk. One night five years ago Sidney had simply run a bath, knocked back a bottle of sleeping pills and cut her wrists. Darla – eleven at the time – had been asleep in bed, Hopper out in some bar. It had been his horrified yells that had woken her; she could still hear his ragged voice screaming at her not to come into the bathroom, the door slamming shut in her face. He had protected her from that, if nothing else.

Darla turned away from the creek and walked slowly back towards the house. Her mind was overcast with shadows – thinking about her mom did that to her. As she passed a house on the other side of the road, she heard wind chimes nudging one another in the warm breeze. Darla glanced over to the verandah and saw an empty glass pitcher on the table. She had been wrong, it seemed – there was at least one other house on the creek road that was occupied.

Then, from somewhere in the house, Darla heard a voice cry out.

It was so faint that at first she thought she had misheard it, but as she froze the voice called out again. Darla looked up and down the empty lane. Perhaps an old lady had fallen and couldn't get up. She thought about running back to the house and getting Hopper, but he was probably still drunk, and what if this was an emergency?

Darla opened the gate and hurried up the path to the verandah, the wooden boards creaking beneath her feet. She rang the doorbell, heard its shrill ricochet inside the house. No answer. The voice called out for a third time, and this time Darla heard it say: "Echo!", like some kind of playful children's game. It was coming from the backyard. Stepping down from the porch, Darla edged around the side of the house.

"Hello?" she called out softly. "Anyone there?"

Silence.

She peered round the corner, and looked out over a yard ringed by trees. In the middle of the lawn there was a small, half-built hut, missing a roof and one of its walls.

"Hello?" Darla called out again.

"Echo!" a girl's voice replied, from within the hut.

A bird took to the air from the trees with a violent flutter of wings. Darla edged across the grass towards the hut. Pressing herself against the wall, she peered inside.

A host of Darlas peered back at her.

Every surface inside the tiny house had been covered in mirrors, casting a dizzying series of reflections. Light danced across the bright surfaces, illuminating a hundred of her own faces. As she stared in wonder into the empty house a voice cried out "Echo" once more, and Darla realized the sound was coming from tiny speakers mounted in each ceiling corner.

"Excuse me?"

Darla whirled around, her heart thumping in her chest. A woman had appeared on the back porch of the main house. She was in her late thirties, tall, with strong but attractive features, dressed in jeans and an oversize man's white shirt, her red hair tied up beneath a patterned scarf. She was carrying a large mirror, thick protective gloves covering her hands.

"S-sorry..." Darla stammered. "I heard a voice and I thought... I rang the bell but no one answered, so I came back here and—"

"Hey, it's all right!" The woman smiled. "I'm sorry I scared you. I was just testing the speakers, and I never hear the doorbell when I'm working. Never hear much of anything, if it comes to that. My house could blow away in a storm and I wouldn't notice."

"What do you do?" asked Darla.

"I'm an artist."

Darla's eyes widened. "Really?"

The woman nodded.

"That's so cool!" Darla had never met a real-life artist before.

"Thank you!" laughed the woman. "Though believe me, there's absolutely nothing cool about me."

She hauled the heavy-looking mirror across the lawn and laid it carefully down against the side of the hut.

"Annie Taylor," she said, taking off a glove and offering her hand.

"I'm Darla."

"Nice to meet you, Darla," said Annie. "You new in town?"

"Yeah. Me and my daddy just moved in across the street."

"Well, I guess that makes us neighbours, then, doesn't it?" Annie said brightly. "I just moved back to Saffron Hills from New York myself, six months ago. I've got a little gallery in town, and I teach a couple of classes at the Allan West Academy."

"Echo!"

"Hold on," she said, "let me turn this thing off."

She disappeared inside the building and began

60

fiddling with one of the speakers.

"Did you build this?" Darla asked her.

"With my own bare hands," Annie called back. "It's a new piece I'm working on. I call it the House of Narcissus."

"The House of what?"

Annie reappeared through the doorway. "In ancient Greek mythology there was a nymph called Echo who fell in love with a beautiful boy called Narcissus," she explained. "When Narcissus rejected her, Echo was so heartbroken she dwindled away until only her voice remained, echoing around the glens. The gods punished Narcissus for his cruelty by making him fall in love with his own reflection."

In Darla's mind artists drew pictures and made paintings, they didn't build small houses in their backyard and fill them with mirrors. Her puzzled expression must have shown, because Annie burst out laughing.

"Don't worry, hon," she said dryly. "I get that look a lot."

"I didn't mean to be rude," Darla said quickly, blushing. "I just haven't seen anything like this before."

"Perfect! That's a great compliment. Now how about I put up this mirror, and then maybe we can have a lemonade on the porch? Hauling these mirrors around is thirsty work."

Darla nodded eagerly. It had been a while since she had talked to anyone apart from Hopper, and she guessed Annie must have some pretty cool stories from New York. She stood back as the artist picked up the mirror.

And saw something in the glass.

The yard and the house of mirrors melted away, and Darla was overwhelmed by the sickly feeling of being in someone else's skin. She was back in the small windowless room filled with red light, sitting at a desk and turning pages in a photograph album. Hoarse breaths of anticipation rose in her throat. Every time her gloved hands turned the page to reveal a new photograph, Darla heard the click of a camera inside her head.

Click.

A gated mansion at night, windows black rectangles in the dark.

Click.

A lone light on the second floor of the building.

Click.

A flash of blond hair in the window, a drape half-closing.

Click.

An empty page.

The album slammed shut, and at that moment Darla knew with icy certainty that she was going to kill someone. She opened her mouth to try to scream, but the dark room vanished and suddenly Darla was standing back in Annie's yard, staring at her own reflection as she crumpled to the floor, her world lurching violently into black.

Chapter Five

Darla opened her eyes to find her daddy's face looming over her. Hopper's cheeks were rough with stubble and his hair was sticking up – he had obviously got dressed in a hurry. Annie hovered behind him, her arms folded and her expression creased with concern. Darla was lying on a couch in what she guessed was Annie's front room. Paintings daubed with violent slashes of colour hung on the walls; weird, shapeless sculptures perched on shelves and surfaces. A fan turned silent circles on the ceiling.

Hopper smiled. "Welcome back, darlin'," he said. "You had us worried for a moment there."

Darla sat up with a groan, rubbing a hand across her face.

"Is she OK?" asked Annie.

"She'll be fine in a moment or two," Hopper replied breezily. "She musta just fainted, nothin' to worry about." He patted Darla's hand. "Ain't that right?"

She nodded quickly. What else was she going to tell them? That she'd had two disturbing visions in twenty-four hours, and she was worried she was going crazy?

"You see – right as rain," said Hopper, flashing Annie his salesman's smile. "I'll take her back to the house where she can rest. Please accept my apologies for giving you such a dreadful fright."

"It's fine," said Annie. "I'm just glad that Darla's all right. Are you sure she shouldn't rest here for a while?"

"That's mighty kind of you but I'll take her home – we're just across the street."

Hopper helped Darla to her feet, and led her gently out on to the front porch.

"You take care now, honey!" Annie called after her.

"I will," Darla said weakly. "Thanks."

She could feel the artist watching them from the doorway as she and Hopper walked slowly down the creek road back to the house.

"Darla, darlin'?" muttered Hopper, out of the

corner of his mouth. "By all means introduce yourselves to the neighbours, but try not to faint on their lawns. It makes them kinda nervous."

"I didn't do it on purpose," Darla hissed.

"Lord knows what that woman makes of us," he said, glancing back towards the verandah. "Prob'ly thinks we're crazies."

"Annie."

"What?"

"Her name is Annie."

"Oh, OK."

"She's an artist," Darla told him.

"That so?"

"She's nice. I like her."

"Well maybe we'll invite her round for dinner sometime," said Hopper. "Only you gotta promise not to pass out at the table."

"Hey!" protested Darla, giving him a push. "That's not funny!"

"I wasn't joking," he replied. "Word gets around fast in this kind of town."

Darla didn't think that Annie was the type of person who went around gossiping, but she knew that Hopper wouldn't be taking any chances. He was paranoid about teachers or care workers or the police poking around in their business and asking questions. Darla knew she could get her own back on him by bringing up Shooters and the quart of whiskey, but she had a headache and didn't want another argument. When they got back to the house she lay on the couch watching TV re-runs while Hopper showered and shaved. He emerged from the bathroom looking clean and refreshed, the smell of cheap liquor replaced by the smell of cheap aftershave.

"You feeling up to a trip into town?" he said. "I figured we should take a look around."

Darla shrugged, her eyes glued to the screen.

"I'll take that as a yes," Hopper said. "Come on, darlin', let's go."

On the way into Saffron Hills they drove past a group of riders on horseback, who stared down disapprovingly from their saddles at the Buick and its coughing engine. When they reached the town mall they parked in the underground lot, leaving their car skulking in the shadows away from the rows of soft-top convertibles. Hopper fooled around, making a big show of checking that the car was locked – as though anyone was going to steal the rusty Buick.

They took the elevator up from the underground lot, blinking as they emerged into the light. The mall was several storeys high, each walkway connected by a network of escalators and elevators. Sunshine poured in through the glass ceiling, drenching shoppers as they bustled along the main arcade. On the rare occasions Hopper took Darla shopping it was usually to the thrift store, and she was used to rummaging through jumbled racks in search of cheap clothes. But the stores here were all expensive boutiques: hollow spaces with whitewashed walls and only a handful of items for sale. There were jewellers and sleek electronic goods stores, a movie theatre and a gym. Darla stared through the window at the rows of blank-eyed people jogging on running machines, their faces red and bathed in sweat.

"Look at this place!" Hopper laughed. "This must be where shops go when they die."

As they wandered through the mall, Darla looked up and saw a huge banner stretched across the roof, advertising the upcoming 'Miss Saffron

Beauty Pageant'. A group of teenagers had gathered underneath it by the escalator on the first floor. There were five of them, a line-up from a clothing catalogue, the three girls in skinny jeans and crop tops revealing their toned midriffs, each strand of hair hanging perfectly in place around golden hooped earrings; the two boys in casual shirts and low-riding jeans. Either they were models hired to promote the pageant, or the most beautiful group of friends Darla had ever seen.

As the teenagers looked down over the mall, a blond girl nudged the dark-skinned, shaven-headed boy next to her and nodded at Darla. He raised an eyebrow, and she burst out laughing. *Great*, thought Darla – she had barely stepped foot inside Saffron Hills, and already people were sniggering at her. Resisting the urge to flip them the bird, she looked round for Hopper and saw that he was making for a store on the other side of the restaurant forecourt. With its gloomy interior and faded posters plastered across the windows, it looked as though it had been teleported into the mall from some other, darker dimension. The sign above the door read 'Criminal Records', in bright pink graffiti.

"Come on, Darla!" Hopper said excitedly, ducking inside the record store.

Heading after him, she pushed through the door and found herself in a long, dingy room filled with stacks of vinyl records. Ripped posters of snarling singers and guitar players clung to the wall. Loud music was crashing out from the speakers behind the counter at the far end of the store, where a dark-haired girl sat with her feet up and her eyes closed.

Immediately Hopper dived into the nearest stack of records and began flicking through them. Darla wandered hesitantly around the store, her sandals sticking to the dirty floor. She liked music, but she didn't love it like her daddy did; she never knew what the cool band was, or the next big thing. Without a computer or an iPod, the only time she heard music was on the crackling radio in the Buick. As she stared at the unfamiliar record sleeves, it felt to Darla like she was being set some kind of test – and failing miserably.

"Can I help you?"

The girl had emerged from behind the counter and was leaning over the other side of the rack, eyeing Darla with amusement. Her hair was dyed black and cropped in a rough, boyish cut with a long fringe and a shaved undercut. A silver stud gleamed in her nose and her lip was pierced, her eyes ringed with black eye shadow. She straightened up as Darla stared at her, revealing herself to be a full head taller – and skinny with it, dressed in ripped jeans and a white sleeveless T-shirt with a band name Darla hadn't heard of. She was strikingly beautiful.

Jesus, thought Darla. *Even the punks in this town look like models.*

"Um, no, I'm fine," she said, painfully aware how lame she sounded. "Thanks."

"But *are* you fine, though?" the girl replied. "That is the question."

Darla stared at her, at a loss. The girl nodded, as though her worst suspicions had been confirmed.

"This place is *incredible*!" Hopper's voice echoed around the store as he hurried over to Darla. "I swear I'm in hog's heaven."

The girl gave him a look of barely disguised contempt.

"I wasn't sure anyone even listened to vinyl anymore," continued Hopper. "I thought all you kids did these days was watch videos on YouTube."

"Congratulations," the girl said. "You're officially on speaking terms with the twenty-first century."

If Hopper had noticed the icy tone in her voice, he chose to ignore it. "Takes me back to my own playing days," he said. "One of these records might have me strumming away somewhere in the background."

She shrugged, unimpressed.

"I took my guitar on a few tours across the South, in backing bands and the like," Hopper continued. "No stadiums, but a coupla names you might have heard of."

"How about Elvis?" the girl said sardonically. "I've heard of Elvis."

Hopper laughed and shook his head. "The King was a little before my time," he said. "I ain't *that* old, darlin'."

"I'm no one's darling," she shot back. "Especially not yours."

Hopper smiled ruefully, scratching his stubbled cheek. The song blaring out around the shop came to a sudden end, replaced by a pointed silence.

"Can we go now, please?" Darla asked Hopper.

He nodded slowly, pausing as they walked out of the shop to give the dark-haired girl an exaggerated farewell bow. She ignored him and returned to the counter, the music erupting back to life as the shop door closed behind them.

"Brr!" said Hopper, pretending to shiver. "Don't know about you, Darla, but I feel awful cold all of a sudden."

"You are *so* embarrassing," Darla groaned. "I wish I was dead."

"Don't say that," Hopper told her. "You might end up like the Zombie Bride back there."

"I don't think she liked me very much."

"I wouldn't worry about it. I doubt she likes anyone very much."

"Did you *really* play in backing bands across the South?"

Hopper looked wounded.

"Darla! There are some things in this world that a man just does not lie about. Music is one of them."

"Anything else?"

"Nothing springs to mind," Hopper admitted.

He glanced at Darla and laughed, wrapping his arm around her shoulder. For once she didn't try to shrug him off. Hopper took her to a sandwich shop where they bought subs and sodas, eating them at a table by the window. As they watched the stream of people wash past them, giggling at the rich housewives with their giant bags of designer clothes and tiny designer dogs, Darla felt the tension in her shoulders begin to ease.

Hopper slurped loudly on his soda as he drained it, and went over the counter to settle up the bill. As Darla waited for him outside, she had the uneasy sensation that someone was watching her. She turned around. It was the hot shaven-headed boy she had seen standing beneath the pageant banner. He was alone now, sat on the backrest of a bench and nodding his head in time with the music coming through his headphones, staring at Darla with an unreadable expression on his face. As their eyes met her mouth went dry, and she could feel her cheeks burning.

The boy slipped his headphones down around his neck and jumped off the bench, walking slowly and deliberately towards her. The hum of the mall melted away into the background. He pulled out his phone as he neared, and put his arm around an astonished Darla.

"Hey, I'm TJ," he said. "Take a photo with me."

That was it. Not a question. Before Darla could say anything the boy had leaned in close to her, his smooth cheek brushing against hers, his expensive aftershave enveloping her. He held up his phone and took a picture. Darla stared at him as he pulled away, a glimmer of amusement in his eyes. TJ brushed a finger against her cheek, and then he was gone.

Chapter Six

Darla pulled the sheets up over her head and burrowed deeper into the bed.

"But I don't want to!" she groaned.

Hopper folded his arms. "Tough," he said. "You're going and that's that."

A week had passed since they had driven through the night and washed up in Saffron Hills. Just seven days – and yet in that time, Darla's whole world had changed completely. It had started on the third morning, when Hopper had driven into Saffron Hills to pick up some groceries. But he had returned with something else, something entirely unexpected.

A job.

"I cannot believe it, Darla!" he had said excitedly. "There I was at the music store, checkin' out the guitars—"

"I thought you were supposed to be grocery shopping."

"I was! That mean I can't stop off along the way? Anyway, I was playing some licks on a baby-blue Epiphone when I heard the manager grousing about a salesman who'd walked out on him, hadn't given notice or nothin'. I know an opportunity when I hear one, so I marched straight up to him and offered my services and he hired me on the spot!"

"He gave you a job?" Darla said dubiously. "Just like that?"

"OK, a two-week trial, but that's good enough for starters, right?"

"Sure. If you think you can do it."

Hopper gave her a reproachful look. "Darla, there are two things your daddy knows about in this world· one is guitars, the other is sellin'. You just wait and see – our luck is changin' for the better."

Although Darla was pleased for him, she wasn't going to get her hopes up. Hopper had talked his way into jobs before – it was *keeping* them that was the hard part. He was still sneaking out to bars after she went to bed, coming back drunk early in the morning. Darla wondered whether he thought she couldn't hear him stumbling around the house, or whether he was just hoping she wouldn't say anything. She decided to keep quiet for the time being. After all, she had her own secrets to keep.

Thankfully there had been no more mirror visions since the incident in Annie's backyard. Darla had pushed them firmly to the back of her mind. They were a blip, nothing more – their flight from Marvin back at the trailer park must have unsettled her more than she had realized. Real life was hard enough without dreaming up things to worry about. Darla was still annoyed about what had happened in the mall with TJ. She should have pushed him away or told him to drop dead, but instead she had just stood there like a dummy and let him take a picture of her. There was something amazingly arrogant about the way TJ had moved in on Darla, as though there could be no doubt whether she wanted to be in a photograph with him or not. If she saw him again, Darla swore to herself, she would tell Mr High and Mighty exactly what she thought of him.

Now that Hopper had a job – even if it was only for a trial period – he was trying to arrange a rental agreement with Luis so they could stay in the house by the creek. Darla was pretty sure the realtor would have preferred them to leave town and never come back, but as long as Hopper kept threatening to tell Luis's wife all about New Mexico he didn't have much choice – and some rent money was better than nothing. In just seven days, they were looking at putting down some real roots.

But now Hopper was threatening to ruin everything. He was making Darla go to school.

The news that she had been enrolled at the Allan West Academy had come as an unpleasant surprise. It seemed Darla had Annie to blame for that – the art teacher had apparently pulled some strings to help get her registered. Hopper had kept quiet about the whole thing, aware that Darla would take some convincing. It wasn't that she didn't want to learn; she could read just fine and even secretly enjoyed math. It was the other students that were the problem. Hopper moved her around so much that Darla barely had enough time to make friends before she had to leave again. She wasn't funny or pretty or confident or good at sports – she needed time to settle in. Instead she was doomed to be the New Girl, always behind, always out of fashion, always alone.

But as hard as Darla protested, Hopper wasn't

listening. He bullied her out of bed and into the bathroom, telling her to hurry up or else they'd both be late. Darla glumly showered and dressed, digging out an old bag for her schoolbooks. She couldn't eat any breakfast, her stomach tightening into a knot. All she could think about was that moment when she would walk into a strange classroom and everyone would turn and stare at her.

Hopper turned up the Buick's radio on their way to school, insisting on driving Darla up to the front entrance despite her pleas for him not to. They drove through the front gates and up a broad driveway towards a cluster of imposing white buildings gathered on a hilltop. The Stars and Stripes rippled proudly in the breeze at the top of a flagpole. There was a clock tower above the main entrance, a sports field and tennis courts visible in the distance. Darla had never seen a school like it. She sank lower into the front seat as the battered Buick rolled to a stop, praying that nobody would see her.

"Would you take a look at this place?" said Hopper. "It's the nicest damned school I ever saw!"

"You go, if you like it so much," Darla replied.

"Look, I know this ain't easy, but at least try to

give it a shot, darlin'," he told her. "For me?"

Hopper grinned as Darla climbed out of the Buick. "Atta girl!"

She had a retort ready on her lips but he was already driving away. The school steps were empty – the bell for homeroom must already have rung. Darla wandered through the empty hallways in search of the office, past a trophy cabinet filled with glittering awards. From football to gymnastics and lacrosse, there didn't seem to be a sport the West Academy didn't compete – and win – in. To her surprise, Darla also saw several photographs of beautiful, smiling girls in gowns wearing tiaras. Looking closer, she saw that they were all wearing sashes with 'Miss Saffron' written on them. Darla shook her head. Beauty pageants were obviously a big deal in this town.

When she finally found the office, Darla was taken along the corridors to her homeroom, where twenty heads swivelled and stared at her as she entered. The worst moment – it was always the worst moment – was when Darla had to stand at the front of the class and introduce herself, her cheeks burning as she mumbled into her shoes. She was convinced that people were giggling at her, but she told herself it was OK, just first day nerves.

At lunch Darla ate alone in the canteen, staring down at her tray. When she had finished she went in search of her new locker, only to stop at the sight of the punk girl from Criminal Records. She was rooting through her locker, tossing old T-shirts and dog-eared textbooks on to the floor. A good-looking blond-haired boy was leaning against the locker beside her, his eyes twinkling with amusement.

"Have you ever thought of getting a maid, Sasha?" he said. "I'd give it some *serious* consideration, because there are health and safety implications for a locker this dirty."

Sasha didn't even bother to look up. "I'm busy, Swim Team."

"Please, call me Ryan," he said mildly. "Everyone else does."

"Go away, Swim Team."

"I've got it," said Ryan, snapping his fingers. "You could ask Frank to be your maid. We all know how much he likes to follow you around, and I've got a hunch he'd enjoy the outfit—"

Sasha snatched up a hairbrush and threw it at Ryan, who narrowly ducked out of the way as it cracked into the locker behind his head.

"I'm kidding, I'm kidding!" he said quickly, holding his hands up. "Jesus, tough crowd."

He was still smiling though, which only seemed to infuriate Sasha even more. She reached inside her locker for another missile. As Darla looked on, intrigued by the exchange, she felt a sharp elbow in her ribs. A trio of tall, willowy girls in designer clothes stalked past her towards Sasha, their hair seeming to swish in time together. Darla recognized them from the mall: two blondes and an African-American girl with thick black curls. All three of them were astonishingly beautiful. They sashayed down the hall, barely looking at the crowds as they parted for them. None of them were smiling.

The lead girl, the slightly taller of the two blondes, came to a halt by Sasha's locker and slowly looked her up and down.

"Nice outfit," she said. "Halloween's come early this year."

Sasha smiled sweetly, and raised her middle finger. "Drop dead, Natalie."

"You need to show a little more respect," said the other blond girl. "Next month Natalie's going to be crowned Miss Saffron. Everybody knows it."

"Whoop-de-doo, Carmen," Sasha replied, in a bored voice. "Who cares?"

"How about, everybody in this town?" Natalie shot back. "Everybody who matters, anyway."

"I wouldn't count your tiaras just yet," said Sasha. "I hear you have to have a talent to enter Miss Saffron, and I don't think walking in high heels counts."

Darla burst out laughing. She hastily tried to disguise it as a cough, but it was too late. Sasha, Ryan, the three beautiful girls — everyone had turned to look at her

"What are you staring at, you little freak?" Natalie snapped.

"Nothing," Darla said hurriedly.

"This conversation is *way* beyond your pay grade," the dark-skinned girl told her, flicking a dismissive finger. "You run along now."

"You tell her, Gabrielle," said Carmen.

Sasha said nothing, studying Darla with interest.

At that moment, TJ came slouching down the

corridor towards them, his headphones up around
his ears. Perfect. Darla should have guessed he
would also be a West Academy student. Completely
lost in the music, TJ didn't notice her glaring at him
as he walked past. Darla knew this wasn't the time
to say anything, but she was too annoyed to let it
go. She stepped in front of him, forcing him to stop.

"Excuse me?" she said. "You don't know me, I'm
Darla. You took a photo of me in the mall the other
day."

Carmen snorted with laughter. Darla ignored her.

"I wanted to tell you that it was kinda creepy and
I didn't appreciate it," she said to TJ, aware that the
whole corridor was watching her now.

TJ said nothing. She wasn't even sure that he had
heard her over the music in his headphones. He went
to push past her.

"Hey!" Darla reached out and caught his arm.
"I'm talking to you!"

He turned and slowly looked her up and down, as
though examining another species. Then he pointed to
his headphones, shrugged, and walked away from her.

"Fatal error, newbie!" Ryan called out to Darla.
"Lesson one: do *not* try to interrupt my man TJ

when he's tuned in to his beats."

Sasha laughed incredulously. "What is he, six?"

"Stay out of this, Sasha," Natalie warned. She looked Darla up and down. "Newbie, I'll give you lesson two for free: I don't know what mountain top you've come down from, Marla, but that hillbilly chic look just isn't going to cut it around here."

Carmen and Gabrielle burst into spiteful peals of laughter. Darla turned, her cheeks burning, and walked away down the corridor. She went into the girls' toilets and locked herself into a cubicle, banging the wall with irritation. It clearly wasn't going to work here – there was no way Darla could fit in with these rich creeps and snooty ice queens. For a moment she considered walking out of the West Academy, only to picture the look on Hopper's face when he found out. Even after everything, she couldn't bear to disappoint him.

Darla sat down and took a deep, calming breath. It had only been a morning, she told herself firmly, she couldn't give up yet. When the bell rang she emerged from the cubicle and went to her next class, but the afternoon didn't go any better than the morning. Even though Darla kept her head down and didn't say anything, she was convinced that her classmates were whispering about her. Had people heard about her confronting TJ? Did news really travel that fast? She kept staring up at the clock on the wall, but it was as though the minute hand had frozen.

Finally the lesson ended, and Darla could throw her books into her bag and hurry out of the classroom. At the end of the corridor she burst out through the doors into the warm afternoon sunshine, feeling like a prisoner let out of jail.

Down amongst the cars, Sasha was leaning against the bumper of a rusting black pick-up truck, idly picking at her nails. Beside her a boy with sandy hair and glasses was engrossed in a paperback book. At the sight of Darla, Sasha put her fingers in her mouth and made a piercing whistle.

"Hey, new girl!" she called out. "Over here!"

Darla hesitated. Sasha rolled her eyes, and waved her over.

"Come on, I don't bite!"

Reluctantly Darla walked down the steps and headed over to the pick-up.

"Your name's Darla, right?" said Sasha. "You know who I am?"

Darla nodded.

"This is Frank," said Sasha, gesturing at the boy with her.

"I'm the chauffeur," Frank added archly.

"You're more to me than that," Sasha told him. "You do my math homework, too, remember?"

"I *am* multi-talented," Frank agreed.

"Frank's driving me home," Sasha said. "Come with us."

It wasn't, Darla couldn't help but notice, a question. Everyone around here seemed to act like they were kings and queens, expecting to be instantly obeyed. But it had been a long, miserable day and all Darla wanted to do was go home and try to forget about the fact that she would have to come back to this horrible place tomorrow, and the day after that.

"I'm sorry, I can't," she said apologetically. "My daddy's expecting me home."

Sasha reached out and grabbed her firmly by the wrist. "I don't think you understand," she said. "We *really* need to talk."

Chapter Seven

The wind picked up as Natalie McRae jogged home alone through the hills, her long blond ponytail bouncing against her back. Dark clouds gathered high above her head. The air was thick with the threat of the rain. Natalie couldn't hear her panting breaths over the dance music in her earphones, but her back was damp with sweat and she could feel her chest burning. As the road skirted around the overgrown grounds of the old West house, the incline got suddenly steeper. Natalie forced herself to keep running, keeping her feet in time with the pounding beat.

She had waited until the others had left school before changing into her running gear, tying back her hair and swapping her designer mules for a pair of pink sneakers. Usually Ryan drove her home – Natalie wondered how long he had waited by his convertible before realizing she wasn't coming.

That would teach him to hang round Sasha's locker, flashing that smile of his at her. Ryan Cafferty was *her* boyfriend; what did he think he was doing? Natalie couldn't understand why he even gave Sasha a second glance. She thought she was so *smart*. Well, if the captain of the swim team wanted to date some dirty goth he could have her. Ryan's wasn't the only ride in town, and there would always be a line of guys willing to drive Natalie wherever she wanted.

Thinking about Ryan had made her angry, giving her a second wind. She speeded up, the soles of her sneakers biting into the side of the road with a satisfying crunch. The road began to level out: she was in the home stretch now. The McRae house was built on one of the highest hills in the town, overlooking even Tall Pines. Natalie's father, Benjamin McRae, came from a rich Southern family flush with oil money, and he had lived in Louisiana before Allan West had persuaded him to move to South Carolina. Natalie staggered to a grateful halt outside the front gates, leaning against the railings as she took in great lungfuls of air. She pulled out her earphones but the music continued to play, a small, tinny racket. When she had caught her breath Natalie fished her keys out of her pocket and beeped open the front gate. It swung smoothly open and she slipped inside.

The driveway stretched out before her like a paved catwalk, sprinklers drenching the grass with liquid applause. As she walked up towards the front door, checking her neck for her pulse rate, Natalie had the sudden sense that she was being watched. She turned around, glancing sharply up and down the road. There was no one there.

She slid the key into the front door and went inside, hurrying over to the alarm and tapping in the code before it could explode into life. The previous year, one of her father's friends back in New Orleans had been the victim of a home invasion – a gang of thieves had broken into his home and threatened the whole family with knives until the safe had been emptied. Now the McRae residence was protected with electronic gates and state-of-the-art alarms that automatically alerted local law enforcement every time they went off. But in a strange way the new security made Natalie feel more vulnerable – protecting her from a threat she hadn't even considered before.

She went straight to the kitchen and opened the fridge, taking out a small plastic bottle of water. Natalie pressed it against her cheek, relishing its cool kiss against her skin. No one else was home. They rarely were. Her father was always on business somewhere, in Memphis or Houston or Atlanta – anywhere, it seemed, but Saffron Hills. Her mom Kimberley spent most of her days in the country club lounge with all the other 'business widows', swapping bitchy gossip over gin and tonics. Juanita the maid came Tuesdays and Thursdays, but she didn't speak any English and Natalie avoided her whenever she could.

A photo of Natalie and her friends was stuck to the fridge door: her, Carmen, Gabrielle, and Ryan and TJ all bunched in close together, smiling for the camera. Carmen was obsessed with taking selfies, and they couldn't go anywhere without her pestering them to join in. This one had been taken in the mall the day TJ had photographed himself with the new girl. He and Ryan had been taking pictures like that all summer. Natalie had found it funny at first – they all had – but now she wasn't so sure. They had all seen the way the new girl – the one with the thrift-store stylings, Marla, was it? – had tried to confront TJ in the hallway. Gabrielle and Carmen had found it hilarious but Natalie thought it was a bit pathetic. It wasn't that she felt sorry for Marla; it was more that she was aggrieved that she couldn't see the obvious social order. Natalie knew that not every girl could look like Taylor Swift or Katy Perry. But some girls didn't even *try* to look nice, and as far as she was concerned, that was just plain lazy.

She wandered through the cool house taking sips of water, coming to a halt by a large glass case at the foot of the stairs. Nearly half the size of the West Academy's trophy cabinet, it contained the mementos of Natalie's mom Kimberley's teenage pageant triumphs. There were photographs and certificates, sashes and tiaras, and – at the very heart of the cabinet – the beautiful red sequinned dress Kimberley had worn the night she had been crowned Miss Saffron. It was impossible to walk through the house without seeing it, a constant reminder that in her day Natalie's mom had been the prettiest girl in the county. "Pretty enough to model in New York," Kimberley used to tell Natalie, with a hint of sourness that suggested it was somehow her daughter's fault that she had married Benjamin McRae instead and never left Saffron Hills.

When she was little Natalie would sit at the top of the stairs and watch her mom stand motionless in front of the cabinet, lost in its reflection. Kimberley would beckon her down and take her little hand in hers.

"When you grow up," her mom used to whisper, "you're going to win that pageant and bring that title back home where it belongs."

She had never asked Natalie whether she actually *wanted* to enter Miss Saffron, or any beauty pageant for that matter. It wasn't really about her, Natalie knew. The only thing that mattered was that Kimberley McRae's daughter was as pretty as Kimberley McRae had been.

Turning her back on the glass case, Natalie trudged up the stairs and went into her bedroom. Even though she was alone in the house, it was still a relief to close the door and shut out the world. Her room was shrouded in gloom, the windows filled with sullen rainclouds. She turned on her bedside lamp and went straight to her dresser mirror, pushing a stray lock of blond hair behind her ear. On the dresser beside her closet, a carved wooden Japanese box lay open filled with jewellery: diamond ear studs, delicate gold bracelets and rings of fiery ruby and cold sapphire. So many expensive things, all of them bought by her father – part of his continual, unspoken apology for leaving her alone with her mom.

Opening the closet, Natalie reached up and sifted through the stack of shoeboxes on the top shelf. Her hands alighted upon a brown Louis Vuitton box at the bottom of one of the piles, and she carefully manoeuvred it free. She was alert now, her ears pricked for the sound of anyone unexpectedly coming home. Natalie carried the shoebox over to her bed and opened it. Inside there was an instant image camera, on top of a sea of photographs. She had secretly bought the camera online – her friends would have scoffed at the old-fashioned technology but Natalie didn't want to leave the pictures she took on her phone where anybody could find them, and there was no way she would ever put them on the internet. The contents of the Louis Vuitton shoebox were her secret, for her eyes only.

She took out the camera and sifted unhappily through the photographs at the bottom of the box. Every shot was a near-identical picture of her own face. Natalie had photographed herself every day for two years, carefully examining her features for the slightest blemish. She didn't take the photos because she *liked* the way she looked — it was exactly the opposite. Every faint line, every patch of greasy skin was a fresh nightmare. But if she examined herself for imperfections, maybe one day she would be able to take a perfect picture. Maybe then, Natalie told herself, her mom would be happy.

Her face was still red from the jog home, her hair in a sweaty tangle. Any photo she took now would only make her even more miserable, but Natalie knew that she couldn't wait until she had showered and changed and put on make-up. It was almost as though she was punishing herself — although for what, exactly, Natalie couldn't say. She wondered what Sasha would say if she could see her shoebox. She'd probably be laughing too hard to speak.

Natalie held out the camera and trained it on herself. She composed her face and took a picture. There was a bright flash, followed by a click and a whirr as the photograph slid out of the camera. Natalie took it by the edges, waving it dry in the air.

A loud beep came from downstairs. Natalie glanced up, and heard the electronic voice of the alarm announce that it was re-setting. She frowned.

"Mom?" she called out. "Is that you?"

She put the drying photograph down on her desk and went over to the window. Through the glass, she caught a glimpse of a red pick-up truck parked across the street. Natalie couldn't remember whether it had been there when she came home, but she remembered the feeling of being watched in the driveway. Had the pick-up followed her home? Briefly she thought about calling security. But what would she tell them – that she was worried because the alarm had reset and someone had parked outside her house? Most likely by the time the guards turned up the pick-up would be gone, and it would take Natalie for ever to get rid of them. They loved to poke their noses around the mansions, to see how successful people lived. They weren't even proper cops, Natalie thought disdainfully.

Distracted, she went back over to her desk and

picked up the photograph. As Natalie stared at it, the room suddenly went very cold. Her face was red and there was a cluster of pimples on her forehead. But that wasn't why the sweat had frozen on her skin. Behind Natalie's shoulder, through the open closet door, there was a pale, blurred oval in the shadows.

Another face.

The photograph fell fluttering from Natalie's fingers. She backed slowly away from the closet, and felt her back bump against her desk. Scrabbling through her things, she snatched up a pair of scissors, her hands shaking as she held them out in front of her.

"Who's there?" she called out.

The bedroom stayed silent, the closet door remaining tight-lipped. Whoever was in there must have been hiding behind the racks of clothes when Natalie had brought down her shoebox, close enough to touch her. The thought sent a shiver of horror down Natalie's spine. Running her tongue nervously over her lip, she glanced towards her bedroom door. Four, five paces and she would be away – no one would catch her when she started running.

So why was she still standing there?

"Come out, whoever you are," she said. "I'm not scared of you."

She was — more scared than she had ever been. But Natalie was also angry: at her lousy boyfriend, her cold, bitter mom and her coward of a dad, and now whichever creep was hiding in her wardrobe.

Wait a minute.

Her lousy boyfriend.

Whom she had stood up only an hour earlier, and might be looking for a way to pay her back…

Natalie laughed with disbelief. "Ryan?" she said. "If that's you hiding in there, we are *so* over."

Marching over to the closet, she raised the scissors above her head and yanked open the door. A dazzling light exploded in her face, blinding her. Natalie stumbled backwards, opening her eyes just in time to see a silver blade slicing down through the air, slashing her face. She screamed, hot blood pouring from her cheek.

Natalie dropped the scissors and staggered out of her bedroom clutching her face. There was no pain, her senses numb with panic and adrenaline. Glancing over her shoulder, she saw the knife swinging towards her again – instinctively she ducked, and heard the thud of the blade as it buried itself into the landing wall. Sobbing, Natalie ran down the stairs, focusing on the front door and the safety that lay beyond it. She had almost reached the bottom step when she felt a rough hand in the small of her back. Natalie went flying forwards, careering headfirst into Kimberley McRae's trophy cabinet amid an explosion of shattered glass.

Things went very still for a time: Natalie must have blacked out with the pain. When she came to, she found herself lying on her back on the hallway floor, surrounded by glass shards and torn pageant sashes. There was blood on her face and hands and she was in so much pain she could barely move. A crunch of broken glass alerted her to the fact that someone was standing over her. There was another flash of light – had they taken a picture of her? Her eyes were swimming with blood and tears, it was hard to tell. Natalie could just make a figure dressed all in black as it knelt down beside her and carefully sifted through objects from the destroyed trophy cabinet.

Something glinted in the light – one of her mom's diamond tiaras. She wanted to beg for her life, but all that came out of her throat was a wet bubbling sound.

The last thing Natalie McRae saw was the tiara's brilliant gleam as her attacker raised it high into the air, and then everything went black.

Chapter Eight

Darla sat quietly in the backseat of the truck as Frank
drove it out of the school lot, battling a cranky stick
shift. Sasha had ignored Darla's polite attempts to
turn down her invitation, all but dragging her into
the truck. The spiky punk sat in the front passenger
seat fiddling with the radio, jumping from station
to station.

"Hey, stop!" said Frank. "I like that song!"

Sasha gave him a cold stare. "Franklin K
Matthews," she said, "you may be driving but this
is my vehicle, and while I have breath left in my
body, on no account will there be *any* country music
played in it. Understand?"

"Loud and clear," said Frank. "But at some stage,
you do realize you are going to have to accept that
you live in the South, don't you?"

"Maybe," Sasha accepted. "But not today."

Something about Sasha's defiant attitude and

look – and her beat-up truck, and her job in the record store – had made Darla assume she lived in the poorer neighbourhood of the town, somewhere close to her and Hopper. But to her surprise the pick-up headed up into the hills, its engine grumbling as it struggled up the steep road past all the expensive properties. Giving up on the radio in disgust, Sasha looked through the window at the glowering sky.

"Storm's coming in," she said.

"Good job we're here, then," replied Frank.

He turned into a driveway through a set of automatic gates, following the black tarmac as it swept around a grassy expanse towards the house. There was a swimming pool at the back, tables and chairs arranged neatly across a paved terrace. As Frank parked the pick-up in front of a twin garage, besides a bright yellow sports car, Darla gazed around in wonder.

"You really live here?"

"No, Darla, I'm training to be a realtor," Sasha said sarcastically. "Of *course* I live here. Come on inside."

She cut across the lawn towards the house,

stomping across the grass in her heavy boots. As Darla followed behind, Frank jogged up and slipped his arm through hers. Up close, Darla noticed that his eyes were a sparkling blue colour. He didn't look anything like Ryan or TJ, with their brash style and expensive clothes, but in his own quiet way Frank was almost as attractive.

"Not quite what you were expecting, is it?" he whispered. "No shabby trailer down by the creek for Sasha Haas, no sirree. She might prefer that, but her mom and pop have got used to a certain lifestyle, if you know what I mean…"

As she looked around at the immaculately manicured lawns, Darla couldn't imagine anyone who would prefer a trailer to this. She bet that Sasha had never had to put out buckets to catch the drips from a leaking ceiling, or chase raccoons away from her trash in the middle of the night.

The interior of the house was just as luxurious as the exterior, the entrance hall leading out into a huge open-plan living space with polished wooden floorboards and thick rugs. Bookshelves lined the walls, and a vast widescreen TV hung over the fireplace.

"Sasha, honey?" a woman's voice floated out from somewhere deep within the mansion. "Is that you?"

"Yes!" Sasha shouted back. "I'm going upstairs, don't bother coming out!"

She grabbed Darla's arm and quickly steered her up the stairs, stopping on the landing outside a door with a padlocked latch. Fishing out a small key from the depths of her bag, Sasha opened the padlock.

Inside the room the drapes were drawn, and it took Darla's eyes a few seconds to adjust to the gloom. Sasha's bedroom, she realized, was a complete mess. The floor was strewn with old clothes and plates with pizza slices and half-eaten sandwiches on them. There was no furniture, not even a bed — just a mattress in the corner of the room, the pillows strewn about and the covers thrown back, a pile of books, and a stack of records by an ancient-looking record player. The walls were covered in scrawled graffiti, slogans and song lyrics written in block capitals. There was no mirror; in its place Sasha had drawn a rectangular outline in marker pen on the wall and stuck a magazine cutout of a woman inside it. The woman

105

was beautiful, in a slightly haunted way, wearing thick black eye shadow and bright pink lipstick, her bare arms covered in tattoos. She looked like she might be famous, but Darla didn't recognize her.

"Welcome," said Sasha, collapsing on to her mattress. "Make yourself at home."

"Can we start by opening a window?" asked Frank, pinching his nose. "It smells like used gym socks in here."

Sasha shrugged. "Be my guest."

He pulled back the drapes and pushed open a window, allowing a welcome gust of fresh air inside the room. Darla moved an empty pizza box and sat on the floor, her back against the wall. Blobs of used chewing gum clung to the wall like tiny snails. She couldn't understand it. If Darla had been given a room in a beautiful house like this, she would have kept it neat and clean and fresh. Why had Sasha destroyed hers?

She glanced up again at the woman in the 'mirror'. It felt as though she was watching Darla.

"Her name's Brody Dalle." Sasha paused, waiting to see if Darla knew who that was. "She's a singer and guitarist. Her stuff's pretty cool."

"Oh," said Darla politely. "I don't know much about music."

"You and Frank should get on just fine, then." Sasha stretched out across the mattress. "So what's your story, Darla? Where are you from?"

"Round and about," Darla replied cautiously. "We move about a lot because of my daddy's work. Don't tend to stay in any place too long."

"You like Saffron Hills?"

"I guess. It's really pretty, all these amazing houses."

"Shame about the people who live inside them," Sasha replied. "Sorry for all the drama by the lockers today, that was a pretty rough introduction to the Picture Perfects."

Darla blinked. "The Picture Perfects?"

"Natalie and her friends," Frank explained. "It's how they're known."

"Know your enemy, Darla," Sasha said seriously. "Chief Perfect is Natalie McRae. She's from a super-rich family and her mom is a psycho ex-beauty queen who practically runs the local country club. Natalie's spent her whole life being told she's beautiful and better than everyone else and now she believes it. The other blonde is Carmen Russo. Her dad is the CEO of a cosmetics company who's made a fortune out of pressuring girls to look pretty. So maybe he got the daughter he deserved."

"How so?" asked Darla.

"I'm not saying Carmen's stupid, but she thinks a menstrual cycle is something you ride in the gym. Then there's Gabrielle Jones. Straight-A student. Member of the state girls' volleyball team. Sings at Pastor James's church every Sunday. In fact, Gabrielle's practically perfect in every way. Oh, apart from the fact she's a complete bitch."

"What about Ryan and TJ?" Darla said. "When I saw them at the mall, they were all hanging out together."

Sasha nodded. "Natalie and Swim Team have been going out since, like, whenever, and TJ Phillips is Ryan's best friend."

"They're jerks," said Darla, with feeling. "If I'm not good enough to even speak to TJ why did he take a photo with me? Just to mess with me?"

Frank and Sasha exchanged a glance. Then Sasha shrugged her shoulders, and pulled out a laptop from under her bedcovers. The laptop, Darla couldn't help noticing, was brand new and ultra sleek. It appeared that there was at least one expensive item Sasha didn't mind having. Her internet browser opened on her Instagram page, which was filled with selfies: Sasha standing in the front row of gigs; messing around with Frank, wearing his glasses; alone in her room, moodily staring back at the camera.

Sasha quickly moved to another Instagram page and handed Darla the laptop. The new site was filled with photographs of teenage girls – not girls like Natalie and Gabrielle and Carmen and Sasha. These were normal girls: overweight girls and girls with thick glasses and girls with frizzy hair.

Or, as the site called them, 'Plain Girls'.

In every photograph, either Ryan or TJ was standing with the girls, their arms draped around their shoulders. The girls had the same expression of startled amazement, as though they couldn't believe these good-looking guys were having their photo taken with them.

Which was the joke, of course.

Her heart sinking, Darla scrolled down to the second row. Sure enough, there was the selfie of her and TJ in the mall. She was squinting into the camera, her eyes half-closed and her mouth twisted into a weird grimace. Beside TJ's polished features, her face looked frecklier than ever, her ears sticking out through her hair. But even worse than the photo were the comments beneath it.

This dirt-eater has got it all over her face LOL!!!
Ugh.
Hillbillies don't wash: FACT.

Darla pushed the laptop away. No wonder she thought people had been whispering about her in class. She had been humiliated before she had even walked through the door.

"I don't understand," Darla said slowly. "Why would they do that?"

"Because they can," replied Sasha. "Because they're rich and good-looking and nobody ever tells them no. Because they're not very nice people. Look, I didn't want to make things worse for you, but I thought you should know."

"Yeah," Darla said hesitantly. "OK." What did Sasha want Darla to say to her – thanks?

110

Darla wasn't sure she was better off for knowing about Plain Girls, she certainly didn't *feel* any better. She stood up. "Listen, I have to go. Hopper will be wondering where I got to."

"I'll give you a ride home," said Frank.

Sasha nodded. "Take care of yourself, Darla," she said softly. "There are wolves in these hills."

She shut her computer and lay back on her mattress. As Frank and Darla went down the stairs, loud guitar music came crashing out from Sasha's room. A woman appeared in the hallway below. Like Sasha, she was strikingly pretty, with sharp cheekbones and cropped dark hair.

"Hey, Patti," Frank said easily. "Just taking Darla here home."

Mrs Haas peered up the staircase toward them. "Where's Sasha? It's nearly time for dinner."

"She's in her room," Frank replied, pointing back toward Sasha's bedroom door. "Don't you remember saying hello when we got in?"

Patti looked vague for a second. The she smiled quickly. "Well now, of course I do, Franklin. You kids come in and out so often, it's just hard to keep track sometimes." She nodded toward the window.

"You drive carefully, now. It's raining."

As Patti disappeared off into the kitchen, Darla shot Frank a questioning look.

"She's fine," he whispered. "Sometimes she can zone in and out a bit."

The storm clouds had brought a premature evening to Saffron Hills. Raindrops were hammering down on to the driveway, and even though they ran to the pick-up truck Darla's clothes were wet through by the time she had climbed into the passenger seat. Frank took off his glasses and wiped them dry, running a hand through his damp hair. He turned on the engine and sent the wipers creaking across the windshield, before reversing the pick-up out of the driveway.

"So do you live around here too?" Darla asked him.

Frank snorted. "Hardly. I live on the budget side of town. But I spend most nights at Sasha's."

Darla's eyes widened. "Her parents let you?"

"Let me? They positively beg me to stay over. Occasionally I even persuade Sasha to come out of her room and talk to them."

Darla couldn't imagine Hopper being so relaxed about a boy staying over at their place, but then again she wasn't sure there was anything going on between Frank and Sasha. They were thick as thieves, but there was nothing romantic about the way they were with each other – more like best friends, with a host of secrets that they knew and weren't going to share with anyone else.

"So this is Sasha's truck?" Darla said. "Don't you get bored driving her about all the time?"

Frank shrugged. "I haven't got a ride, and it's not like Sasha can drive. A few months back the rent-a-cops caught her behind the wheel with a forty of bourbon. Her pop's some kind of high-powered lawyer, and he managed to persuade them to keep it off her record on the understanding that she wouldn't drive for a year."

"Really?"

"That's how things work in Saffron Hills," Frank told her. "If you've got money, there ain't much you can't get away with."

"Explains a lot about the people around here," Darla said dryly.

"I know what you mean, but let me tell you a little secret about Sasha," Frank said. "As hard as she tries, and as much as she wants to be … she's not a *total* bitch."

Darla giggled.

"There are even times – brief moments, admittedly – when she's almost nice," Frank continued. "I remember once— Hey!"

A pair of headlights exploded out of the gloom, shining right in their eyes and dazzling them. Frank swerved to the side of the road, the pick-up's tyres skidding in the wet. A red truck hurtled past them through the darkness, its engine growling like a creature on the prowl. Sasha's warning echoed in Darla's head: *There are wolves in these hills…*

"Who the heck was that?" muttered Frank. "That was *not* cool."

Darla barely heard him. They had come to a stop outside a set of long railings in front of a mansion. The electronic gate was wide open, the building behind it shrouded in darkness. But Darla recognized it at once. During her vision in Annie's backyard, there had been a series of photographs of the mansion in the eerie album – the single lit window in the darkness, the flash of bright blond hair. Someone had been watching this house.

"Whose house is that?" she asked quietly.

114

"That's Natalie's place," Frank told her. "The Picture Perfect Palace."

"The gate's open," said Darla.

"So?" said Frank.

She stared at the house. Maybe it was all just a coincidence – her vision, this house, the red truck hurtling out of the rain. It was just an open gate, there was no reason to think that anything was wrong. So why was her skin crawling as though she was covered in a thousand tiny insects?

Darla opened the truck door.

"I'll be back in a second," she said.

"Wait, what?"

She was already out of the truck, hurrying through the rain towards the McRae house. As she slipped through the open gate, Frank jumped out and chased her up the path.

"Are you crazy?" he called out. "Come back!"

Darla couldn't have explained if she'd wanted to. But the terrible feeling that something was wrong wouldn't leave her. Her clothes were wet through by the time she had reached the shelter of the porch, rain hammering down upon the eaves. As she reached for the doorbell Frank caught up with her.

"You're going to call on *Natalie McRae*?" He laughed in disbelief. "Are you kidding me? You do remember her, right — tall girl? Blond? Composed entirely of evil?"

"Wait in the truck if you want," Darla said.

He muttered something under his breath, but didn't move. Darla pressed the doorbell, a melodic chime ringing out. No one came to answer. She cautiously tried the handle, and the door swung open.

"Hello?" she called out. "Natalie? Y'all home?"

The hall was dark, the only sound an electronic beeping coming from a box on the nearby wall. Shards of glass covered the floor around the foot of the stairs. Everything about the stillness of the house was wrong. Glancing at Frank, Darla stepped inside the hall. A piercing alarm went off, electronic shrieks of distress echoing through the mansion. The lights blinked on above Darla's head as she hurried towards the stairs, only to stop and stare in horror at the scene before her.

Natalie McRae was strung up in the shattered remains of a display cabinet, her wrists tied with silk pageant sashes and her arms jutting out awkwardly at her side. She was dressed in a flowing red ballgown, her bare arms covered in cuts and scratches and her beautiful face disfigured by a wicked diagonal cut across her nose and cheek. She looked like a broken doll on puppet strings. Behind her, a series of old photographs of a smiling and victorious beauty queen were now flecked with Natalie's blood. Something was protruding out of her chest. Bile rose in Darla's throat when she realized what it was.

A diamond tiara.

Chapter Nine

The next few hours were a nightmarish blur. Darla remembered a hand on her arm – Frank, his face as white as a sheet, dragging her out of the McRae house. She stood in the rain, staring vacantly into space as he threw up in the bushes. Suddenly the hills were alive with flashing blue lights – Darla later learned that the local security guards had been automatically alerted when the McRae's alarm went off. But there was nothing they could do now. There was nothing anyone could do. Someone wrapped a blanket around Darla as she sat on the kerb. Voices asked her questions. She wasn't sure what she said back. All she could think about was Natalie's body hanging inside the display cabinet, the malice and the effort it must have taken to arrange her just so.

Darla and Frank were driven to the local police station down on the strip, where they were split up and Darla was taken to a room with mirrors running the length of the wall. She avoided her own reflection, suddenly scared what else she might see. Someone gave her coffee; she didn't drink it, but she remembered the feeling of the warm polystyrene cup in her hands. There were more questions, men scribbling her replies down in their notepads. Finally the door to the interview room opened and Hopper appeared, his eyes glancing warily towards the long mirror and whoever might be watching them from the other side.

"You all right, darlin'?" he asked.

Darla nodded quickly. She knew that her daddy wouldn't want to spend a second longer in the police station than he had to — fortunately the questions had ended for now, and they were allowed to leave. Hopper drove home slowly through the teeming rain, deep puddles forming on the creek road. Darla was glad when their house came into view, lights burning brightly in the front window. When Hopper parked the car and turned off the engine she didn't move, her brain whirring as she gazed towards the lights.

Darla looked up to find Hopper studying her

thoughtfully. "Something on your mind?"

"It's nothing," she said quickly.

"You sure? You've had a hell of a fright, darlin', a *hell* of a fright. I can't believe what's happened. It's a terrible tragedy. And if there's anything you want to talk about, that's what I'm here for."

"It's just…" Darla hesitated. "Before we went by Natalie's house, this red truck came shooting past us, shining the headlights right into our eyes. It reminded me of when we came to Saffron Hills that first morning, and that guy who nearly ran us off the road."

"I believe the man's name was Leeroy Mills," Hopper said.

"What if it was him again? Luis said he lived in a trailer down by the creek – what was he doing up in the hills?"

"No crime in driving down a road, Darla, no matter how rich the neighbourhood."

"I know, but—"

"Luis said Leeroy had a record, right? Listen, the first thing the cops are going to do is pay a visit to all the known criminals in the area and see if they can put them near the McRae house. If Leeroy was hanging around they'll find out and he'll be in a jail cell before the end of the week. Trust me on this one."

A nasty thought occurred to Darla. "What about you, Daddy? The cops won't come looking for you, will they?"

"I sincerely hope not, darlin'," Hopper replied. "I ain't never done anything that could make a man think I'd kill a girl. But it might be an idea to try to keep a low profile from now on. Both of us."

He squeezed her hand.

"Come on," he said. "We can't sit out here all night."

All of a sudden Darla felt utterly exhausted, as though her insides had been scooped out. She went to her room and climbed into bed fully dressed. But her mind was racing too fast to sleep, and an hour later she heard Hopper creep out of the house. Darla was still awake when he came back, announcing his return with the familiar fumble of the key in the lock, muffled swearing and clinking bottles.

The next day Darla got up late and didn't go to school, while a bleary-eyed Hopper called in sick. They sat on the couch, watching TV in silence.

A breezy knock on her bedroom door woke Darla up the next morning. Hopper came into her room, fiddling with his tie, and pushed open the drapes.

"Rise and shine, Darla!" he said. "Day's a wastin'!"

He was acting cheerily but Darla knew that it was just a façade. It was the day after the day after; Hopper *always* felt guilty then.

"I don't feel well," Darla said feebly.

"Ain't takin' no for an answer. Come on."

He hauled Darla out of bed, guiding her towards the bathroom and shutting the door behind her.

"Don't forget to scrub between your toes!" he called through the door, as if she was a little girl.

As she showered Darla dreamed up morbid ways she might avoid having to go to school. Hopper could crash the Buick on the way, killing them both. There might be a bomb scare; the West Academy might actually blow up. Or maybe someone might stumble across a body in the classroom... Darla shook her head. It was too horrible to think about. When she had dressed she came out of her room to find Hopper waiting impatiently for her.

"I was going to offer you a ride to school," he said, peering out of the window. "But it looks like someone already beat me to it."

When Darla trudged over to the window, she saw Sasha's black pick-up parked outside their front lawn. Frank was sitting behind the wheel, engrossed in a book, while Sasha sunned herself on top of the truck, her back against the windshield. She was wearing a pair of large sunglasses, an oversized plaid shirt and denim shorts, her bare legs stretching out across the hood.

"Well, I'll be damned," said Hopper. "That's the girl from the record store, isn't it? Is she a friend of yours now?"

"I don't know," Darla replied truthfully. "Maybe."

"Good for you. Can't never have too many friends – even if they are, you know, psychos." Hopper clicked his fingers. "I almost forgot," he said. "Annie, the artist lady across the road – I invited her round to dinner tomorrow night."

Darla blinked with surprise. "Really?"

"Looks like we might be here for a while, so no harm in making nice with the neighbours. But make sure you're here in good time. I don't want her thinking I'm trying to romance her on the sly."

"Why ever would she think that, Daddy?" Darla said innocently. "She doesn't know you yet."

Hopper left the house, and she watched through the window as he marched down the path and unlocked the Buick.

"Morning, folks," he called out to Frank and Sasha. "Darla'll be out in just a moment."

Sasha flicked him a lazy salute.

Darla waited until Hopper had driven away before grabbing her schoolbag and heading outside. The sun was a yellow disc in a cloudless blue sky, the trees alive with birdsong. It seemed impossible that this could be the same town where a girl had been brutally murdered.

"Hey," said Sasha, slipping down from the hood.

"What are y'all doing here?" asked Darla. "How did you find me?"

"It was easy," Frank said airily. "We just followed the trail of blood and dismembered body parts."

Sasha pushed up her sunglasses and stared at him. "Really?" she said.

He looked a little sheepish. "Too soon?"

"Maybe a little," Darla said.

"You gotta admit, Darla, as first days go, that was *pretty* intense," said Sasha. "When you didn't show up at school yesterday Frank got worried, so we thought we'd swing by and see how you were doing."

"Hey!" Frank protested. "You were worried too!"

"I was concerned," corrected Sasha. "There is a difference, Franklin."

"Does everyone know?" Darla asked them. "You know, about Natalie?"

Sasha laughed incredulously. "Does everyone *know*? The Prom Queen In Waiting was savagely murdered in her own home, Darla — so yeah, it's cropped up in the occasional conversation."

"School was unbelievable yesterday," added Frank, with a hint of ghoulish glee. "Guys arguing, girls running crying through the halls. Everyone talking about angels and…"

Sasha shot him a warning look, and he fell silent. Darla couldn't help thinking back to the moments after they had found Natalie's body — Frank throwing up in the bushes outside the McRae's house, his face as pale as a ghost. She wondered if he was really being insensitive, or whether it was just an act to show Sasha that he hadn't been scared. Either way, she was too grateful that they had come to pick her up to say anything.

As soon as they pulled up outside the West Academy, Darla knew she was in for a long day. Heads instantly swivelled in her direction. Mouths dropped open. In the halls, in the homeroom, people openly stared at her, nudging one another and whispering behind their hands. It was like her first day all over again – only ten times worse.

"I guess people know it was Frank and me who found the body, then," Darla said to Sasha.

"Ignore them," she replied breezily. "That's what I always do."

After homeroom the entire school was summoned to the gym for an emergency assembly. Darla huddled between Sasha and Frank on the top bleacher, wishing she could melt like ice through the cracks in the seats and flow out of the gym. It looked like the entire teaching faculty had taken seats behind a microphone stand set up in the middle of the court. Darla caught a glimpse of Annie: the art teacher was gazing off into the distance, her hands clasped together in her lap. After a couple of minutes Principal Bell entered the gym and took the microphone. His face was drawn, and he hadn't shaved that morning. He began to talk gravely about Natalie's death – careful, Darla noted, not to use the word 'murder'. It was a terrible shock, a tragedy. Grief counsellors would be available for any student who wanted to talk about what had happened. The West Academy would be closed the following day to enable any students who wished to attend Natalie's funeral to do so. Principal Bell shuffled his notes, and coughed.

"Now," he said. "I'm aware that there are lurid rumours going around the school about exactly what took place on Wednesday night. Please, I'd like you all to think about Natalie's family and friends. They've suffered enough with this tragic loss without malicious gossip causing them further distress."

The principal dismissed them, and the students began to file out of the bleachers. As Darla went down the steps someone shoved her in the shoulder, pushing her into Frank.

"Hey!" she said.

Gabrielle was standing on the step behind her, her hands on her hips and a cold expression on her face. Behind her TJ had wrapped a protective arm around Carmen, whose eyes were red-rimmed with tears. Ryan's face was pale, his knowing smile extinguished. But if anything, their grief had only made them look even more beautiful, lending an elegant shadow to their perfect faces.

Sasha stepped quickly in front of Darla.

"Back off, Gabrielle."

"I just want to make sure your little friend heard what the principal said," said Gabrielle. "She needs to stop talking about Natalie. Have you heard what people have been saying – that Natalie was stabbed with her mom's tiara? It's disgusting!"

"It's a pretty creepy way to try to make yourself popular, Darla," added Carmen. "You want to watch yourself."

"I didn't say nothing!" Darla shot back.

"We know it was you and Frank who found her," said Gabrielle. "It must have been one of you."

"Is that a fact?" Frank retorted. "And what about the cops? You think maybe one of them might have had a few beers and started talking?"

"Listen, ladies," said Sasha. "Go shake some pompoms, get a pedicure, buy some shoes – whatever it is you do when you need to calm down. But leave Darla alone."

Gabrielle turned angrily to Ryan. "Are you going to let her speak to us like that?"

He rubbed his face wearily. "I can't deal with this right now," he said. "Fight all you want. I'm out of here."

Ryan pushed his way through the crowd and down the steps, leaving the rest of the group to hurry after him. As Darla watched the four Perfects leave the hall, her cheeks burning with the injustice of it all, she felt Sasha drape an arm around her shoulder.

"Don't let them get to you," she said. "They're just looking for someone to blame."

"Glad I could help out," Darla said bitterly. "I'm telling you right now, I ain't going to Natalie's funeral. If the Perfects are telling people it was me going around gossiping, everyone there's going to hate me!"

"That's entirely possible," agreed Sasha. "Which is why *we're* not going to be anywhere near it."

"You heard the principal," said Frank. "School is

closed. Why waste it going to a funeral?"

"OK," Darla said slowly. "So where *are* we going, then?"

Sasha grinned.

Chapter Ten

The next day, Darla woke to a strange scratching noise coming from below her room. Rubbing sleep from her eyes, she padded down the stairs and into the kitchen to find Hopper scrubbing away at the worktops. He had rolled up his shirtsleeves and put on a pair of bright yellow kitchen gloves, his leather jacket hanging from a peg on the back of the door.

"There's coffee in the pot," he told Darla.

"Great. How long have you been up?"

"A while," replied Hopper. "I wanted to make sure the place was shipshape before Annie came round tonight. Don't want her thinking we're hillbillies, do we?"

"She's an artist, Daddy," said Darla, pouring herself a mug of coffee. "She'd probably love it if we were hillbillies. We could be the subjects of her next artwork."

Hopper looked up sharply. "Don't you go spilling

anything on my nice clean surfaces now," he warned.

Darla hid a smile. Hopper wouldn't think twice about walking up to a pretty woman in the street and asking for her number, but the prospect of a neighbour coming round for dinner had turned him into a bundle of nerves. She yawned, blowing the steam from the surface of her black coffee.

"Shouldn't you be getting ready for school?" Hopper asked her.

"I told you last night," she said. "It's the funeral today. School's closed."

"Oh. Right." Glancing up at the clock, Hopper peeled off the rubber gloves and rolled his sleeves down. "I'm goin' to be late, darlin'. Gotta rush." He kissed the top of her head as he hurried out of the house. "See you tonight!" he called out, as the screen door banged shut behind him.

Darla finished her coffee in the backyard, wandering barefoot through the tangled grass and listening to the gentle trickle of the creek. By the time she had showered and slipped into a T-shirt and jeans it was well after ten – the funeral would soon be starting. In her bedroom, Darla avoided the blank gaze of the ornate mirror on the wall. It was bad enough that she saw Natalie's maimed corpse every time she closed her eyes, without worrying that she might be taken back to the sinister dark room and the hateful presence that lived there. Even worse was the gnawing sense of guilt that she should have gone to the cops and tried to tell them that someone was watching the McRae house. Maybe if she had, Natalie would still be alive.

Outside in the lane, a car horn beeped. Hurrying out of the house, Darla saw Sasha's pick-up parked outside her gate. She ran over and got in the back. Frank and Sasha were dressed somberly – Frank in a dark suit and sunglasses and Sasha in an unusually conservative blouse and knee-length skirt. Darla had a moment of sudden panic. Had they changed their minds? Were they going to the funeral after all?

"Relax, Darla," said Sasha. "We had to put the uniforms on to slip past the guards at Castle Haas."

"But if you think *we're* dressed up, you ain't seen nothing yet," Frank said slyly. "Show Darla the picture, Sasha."

Sasha passed her phone to Darla. On the screen was Carmen Russo's Instagram page, the most recent photo showing her sitting at her dressing table. She was wearing a velvet black dress with lace trim and a cardigan, a silver crucifix glinting around her neck and a large pair of dark glasses covering her eyes. Beneath the photo, Carmen had written: '#Beautifulgoodbye' and '#SleeptightNataliexxx'.

"Just when you thought it was safe to go to the cemetery," Frank boomed, in a dramatic movie-trailer voice. "Along comes the funeral selfie."

"Hashtag: Gross," muttered Sasha.

Darla handed back the phone and wound down her window, feeling the breeze run its fingers through her hair. At the main strip the pick-up turned right, heading away from the heart of the town and bouncing up a series of dirt tracks into the hills.

"We're taking the scenic route, OK?" Frank told Darla, his blue eyes glancing into the rearview mirror. "Don't want to run into anyone wondering why we're not at the funeral."

No one seemed willing to tell Darla where they were headed, but she knew better than to ask. She was the New Girl – it was her role to follow Frank and Sasha around and to be surprised and amazed by whatever they showed her. So she sat quietly and looked out of the window at the woods and the crisscrossing pony trails. The pick-up rattled past the entrance to the Saffron Hills Country Club, a set of imposing gates barring off a paved driveway. The road grew bumpier.

Finally Frank parked the pick-up in a patch of scrubland on the edge of the woods. He stretched as he got out, scanning the area through his sunglasses as Sasha kicked off her shoes with a sigh of relief and hopped barefoot into the dirt. They linked arms and headed down the hillside into the trees. Darla followed behind, stepping over snagging roots and skirting around stinging plants. The heat seemed to thicken amongst the pines, sweat trickling down her back. Leaves rustled with unseen creatures. A sudden flap of wings startled Darla; she glanced up to see a bird climbing into the air. The chirrup of the crickets was deafening.

Ahead of her, a set of rusted railings rose out of the undergrowth. Moving quickly, with the ease of someone who had come this way many times before, Frank cut through the weeds and pushed aside a giant fern, revealing a yawning gap in the railings. He ducked down and slipped through,

Darla following closely behind. Sasha, taller than both of them and struggling in her skirt, cursed loudly as she caught her blouse on a rusty railing.

"I *told* you to bring a change of clothes," Frank told her.

"What are you, my mother?" retorted Sasha. She inspected the hole in her sleeve. "If anyone asks, I caught it on one of Carmen's earrings, OK?"

Frank snickered in reply.

The plants were even wilder on this side of the railings, and Darla found herself wading through waist-high grass. Gradually a house emerged from the thick greenery. It was a sprawling, dilapidated building with smashed windows, jagged glass teeth jutting up from the sills. Flies hung in clouds among the rusting ceiling fans and rotten balustrades on the second-floor balcony. Nesting wood pigeons fluttered around the eaves, vanishing through the missing roof tiles into the darkness within. Creepers wrapped sinuous green fingers around the walls, trying to drag them down into the earth. The entire building was shrouded in fading grandeur and dying dreams.

Frank and Sasha went straight to the nearest

window, where Darla saw the glass had been cleared from the sill and a crate had been placed on the ground beneath it. This time Sasha took the lead, using the crate as a stepping stone as she hopped through the window. Darla hesitated, glancing up at the building's grim façade before climbing up on to the sill and disappearing inside.

It was like plunging into a dank, chill pond. Darla could almost taste the mould in the air inside the house. Browning wallpaper peeled off the walls like dead skin, white rectangles shining where paintings and photographs had once hung. Plants and weeds poked up through the floor, and as they wandered through the mansion's gloomy corridors Darla had the eerie sensation that she was moving around inside the trunk of some unimaginably vast tree. She stayed close to Sasha and Frank, carefully skirting the splattered bird droppings and rotten holes in the floorboards. Finally they came into a vast dining room, dominated by a long table that was chipped and covered in knife scars. Sasha collapsed into a seat at the head of the table, draping a leg over the mahogany. She produced a small hip flask from her skirt pocket and took a sip.

"Sasha, it's still morning!" said Frank, appalled. "Do I need to take you to a meeting?"

"TGI Friday, Frank," she replied, raising her flask in a toast.

He rolled his eyes.

When Sasha offered her the flash, Darla shook her head. "No, thanks."

"Suit yourself."

Darla took a seat at the table, the rotten chair groaning and teetering beneath her weight. She ran her hands over her bare arms, trying to brush away the goosebumps.

"Welcome to Tall Pines," Sasha announced grandly, throwing out her arms. "Make yourself at home."

Darla shivered. "What is this place?"

"Once upon a time, it was the most luxurious property in the county," Frank told her. "It belonged to Allan and Madeline West, the first couple of Saffron Hills. This whole town is founded on West money: the mansions in the hills, the school, the hospital. Allan built it all, and then persuaded a bunch of other rich people to come live here. His son Walter went to the

West Academy – he was like the Ryan Cafferty of the mid-1990s: wealthy, popular, good-looking. Everything seemed perfect." Frank smiled thinly. "Then one day they pulled a girl out of the creek. Her name was Crystal – Miss Saffron, 1995. Her skull had been caved in with a blunt instrument. It turned out that she was a classmate of Walter's, and that he'd invited her up to Tall Pines to take some pictures of her. Only things had gotten a little out of hand: he beat her to death halfway through the shoot."

Darla's stomach lurched. Once more she was staring through a killer's eyes at a photograph album filled with screaming faces. "But why? Why did he kill her?"

"At first no one could figure it out. But when the cops searched Walter's locker at school they found a diary filled with some pretty sick stuff. He wrote pages about trying to photograph beautiful things, only it turned out that he found a dead beauty queen prettier than a live one. After he killed Crystal, Walter started to call himself the Angel Taker, and drew pictures of wings all over his diary."

"A dead beauty queen," Darla repeated faintly. She looked up at Frank. "Everyone said Natalie was going to be the new Miss Saffron, and now she's... I mean, it couldn't be the same guy, could it? Walter couldn't have come back?"

"Not from where's he's gone," Frank replied. "The cops were on their way here to question him when Walter's dad found him dangling from a rope under one of the pines out back – I guess Walter knew he wouldn't get to photograph any more angels in jail. After his funeral Allan and Madeline became recluses, wouldn't leave Tall Pines. Then, on the tenth anniversary of Walter's death, they locked themselves in the garage and turned on the car engine. It was two months before anyone found their bodies."

"So as you can see, there is some seriously bad voodoo about this place," said Sasha, taking another sip from her flask. "Which makes it perfect for us."

"But if this Walter guy is dead," Darla asked, "who killed Natalie?"

Frank laughed. "Jesus, Darla, how should I know?"

"Maybe we could hold a séance and ask Natalie

herself," Sasha suggested. "Call up the hotline to hell."

The table fell silent.

"What?" Sasha said defensively. "Look, what happened to Natalie was horrible, and I hope they catch the whack-job who did it. Just don't ask me to start crying and pretending like we were best friends, because we weren't. Truth was, she thought everyone outside her little circle of friends was some kind of inferior product. You want to know why most of the people in this town are so upset? Because their precious beauty pageant is ruined. Natalie was going to be Miss Saffron just like her mommy before her, and everyone was going to be happy. But it's not like they can make the contestants wear black swimsuits in mourning, is it?"

Frank frowned. "Do they even wear swimsuits at pageants now?"

"Of course not," she said irritably. "I was *trying* to make a point. All these pageants are about is putting pretty teenage girls on stage and having a bunch of dirty old men stare at them and judge them. It's sick."

Frank waved dismissively. "You're no fun sometimes, you know that? It's harmless! You know what would be fun? *You* should enter."

Sasha stared at him. "Me."

"Why not? I think you'd look simply divine in sequins, darling."

Darla tried to imagine Sasha standing on stage in a pretty frock, making a speech about world peace. She laughed.

Sasha gave her a sharp look. "Something funny, Darla?"

"Not really," she said. "I just can't imagine you in a beauty pageant, that's all."

"I'm guessing your family would be experts on girls, wouldn't they?" said Sasha.

"What do you mean by that?"

"Put it this way: Hopper gave me a pretty thorough inspection when I was waiting outside your house yesterday morning."

"You were sunbathing on the hood of your truck!" said Darla. "What was he supposed to do, ignore you? Can we drop it, please?"

But Sasha didn't want to drop it. "It seems to me that you're in denial about your darling daddy," she said. "Don't you remember how he talked to me at the record store?"

"He was just trying to be friendly," Darla said stubbornly. "He don't mean nothing by it. You were the one being rude."

"It was *my* fault? He was hitting on me right in front of you!"

"Stop it! Don't say that!"

"He's a creep!"

"Go to hell!" shouted Darla.

Pigeons fluttered up from the rafters in surprise as Darla sprang up from her chair and stormed out of the dining room, her footfalls thudding on the rotting floorboards. She was looking for the window they had climbed through but the labyrinth of corridors confused her – pushing open a door, she found herself at the top of a set of basement steps. Darla went to turn back, only to hear Frank's voice calling her name from the corridor outside. Closing the door as quietly as possible, Darla crept down the stairs. She needed space, room to think and catch her breath. More than anything, she needed to be where Sasha wasn't.

The basement was wrapped in shadow, a thin ray

of sunlight slicing down through a window high up on the wall. Cobwebs gathered in the corners. The room was empty, save for an old desk and a couch in which a family of possums was nesting. Darla flicked the light switch but the bulb stayed dark. There were photographs hanging on the wall near her hand – she brushed the cobwebs away from the frames and found herself staring at a series of eerily beautiful landscapes. Photographs. This must have been Walter West's old studio. Was this where he had killed Crystal? Almost against her will, Darla's eyes flicked towards the flagstones, searching for faded bloodstains. She had to remember what Frank had told her – Walter West had been dead for twenty years. But it didn't make Darla feel any easier about creeping through his old house.

As she stepped back from the photographs she knocked into a desk, dislodging an object that had been wedged between it and the wall. Crouching down, Darla pulled free a book and wiped the thick layer of dust from the cover. It was a photograph album. Her chest tightened. What if this was like the albums she had seen in her visions, filled with photographs of screaming faces?

She took a deep breath and opened the album. Her shoulders slumped with relief at the sight of bright teenage faces smiling back at her: in the bleachers at the school football game; sitting on the lawns behind the West Academy; at a pool party in one of Saffron Hills' mansions. Snapshots of normal, happy lives. But when Darla turned over the page and saw the next photograph, her heart stuttered. A pretty teenage girl in a riding outfit was standing in front of the Saffron Hills Country Club, holding on to a pony's reins.

It wasn't possible. She was imagining it.

Voices were calling out her name upstairs but the noise was muffled, as though she was underwater. Darla looked at the photograph again. She wasn't imagining it. She wasn't confused. She could never confuse this face, with its soft eyes and flowing blond hair. The face of Sidney O'Neill.

Her mom.

Chapter Eleven

Darla wriggled out of Tall Pines through the basement window, her mom's photograph clutched in her hot palm. As she stumbled through the grass in search of the gap in the railings, she could hear Frank and Sasha's voices still echoing inside the mansion. Darla didn't care. Sasha might have pretended to be different, but deep down she was just like everyone else in Saffron Hills — spoiled, selfish and cruel.

When she came to the rusted railings Darla squeezed through the gap, brushing the fern out of the way on the other side. She ran into the woods, no idea where she was going or in which direction lay the way out. Stumbling over a tree root, Darla fell to the ground, banging her elbow on a rock. There were tears in her eyes and she was gasping for breath. She pushed herself into a sitting position and stared at the photograph, still unable to believe that

Sidney had once stood outside the Country Club, not ten minutes' walk from where Darla was now. The thought made Darla's heart ache.

Troubling questions ran through her mind, one after the other. Why did Walter West have a photograph of her mom in his basement? Had she known the Angel Taker – had they been friends? Whatever had happened to her mom in Saffron Hills, could it explain why she had chosen to kill herself rather than live on with her family? Beneath the pain, Darla felt anger bubbling inside of her. Not just with Sasha and Frank, but Hopper too. No wonder he had acted strangely back in the diner, when he had first discovered that they were in Saffron Hills. He knew Sidney had been here. Darla could have screamed with frustration. Why hadn't Hopper told her? Couldn't he be honest about *anything*?

Darla walked for hours in maddening circles through the woods, lost among the pines and the turmoil of her own thoughts. She was so mad she almost didn't care whether she found her way out or not. When Darla finally did emerge from the trees back on to the strip, the horizon was beginning to darken. She had spent the whole afternoon stumbling around the woods. Her feet were aching in her flip-flops and her arms were blotchy from the poisonous kiss of stinging nettles, and it was a relief when the turning for the creek road came into view and she could see their house halfway down the lane.

Hopper darted out of the kitchen as Darla pushed through the front door. He had shaved and slicked his hair into style, looking sharp in a freshly ironed shirt and jeans. The house was filled with the warm aroma of pasta bake. Of course – Annie was coming round for dinner. Darla had completely forgotten.

"What time d'you call this?" said Hopper. "I asked you not to be late."

"I got lost," Darla said abruptly. She wasn't in the mood for being shouted at. Not today.

"Lost? What kind of sorry-assed excuse is that? Look at the state of you! Where was the funeral, Darla, down a mine?"

"No."

"So where've you been?"

"Nowhere."

Hopper pointed at her. "We're going to have a little talk about this later, missy, but there ain't time

148

now. Go on and get showered and changed."

Too late: the doorbell rang. Hopper hurried over to answer it, ushering Annie into the house. She was wearing a loose-flowing gypsy skirt and a blouse overlaid with strings of beads.

"How are y'all doing?" said Annie, smiling brightly at Darla. She handed Hopper a white oven dish. "I brought pie. I was going to pretend I baked it myself, but it's from the shop. Don't tell anyone," she confided in a whisper, "but I'm a terrible cook."

"You'll be right at home here, then," Hopper said. "I've been sweating away in the kitchen like a man on death row, but God only knows what's coming out of that oven."

Annie laughed. "I'm sure it will be delicious," she said.

"Come on through," Hopper told Annie. "Darla, honey, at least brush the cobwebs out of your hair before you come to the table."

Darla went into the bathroom and washed her face and hands, muttering under her breath. It wasn't fair that Hopper was making jokes about her; it wasn't fair that Annie had dressed up prettily and was being nice to him. He was a liar and a drunk.

Darla tossed her hairbrush to one side, deciding that the cobwebs could stay where they were. She came into the kitchen to find that Hopper had put a cloth over the table and lit candles. It looked like a photograph of someone else's life – a warmer, happier household.

Hopper was rummaging through the fridge. "I've got water and I've got soda," he called out to Annie. "Which would you prefer? I'm afraid we haven't got anything stronger."

"Makes a change," Darla snorted.

Hopper gave her a sidelong glance, but said nothing.

"Water would be fine, thank you," said Annie.

Darla sat down at the table and folded her arms. The kitchen fell into an awkward silence as Hopper poured water for everyone and dished out the pasta bake. The pasta was burnt around the edges and there was too much chilli but Annie insisted it was lovely. Darla pushed the food around her plate with her fork. She wasn't hungry at all.

"So, Annie..." Hopper said. "Darla tells me you're an artist. Ain't never met an artist before." He grinned. "Coupla con artists, maybe, but I wouldn't trust them with no paintbrush."

"Y'all should come visit my gallery in town," Annie told him. "It's only small but we've got some interesting pieces."

"I'm afraid I don't know much about art," said Hopper.

"You don't have to, I promise!" she laughed. "All you have to do is look and ask yourself how the pieces make you feel — there's no right or wrong answer."

"Well, OK then," said Hopper. "Maybe I'll come down on my lunch break. I work over at the music store."

"Great!" Annie said brightly. "How's business?"

"Pretty slow today, pretty sombre. Ain't many people wanting to buy guitars when they're putting a young girl in the ground."

"Of course," said Annie. "I was at Natalie's funeral today with the rest of the school. I looked out for you, Darla, but I didn't see you." She reached out and patted her hand. "I know it was you who found her body, honey. That must have been so awful."

Darla shrugged.

"Like something outta a nightmare," Hopper said gravely. "I'm just grateful my girl was OK."

"Oh, give it a rest, *please!*" snapped Darla.

Hopper and Annie stared at her, startled.

"I mean it, Hopper," she said, her voice rising. "Quit the act. Stop pretending to be Mr Perfect Dad. Who are you pretending for? Me? I know the truth. Annie? She's not some bimbo you picked up in a bar."

"That's enough, Darla!" shouted Hopper.

"Maybe I should go," Annie said delicately, folding up her napkin. "It's getting late."

Hopper hurriedly rose as she got up from the table. Darla stared moodily down at her plate, listening to their low tones in the hallway.

"I'm real sorry about this, Annie," she heard Hopper say. "Seems like every time we try to act like normal neighbours we make a god-awful mess of it."

Annie laughed. "It's all right, really. I had a lovely time."

"Now you're just making fun of me."

"I did! Maybe next time you'll both come to my house so I can return the favour."

"I'd like that, Annie," said Hopper. "And I know Darla would too – as soon as she stops being, you know, a teenage girl."

"I was once a teenage girl, too; I remember what that feels like," Annie told him. "Darla's had a terrible shock. Give her time – she'll be OK."

Darla heard the screen door close and then Hopper came back into the kitchen. He put his hands on his hips.

"You want to tell me what's going on?" he demanded.

"How about you tell *me* what's going on?" Darla shouted back. She took the folded photograph of her mom from her pocket and thrust it into Hopper's hands. He stared down at it, his eyes widening in amazement.

"Where in hell did you get this?"

"What does it matter?" Darla shot back. "You knew Mom used to live here, didn't you? That's why you tried to shut Luis up when we went to see him. Why didn't you tell me? Why, Daddy?"

"Why?" Hopper's voice was rising. "Because I'm your father and you're my daughter, and I'll tell you what I goddamn please!" he yelled.

Darla made a noise of disgust and stormed up the stairs to her room, slamming the door shut behind her. She threw herself down on her bed, punching her pillow in frustration. The house fell silent. Eventually there came a soft knock at Darla's door.

"Go away!" she shouted.

Hopper came in anyway, carefully placing Sidney's photograph on Darla's bedside table before taking a seat on the edge of her bed. He rubbed his face wearily.

"I've been trying to figure out a way to tell you," he said finally. "You prob'ly won't believe that, but it's the truth. I knew you'd be upset and I knew you'd have questions and I wasn't sure I had any answers for you. That night when we left the trailer park, I was concentrating so hard on losing Marvin that I didn't even realize we were heading to Saffron Hills. I woulda turned back right there at the diner, but then I saw the picture of Luis in the paper and I figured that maybe we had a shot at a way out of this mess."

"So you lied to me."

"It weren't *lying*, Darla, not exactly. OK, so I didn't meet Sidney in Charleston. I was playing with

154

a band at the arts centre here when I saw her. She wanted so badly outta this town it wasn't funny. We left together that night, and she didn't ever talk about Saffron Hills again. I didn't know who her family or her friends were, where she lived, where she hung out. Any time I tried to ask she'd change the subject. She was runnin' away from something, all right." Hopper scratched his cheek ruefully. "Had to be, to take up with a loser like me."

"You're not a loser," Darla said quietly.

"Yes, darlin', I am. Have been for as long as I can remember." Hopper glanced at Sidney's photograph on the bedside table. "I'd say it was losing your mom that did it, but I'm not sure that'd be true. But this time I'm serious about changing, I swear. I'm gonna kick the drinking and work hard at the music store, and maybe we can start to put the pieces back together. Kinda fitting if we could do that here. What do you say?"

Darla nodded.

"Sorry I didn't tell you about your mom," said Hopper.

"Sorry for ruining dinner," said Darla. "Annie's really nice."

"She's one classy lady — too classy for the likes of us." Hopper grinned. "She did leave us pie, though. You want to come through and have a slice? You barely touched your dinner."

Darla smiled. "OK."

She got up from her bed and followed Hopper back into the kitchen.

Chapter Twelve

Darla stayed in the house all weekend, watching TV as Hopper wrestled a rusty lawnmower around the backyard. Part of her wondered whether Sasha or Frank might drive down to see if she was OK, but there was no sign of their truck on the lane outside. Maybe they were too embarrassed – or maybe they hadn't really cared about her in the first place. Darla knew Sasha wasn't the only person who had behaved badly on Friday: she slipped a note underneath Annie's door apologizing for her behaviour over dinner, and immediately felt better about the world. By the time Hopper had finished with the mower the yard looked as good as new, and he celebrated with a lemonade rather than a beer afterwards. He *was* trying to be better, Darla thought, with an unexpected flicker of pride.

The thought of Monday morning cast an unwanted shadow over the weekend. Darla was dreading school more than ever. At least Sasha and Frank had helped to protect her from the Picture Perfects. Now it looked as though she was on her own again. Darla sat quietly in the passenger seat of the Buick as Hopper drove her to school, barely listening to his breezy chatter. She got out of the car and murmured goodbye, trudging up the school steps like a condemned prisoner.

As Darla headed through the crowded lockers to her homeroom, a voice called out behind her.

"Darla, wait up!"

It was Sasha. Darla kept walking.

"Hey, I said wait up!"

A hand grabbed her arm, forcing Darla to turn around. Sasha was dressed for war, in a combat fatigues shirt, black leggings and a pair of heavy army-issue boots – setting off her outfit with shocking pink lipstick. Over her shoulder she was carrying a knapsack covered in bright badges with band names on them.

"Please don't make me run any more than I have to," she pleaded, out-of-breath. "Not in these boots."

"Can I help you with something?" Darla said flatly.

Sasha sighed. "Look, back at Tall Pines," she said, awkwardly fingering the strap on her knapsack. "Frank tells me there was a *tiny* chance I was being a bitch to you."

"Frank was right."

"I know. I'm sorry. Sometimes my mouth just opens and all these things come out without me even realizing it. Kind of like I'm … I don't know… sleeptalking."

"I know Hopper's not perfect," Darla told her. "But if you just gave him a chance, maybe you'd see he was OK."

"I'll do that. Hey, the guy works in a music store – he can't be all bad, right? Friends again?"

Darla nodded. Life in Saffron Hills was hard enough without losing the only friends she had made.

"Excellent!" Sasha linked her arm through Darla's and marched her along the corridor. "And it just so happens I've got the perfect way we can celebrate. You know Ryan, Natalie's douche of a boyfriend? He's throwing a party tonight. OK, he's calling it a wake, but everyone else is calling it a party. We should go."

"Why?" said Darla. "I thought you didn't like Ryan."

"I don't. Hence why I call him a douche. But a party is a party, Darla, and I figure it's about time you actually had some fun in Saffron Hills. So what do you say?"

"I don't know," Darla said dubiously. "Is Frank going?"

Sasha gave her a level stare. "*That's* your answer? OK, I promise to bring Frank along."

"Wait. Don't Natalie's friends all hate me because they think I spread gossip about her?"

Sasha waved her hand dismissively. "Don't worry about *them*. I'll look after you. Tell your dad I've invited you to stay at my house afterwards. We'll pick you up, go to the party and then you can sleep over at mine. What could possibly go wrong?"

Lots of things, Darla retorted in her head. But she nodded. The bell echoed around the hall.

"Gotta rush," Sasha told her, untangling her arm. "Later, Darla."

Darla watched her friend stride away in her heavy boots. Sasha looked utterly fearless, ready to fight the world if need be.

To her surprise Darla did feel better for making up with Sasha, and her day at school didn't turn out to be as awful as she had feared. The students of the West Academy were still shaken by Natalie's death, but the poisonous atmosphere that had hung over the classrooms the previous week had lifted. Darla couldn't say that she was exactly looking forwards to Ryan's party, but maybe Sasha was right. If she and Hopper were going to stay in Saffron Hills, she should at least *try* to enjoy herself.

She wasn't sure what Hopper was going to say about her going to the 'wake' that evening, but if anything he seemed pleased that she had been invited.

"Sure you can go!" he said easily. "Just don't stay up too late. Remember it's a school night."

Darla nodded, trying not to think about all the years that Hopper had rolled back to their trailer in the middle of the night, dead drunk. What was the point in bringing it up now?

Frank and Sasha came by around eight to collect her, driving up into the hills. As the pick-up pulled up beside the gated entrance to Ryan's house, Darla noticed a red truck parked on the other side of the road, a cigarette end glowing inside the dark vehicle. Before Darla could say anything the truck's headlights flicked on, bathing them all in white light, and the vehicle roared away down the hill.

"Looks like someone didn't get their invite," said Frank.

Darla didn't laugh. All she could think about was the last time she and Frank had encountered a set of blinding headlights up in the hills. The roaring engine, an open gate; Natalie's dead body encased in broken glass.

She shook her head. It was just a truck – no point in getting paranoid. Sasha leaned over Frank and out of the window, pressing the intercom by the gates. A voice crackled out of the speaker.

"Who is it?"

"It's Sasha," she said, deadpan. "Open up or I'll kill you."

The gate swung open with a loud buzz. Frank parked the battered pick-up in the shadow of Ryan's huge three-storey house, beside a couple of open-top sports cars and an SUV.

"No valet parking?" he said, with feigned astonishment. "Standards are slipping round here."

"I'll tell Ryan's butler," Sasha replied.

The windows were dark inside Ryan's house, but as she climbed out of the truck Darla could hear music thudding out from the back. Sasha led them through an archway and down a narrow paved path along the side of the house. Lights glowed in the distance; shouts and laughter grew louder.

"I still don't know what I'm doing here," Darla whispered to Frank.

"Welcome to my world," Frank replied. "Sasha has a habit of making people do things they don't want to. You'll get used to it."

They came out on a wide terrace illuminated with strings of Chinese lanterns. About twenty people had gathered around the outdoor pool, splashing and whooping in the warm night air. The guys were bare-chested, wearing only board shorts, while the girls were dressed in bikini tops and cut-offs. Everywhere Darla looked, she saw long legs and flat stomachs. A sound system was pumping hip-hop beats through the open patio doors and out over the terrace. Immediately Sasha elbowed her way to the punch bowl, and returned carrying three plastic cups. She gave one to Frank and offered Darla another.

"No thanks," said Darla.

Sasha grinned. "All the more for me." She took a sip from the cup, and winced. "Ugh, this tastes like gasoline."

"You've *got* to be kidding me," a voice said acidly. "Who invited *you*?"

Her heart sinking, Darla turned round to find Carmen Russo staring at her, her blond hair tumbling gracefully down over her bare shoulders. Gabrielle was at Carmen's side, her eyes narrowed.

"Good evening, ladies," Frank said quickly. "Are we enjoying the party?"

Gabrielle ignored him. "This is a Hills party, Sasha," she said, with a pointed glance at Darla. "No Creekers allowed."

"Nobody told me," Sasha replied with a shrug.

"I didn't see you at the funeral," said Carmen. "Or your little friends. So what makes you think you can show up now?"

"It's not your house, Carmen – or your party,"

said Sasha. "Go shriek at someone who cares."

Carmen spun on her heel and stalked away. Gabrielle went after her friend, shooting Sasha a withering look as she left.

"That's what I love about you, Sasha," an amused male voice said behind her. "You're such a people person."

Ryan had just climbed out of the pool, and was rubbing himself down with a towel. Darla tried not to stare at the water droplets running down his bare, muscular chest. Even she had to admit he was gorgeous. Everyone here was.

"I get on with *normal* people just fine, Swim Team," Sasha said adamantly. "But those girls are part-alien."

Ryan adopted an expression of mock-offence. "Those are Natalie's best friends you're talking about."

"Which explains a lot about Natalie," Sasha shot back. "You really think she's looking down now, enjoying your little soiree?"

"Natalie was a party girl," said Ryan. "It's what she would have wanted."

Darla wasn't sure this was true, but she knew

better than to say anything. Ryan only had eyes for Sasha, anyway. Darla couldn't work out how her friend felt about 'Swim Team'. Sasha was constantly rude about him, behind his back and to his face, but at the same time she didn't seem to mind talking to him. To Darla there was something callous about the way Ryan was chatting up Sasha – this was supposed to be a wake for his murdered girlfriend, after all. But no one else seemed to care. Everyone was too busy having fun, downing cups of punch and bombing the pool, or dancing on the terrace to the music.

Everyone except Darla and Frank.

They perched next to each other on a sun lounger by the pool, on the awkward fringes of the party. Frank barely spoke, his blue eyes intently watching Sasha as she sparred with Ryan. Darla was beginning to suspect that Frank felt more for his best friend than he was willing to let on – not that Sasha would ever reciprocate, she was sure. It was crazy, in a way: in any other town, Frank would have been one of the best-looking boys around. Here, Darla felt as though she was the only one who had noticed how attractive he actually was.

Frank took a sip of punch, winced, and tipped his cup into the bushes.

"I might see if I can find something I can actually, you know, drink," he said. "You want anything?"

Darla shook her head, and he went back to the terrace. As she stared into the rippling pool, she heard a soft giggle behind her. Inside Ryan's gazebo, TJ Phillips had his arm around a girl and was whispering into her ear. The girl giggled again, kissing him and tracing a finger across his cheek. Coyly telling him she had to powder her nose, she got up and headed into the house, leaving TJ to sit back contentedly and sip on his beer. A hot flush of anger came over Darla. She got up from the lounger and went into the gazebo.

"Remember me?" she said.

TJ tapped his beer bottle thoughtfully. "You're the girl who found Natalie's body," he said finally.

"I'm the *girl* you photographed for your stupid website and then ignored in the hall. One of your Plain Girls."

"Oh." TJ reclined back on the cushions, a smile flickering across his face. "Yeah, I remember now."

"That's it?"

TJ shrugged. "It was just a joke. No need to get dramatic. Most of the girls we photographed were happy to get the attention."

"They were *happy*?" Darla couldn't believe her ears. "You can't seriously believe that, can you?"

"Whatever."

She was trembling with anger. "Well maybe someone might take a bad photograph of you someday," she said, her voice rising. "Then we'll see how you like it."

"Are you threatening me?" said TJ, with an incredulous laugh. "Don't you know who I am?"

"Sure I do," Darla retorted. "A grade-A asshole."

She stormed out of the gazebo and went over to Sasha, who had finished both her cups of punch and was starting on Ryan's beer. She giggled as Darla pulled her away, already a little drunk.

"I'm getting out of here," Darla told her in a low voice.

"Now?" said Sasha. "But we only just arrived!"

"I know. It's OK, I can make my own way back."

"But you're supposed to be sleeping over at my house!"

Frank wandered back from the house with a can

of soda. "If she wants to go it's no big deal," he said. "I can drive her home."

"And what am I supposed to do?"

"Hang out with Carmen and Gabrielle," suggested Ryan, who was looking on with open amusement. "They're big fans of yours."

"Go and do some laps or whatever it is you do," Sasha snapped. "This doesn't concern you, Swim Team."

As her friends began to bicker with each other, a loud splash made Darla turn around. The boys had climbed out of the pool to follow the girls on to the dance floor, leaving trails of damp footprints across the terrace. Behind them the water slowly settled, until it was as still and clear as a pane of glass. As Darla stared at her reflection, the loud music and Frank and Sasha's voices faded into the background. The world shuddered.

Slowly colours and shapes swam into focus before her eyes. In her mind Darla was back in the windowless dark room, standing over a photograph developing in a tray of fluid. She wanted to look away but her eyes were no longer her own, and she could feel her breaths quicken with excitement as the image emerged. The picture was a black-and-white blur, a snapshot of a hanged body. The killer used a pair of tongs to fish the photograph from the tray, carefully pegging it on to a line to dry. Beside it was a second picture: another body, this one lying facedown in the still waters of Ryan's swimming pool.

Darla gasped and stumbled backwards into Sasha, knocking her bottle and spraying Ryan with beer.

"Hey!" he cried. "Watch it!"

"I saw something!" she gasped, clutching his arm. "A body, right there in the pool!"

"Okaaaaay," said Ryan. "And exactly how much punch have you had?"

"I ain't drunk!"

"Darla, you're seeing dead people. This isn't *The Sixth Sense*."

She took a deep breath. "You need to stop this party," she told Ryan with a level gaze. "Or something terrible is going to happen."

"Don't tell me," Ryan replied. "Frank's going to dance."

"I'm not kidding!" She wanted to slap that crooked grin off his face, anything to stop him making stupid jokes and *listen* to her. Suddenly Darla was aware that the people around her had stopped dancing and were staring at her. Her cheeks reddened.

"OK, then!" Sasha said brightly. She drained her beer bottle and tossed it into the bushes. "So we're going to leave now. Thank you, Ryan, for a wonderful evening."

Sasha's hand closed firmly around Darla's wrist, dragging her off the terrace before she could argue. Gabrielle folded her arms as they walked past, an icy smile on her face. Sniggers of laughter followed them as Sasha marched Darla down the passageway around the side of the house and out on to the driveway. Frank hurried ahead of them and unlocked the truck, and before she knew it Darla was sitting in the backseat.

"Not cool," Sasha muttered under her breath as she climbed up into the front seat. "So unbelievably not cool."

"You shouldn't have made me leave," Darla told her. "I needed to make Ryan listen to me."

Sasha turned upon her. "You needed to be quiet and stop embarrassing yourself," she said. "If you wanted to go home, you coulda just gone — you didn't have to make up some big drama."

"But I wasn't—!"

"Just stop it, OK?"

"I didn't make it up!" Darla blurted out. "I saw a body in the water, just like I saw pictures of Natalie's house in the killer's photograph album before she died. I didn't say anything then and she got murdered, so what do you think's going to happen now?"

Sasha stared at her.

Chapter Thirteen

Silence fell over the truck. Darla's breaths came quickly and defiantly. She had said more than she meant to. Sasha and Frank had both turned round in the front seat and were watching her carefully.

"You wanna run that by me again?" Sasha said.

Darla looked over at the large shadow of Ryan's house. She swallowed.

"It's kinda hard to explain," she said finally. "I-I've been seeing things."

"Okayyyy," said Frank. "What kind of things?"

"I don't know how to describe it," Darla told him. "My mind takes me to this room, and it's like I'm looking through someone else's eyes."

"Whose eyes?" asked Frank.

"I don't know!" Darla said helplessly. "I never see their face. But this room's a real bad place – there are photos everywhere of dead bodies and people getting murdered. One time I saw this guy looking at an album filled with pictures of Natalie's house – that's how I knew that something was wrong that night. I knew someone wanted to hurt her."

Frank shook his head. "This is pretty out there."

"Out there?" Sasha echoed incredulously. "That's one way to put it. Jesus, Darla! Do you have any idea how crazy this sounds?"

"Why do you think I haven't told anyone?" Darla said bitterly.

"I know sometimes people can say things to get attention, but this isn't the way to do it."

"You can go to hell if you think I'd make this up," said Darla. "I didn't ask for any of this. You think I *wanted* anyone to kill Natalie? You think I *wanted* to see a dead body in the pool tonight? But I did, and I can't ignore it this time. I have to go back and talk to Ryan again."

"He'll be too busy laughing to listen," Sasha told her firmly. "And then he'll get bored and throw you out. We're officially done here, Darla. Come back to my house and tomorrow we'll go to school together, and I *promise* you Ryan and all his friends will be as alive and perfect and irritating as usual. Deal?"

"I think I'd rather go home," Darla said quietly.

Sasha shrugged. "Have it your way." She tapped Frank on the shoulder. "Home, James."

He turned on the engine and guided the truck down the driveway and out through Ryan's gates, which closed behind them with an iron clang. As they drove home, Darla silently fumed. She knew that Sasha and Frank didn't believe her. Did they really think she could have lied about her visions just to get attention? When the truck pulled up outside her house, Darla got out without a word and hurried inside. The lights were off and Hopper's door was closed as Darla went upstairs and crawled into bed. She was utterly exhausted, but it was a long time before she fell asleep.

The party was officially over. Ryan's moonlit terrace was strewn with plastic cups and upturned loungers, an empty bottle of rum bobbing mournfully on the surface of the pool. Inside the house was even worse: the kitchen floor was sticky with alcohol and some douchebag had been hurling damp wads of toilet paper at the bathroom ceiling.

It was a good job Ryan's parents were on the other side of the world – Kenya? Tanzania? Uganda? Somewhere in Africa – else he would have been in a world of trouble. As it was, the worst he had to face was the maid when she came to clean the next day. Ryan would kiss her cheek and tell her she was the best maid in the world and everything would be all right. He knew how to get away with things – especially when it came to women.

Sometimes even that was more hassle than it was worth. During the party one of the West Academy cheerleaders, Harmony, had got drunk and tried to come on to him, grinding up against Ryan on the dance floor and giggling as she rubbed her hand across his bare chest. There was no denying that she was hot, but it was just so … easy. Ordinarily Ryan would have taken her upstairs anyway, just for the hell of it, but tonight was different. For one thing, there was Natalie. Throughout the night Ryan had half-expected her to appear, angrily flicking her hair as she poked him in the chest and shouted at him for hitting on other women. Natalie always came to his parties; it seemed impossible that she wouldn't. That she was … dead. Whenever Ryan thought about that word, it felt as though he was standing on the edge of a dark, dizzying pit that threatened to swallow him up whole. So he tried not to think about it, pushing Natalie to the very back of his mind.

And then, more unexpectedly, there was Sasha. She wasn't the kind of girl Ryan usually went for – she was far too smart-mouthed for one thing, and all that goth stuff was for bedwetters and little boys. But maybe that was the point. Sasha intrigued Ryan in a way other girls didn't. He was pretty sure that she liked him, but any time they started to get close she would pull away. Take tonight: he had invited Sasha to the party, only for her to turn up with her loser friends and leave before the party had even got going. What was the problem? Was she too proud, or did she actually think she was better than him?

Ryan had still been turning Sasha's departure over in his mind when Harmony had leaned in and tried to kiss him. Irritably he had pushed her away – Harmony stared at him, astonished and upset, and then elbowed her way off the terrace. One of her friends gave Ryan an accusatory look.

"What?" Ryan had snapped.

A black mood had descended over him – barging into the house, he had ripped the stereo power cable from the socket and shouted at everyone to get out. There were a few boos, some muttered complaints, but when they saw the look on his face people had started to drift away. TJ had been the only one to stay behind but Ryan had no idea where he had gone – listening to his music, maybe, or throwing up in the bathroom. Leaving Ryan all alone.

Ryan's humourless laughter echoed around the terrace. He was having a little pity party, all by himself. What a loser! He righted a sun lounger and settled down upon it. He was supposed to be going to a swim meet this weekend – he wondered whether it would be going ahead after what had happened. Nothing seemed to be going right any more.

Ryan felt his eyelids begin to droop shut. A second later, they were wide open as music erupted from inside the house. Lil Wayne's voice boomed out across the night sky.

"TJ!" Ryan groaned. "C'mon, dude, turn it down!"

But with the stereo on full-blast, there was no way

that TJ could hear him. The volume was so loud that the music had distorted, the bass a fuzzy mess. If the neighbours complained to his parents Ryan was never going to hear the end of it. He rolled off the lounger and slowly got to his feet. The beer had made his head woozy, and there was a sour taste in his mouth. Groggily Ryan picked his way along the terrace and walked through the French windows.

"TJ? What the hell—?"

The floor trembled under the deafening assault of the stereo. In the middle of the room, TJ was suspended in mid-air beneath the ceiling fan. Somehow his headphone cord had become caught up in the blades, stringing up him up by the neck and choking him. His legs kicked feebly at fresh air as he clutched at the cord around his neck with his left hand. His right was holding his belly, which Ryan saw now was covered in blood. TJ had been sliced open, and was fighting to keep his guts inside his body.

Ryan staggered over to his friend and grabbed his legs, trying to hold him up. He could feel the strength draining from TJ's limbs, but there was no way he could get him down without further opening the yawning red wound in his belly. TJ spluttered, spraying blood over his shirt. Then he stopped kicking.

"TJ?" Ryan said hoarsely. "TJ, man, c'mon!"

He looked up, only to see his friend's head slumped to one side. For a time Ryan didn't move, clutching his friend's body as choked sobs escaped from his throat. The song ended, and in the few seconds of silence before the next one began he slowly let go and took a step back. He was numbly aware that his friend's blood was all over him – on his hands and face and in his hair. Ryan walked over to the stereo and turned down the volume, plunging the house into silence. A breeze stole in through the French windows, sending TJ's body swaying from side to side. Ryan stared out into the night.

Somewhere in the darkness, a light blinked.

There was someone out there.

Crouching down, Ryan picked up a broken bottle from the carpet. He knew, with ice-cold certainty, that he was going to kill whoever had done this. No arrest and no trial: an eye for an eye, a tooth for a tooth. He edged out on to the terrace, scanning the bushes for movement. The pool glimmered under the glow of the Chinese lanterns. Everything was eerily quiet.

"Come on," Ryan muttered, under his breath. "Let's see what you've got."

Click.

The noise came from the gazebo — too late, Ryan whirled around. Someone charged into him, knocking him backwards into the pool. Ryan tumbled with a yell into the water, the broken bottle flying from his hand. He kicked off the bottom of the pool and swam powerfully to the other side, bursting back through the surface and quickly wiping the hair out of his eyes. The terrace was empty. The killer had vanished.

"Is that it?" Ryan called out in a ragged voice. "You think I'm going to drown in my own pool? I'm captain of the swim team, asshole!"

He slapped the water, sending up a great spray into the air. But no one answered him.

Click.

Another sly noise from somewhere in the bushes. Was he being photographed? As the pool rippled around him Ryan felt his fury ebb, replaced by a slow, creeping dread. He shivered violently, his teeth chattering in his skull. Whoever had cut TJ open had to be a stone-cold psycho – what was he doing trying to fight them? He needed to get out of the pool and call the cops.

Ryan was reaching for the side when a shower of sparks erupted from the bushes near the generator and the lights went out around the pool. The power had been cut. As Ryan backed away through the water, a dark snake wound its way across the poolside towards him. The killer had cut the generator cable and was feeding it towards the water.

Fear punched Ryan in the gut with a cold, solid fist. Stranded in the middle of the pool, there was no way he could make it to safety before the deadly cable hit the water. Sasha's friend had been right after all. She had seen a dead body in the pool – maybe if Ryan had known it was going to be his, he might have listened to her.

Ryan's helpless, hysterical laughter rang around the terrace as the spitting electrical cable slipped into the water. There was an angry fizz, and then everything fell silent.

Chapter Fourteen

It seemed like Darla had barely collapsed into bed before her alarm clock brutally woke her up again. She stared up at the ceiling, the fog of sleep taking time to clear from her head. As she sifted through her memories of the previous night, a horrible uneasiness hung over her like a cloud. Forcing herself to get up, Darla went downstairs into the kitchen, where Hopper was sat at the table eating a slice of toast. He looked surprised to see her, but instead of asking why she hadn't stayed at Sasha's he merely pushed back the chair next to him so she could sit down, and nodded at the coffee brewing in the machine.

Darla showered and dressed in a daze, sleep-walking into the Buick and then out of it at the school steps. She barely noticed the jocks as they jostled her in the halls, or Carmen and Gabrielle's giggles as they whispered to one another by the lockers. Usually Ryan and TJ would be with them, but today they were nowhere to be seen. They could have just been hungover and decided to cut class, Darla told herself, it didn't have to mean that something bad had happened to them. But as she sat down at her homeroom desk, Darla realized that Ryan and TJ weren't the only ones who hadn't made it into school. Sasha's chair was empty too.

Darla had to wait for lunch until she found Frank. He was sitting alone in the canteen, a preoccupied expression on his face as he scribbled into a pad of paper. When Darla came over and sat down next to him, he closed it quickly.

"Have you seen Sasha today?" she asked.

He shook his head. "Nope."

"I thought you stayed over at her house."

"She withdrew her invitation. I think she was kinda pissed about the party, so I took her home and drove back to my place. I texted her this morning to see if she wanted a ride but she didn't get back to me. Sometimes her dad drops her at school, so I figured she was OK."

"I'm worried," Darla whispered. "Sasha isn't here, and neither are Ryan and TJ. You don't think... You don't think she went back to the party, do you?"

"How should I know?" Frank said irritably. "You're the one with the crazy visions, not me."

"Hey! That's not fair!"

He took off his glasses and sighed, rubbing his face. "I know," he said. "Sorry. When you told us all that stuff last night I couldn't believe it but now people aren't in school and... I'm just worried about Sasha, is all."

Darla wished she could reassure him. Going back to the party sounded exactly like the kind of thing Sasha would do, even if she had been warned it might be dangerous. *Especially* as she had been warned it might be dangerous. Darla couldn't help feeling responsible, and she agreed to drive over with Frank to Sasha's house after school to check that she was OK.

All afternoon, Darla was haunted by the fear that a shocked teacher would appear in the doorway with news of another murder, or a solemn principal announcement would come over the tannoy, but class went on as usual. She tried to take comfort from the normality of it all.

After the final bell had rung, she hurried down the school steps and met Frank by Sasha's pick-up.

185

Opening the passenger door to the truck, Darla paused. Students were streaming out of the school, parting with their friends as they got into their cars or headed for the school gates. Carmen Russo and Gabrielle hurried towards Carmen's white Cadillac and tossed their bags in the back, barely glancing at the people around them. At that moment, Darla felt utterly alone.

Frank leaned over from the driver's seat. "You OK?"

"Yeah," said Darla. "I'm fine."

She climbed into the truck. As she closed the door behind her, there was a movement in the rearview mirror. A figure sprang up in the backseat. Darla screamed.

"Jesus, Sasha!" shouted Frank.

Darla's hand flew to her mouth. The punk was hunched in the backseat, her face pale and wary.

"What?" she said defensively.

"You scared the hell out of us!" said Frank.

"By sitting in *my* truck? If you've got a problem with that, get your own!"

"Why were you hiding?"

"I didn't want any of the teachers seeing me.

186

Look, something happened last night. Ryan and TJ are dead."

Darla shrank lower into her seat, a wave of nausea washing over her. She had been so desperate to be wrong.

Frank swivelled round in his seat. "What? Are you sure?"

"Dead certain," Sasha replied grimly. "My dad knows a couple of officers inside the local PD, one of them called him this morning to warn him. They said Ryan's house looked like the set of a horror movie. TJ had been strung up and cut open, and they found Ryan's body in the pool. He had been electrocuted. Literally cooked in his own skin."

Just like she had seen in the dark room photographs. Darla was worried she was going to be sick.

"The Angel Taker," Frank said darkly. "It has to be."

"But it don't make no sense!" Darla burst out. "You said Walter West was dead – and I thought he was only interested in pretty girls?"

"Walter may be dead, but it looks like someone's trying to make his memory live on," Sasha replied.

"And Ryan and TJ might not have won any beauty pageants, but they *were* pretty, Darla. When it comes to killing people, it looks like this Angel Taker is a firm believer in equal opportunities."

"Can we stop calling him that, please?"

"If you like." Sasha shrugged. "But we're not the only ones who are going to make the link – the whole town's going to be talking about dead angels when this gets out. The only reason it's still hush-hush is that Ryan's parents are on some kind of safari in Africa and the cops are having trouble reaching them. Man, they are *really* starting to sweat – there's a maniac running around the hills killing students, and some very rich and powerful people are going to want answers."

"Do they have any suspects?" asked Darla.

"Not that I know of," Sasha said. "But let's just say I'm not holding my breath. Three people have been killed in a week – who knows who might be next? Do you really want to cross your fingers and hope that the Donut Patrol catch whoever's doing this?"

"What's the alternative?" laughed Frank. "Go out and catch this guy ourselves?"

Sasha stared at him.

"You've *got* to be kidding me," he said.

"What?

"Even for you, this is a bit … Scooby-Doo." Frank tapped the side of his head. "Seriously, Sasha."

"Just hear me out," Sasha said, leaning closer. "We didn't listen to Darla last night – and maybe if we had, Ryan and TJ would still be alive. But what's she going to do, tell the cops she's having visions of murders before they happen? They'll think she's a total whack-job!"

"Or that she had something to do with it," Frank added.

Darla hadn't even considered that grim prospect.

"Right," said Sasha. "But if Darla really is somehow tuned in to the Angel Taker, maybe we can work out who they are before they attack anybody else."

"But I told you last night, I never see their face," Darla said desperately. "They could be anyone!"

"But you did see a truck though, right?" Frank said suddenly. "We all did."

Sasha frowned. "What truck?"

"You need to stop drinking, girlfriend, you've got

the memory of a goldfish. There was a red pick-up parked outside Ryan's house when we drove up." Frank sat up in his seat. "And the night me and Darla found Natalie, we only stopped by her house because a truck damn-near rode us off the road!"

"Great work, detective," Sasha said sarcastically. "But since there's about... oh, about ten thousand trucks in the county, we might need to narrow it down a little."

"Maybe we can," Darla said slowly. "When we came to Saffron Hills we nearly crashed into a red pick-up, and I kinda thought it might be the same one we saw outside of Ryan's. The realtor told Hopper that the driver was a guy called Leeroy Mills."

"Leeroy Mills?" Sasha scratched her head. "I don't recognize the name."

"You wouldn't," Frank told her. "You live in the wrong part of town. I drive past Leeroy's trailer on the way to school. He's bad news, got a habit of getting into bar fights. A while back he did a couple of years in prison because of it."

"In other words, someone you don't want to mess

with," said Darla. "Tell the police if you want, Sasha, but don't get involved."

"Look, I'm not saying we handcuff this guy and take him in ourselves," she replied. "But let's go and have a look at his trailer, see if he's up to something. At the first sign of trouble, we call the cops. Case solved, to rapturous applause from the grateful townspeople." Sasha made a graceful imaginary wave. "Eat that, Miss Saffron."

Darla was already regretting having mentioned Leeroy's name. But it was useless trying to talk Sasha out of her plan – she was so used to getting her own way that she didn't bother listening to anybody else, especially if they were trying to tell her 'no'. Darla was tempted to leave her to it, but when Frank caved in and agreed to drive down to Leeroy's trailer, she reluctantly said she'd go with them. Hopper wouldn't be home for another couple of hours, and who knew what kind of trouble Sasha and Frank might get themselves into?

The pick-up spluttered out of the school lot and made its way along the main strip and into the countryside, where it rattled along dirt tracks. Birds hooted and chattered in the sassafras trees.

Creek water oozed like a seeping wound. Chewing pensively on a strand of her hair, Darla could sense a creeping apprehension inside the truck. Sasha switched off the radio and they sat in silence. They had to be on the very edge of Saffron Hills itself. Finally Frank pulled over by the side of the lane and turned off the engine.

"We'd better walk the rest of the way," he said. "Don't want Leeroy knowing we're coming."

He looked uneasy, and Darla knew she wasn't the only one regretting coming down here. She stayed close to Frank as he crept along the side of the track, keeping tight to the shadows. Further up the way there was a turn-off, a glimpse of rusted corrugated iron visible through the trees: Leeroy's trailer. As she stepped over a large fallen log, a loud pop made Darla jump. She looked round to see Sasha clumping blithely down the middle of the lane, chewing on a piece of bubblegum.

"What are you doing?" hissed Frank. "Get out of the road before he sees you!"

Sasha sighed and came over to join them in the shadows, resting her foot upon the log.

"Look, you can play commando all you want,

Franklin," she said, "but we're not breaking any laws just walkin—"

"Get down!" squeaked Darla.

She grabbed Sasha and dragged her down behind the fallen log. Just in time. A cloud of dust went up at the mouth of the turn-off and Leeroy Mills' pick-up skidded out on to the dirt track, bouncing past them towards Saffron Hills. Darla pressed herself to the parched ground, holding her breath until the growl of the pick-up's engine faded away. She looked up to find that Sasha had already stood up, and was brushing the dirt from her clothes.

"Well, that makes things a little easier, doesn't it?" she said brightly.

They emerged warily from behind the log and followed Sasha as she marched along the track. The turn-off led on to a small patch of ground scuffed with tyre tracks and ringed with trees. A wooden lean-to secured with a heavy padlock and length of chain threatened to topple over at any moment. Next to it was Leeroy's trailer, a scarred and rusting oblong. Empty beer cans were scattered on the ground by the door, beside a broken cool box lying on its side.

Sasha marched up to the door of the trailer and tried the handle. She made a face.

"Locked," she said.

"That was predictable," said Frank, puffing out his cheeks. "What now?"

As he and Sasha started bickering over whether or not Sasha should kick the door in, Darla sized up the trailer, thinking. More than likely, there was a spare key lying around somewhere – especially if Leeroy liked a drink. She crouched down by the trailer and ran her hands over the tyres to see if anything had been left there. No luck. Darla went round the side of the vehicle and examined the air-conditioning vent to see if a key had been taped to the top or the bottom, but there was nothing there either. Frank and Sasha were watching her now, intrigued. Finally, in desperation, Darla went over to the empty cool box and reached inside. Her fingers closed upon a key taped to the inside of the lid. She smiled, and produced the key with a flourish.

"Here you go," she said. "Problem solved."

Frank blinked with surprise. Even Sasha looked impressed. "Nice work!" she said. "How did you know there'd be a spare?"

Darla shrugged. "Lucky guess." She wasn't about to tell them that she had grown up around trailers – it was nice to be the one with the secrets for once. Darla slipped the key in the lock and turned it. As her hand fastened around the door handle, she glanced quickly back toward the lane to check for any telltale cloud of dust. Then she plunged inside the trailer.

Years of living in trailer parks had also taught Darla that there were pretty much two types of owners – the house-proud, obsessive types who kept everything clean and tidy, and the slobs. Leeroy Mills was not the first type. His trailer was a mess of dirty clothes and half-finished cartons of fast food. The air was sour with cigarette smoke.

"I don't know if this guy's a murderer," said Frank, wrinkling his nose, "but it sure *smells* like someone died here."

Darla went over to the sideboard, where a collection of framed photographs jostled for room. They all appeared to be of the same girl: a pretty teenager with long eyelashes and curly blond hair. In one she was dressed in a West Academy cheerleader's outfit, in another she was wearing a tiara and clutching a bunch of flowers. There was a sash over the ballgown, with the words 'Miss Saffron 1995'. It was Crystal.

"Well, this is ker-reepy," said Sasha, taking the photo of the murdered girl out of Darla's hands. "Stalker's paradise, or what?"

"Jackpot!"

Frank emerged from underneath Leeroy's bed, holding a brown Louis Vuitton shoebox.

"It's only a shoebox, Frank," said Sasha.

"Take a look around," Frank said dryly. "Do you really think that Mr Mills is a regular customer at Louis Vuitton?"

"OK, maybe not. But I'm pretty sure Natalie was."

"Precisely my point."

They sat down on the bed and watched as Frank prised open the box. Inside, to Darla's surprise, there was an old-fashioned Polaroid camera and a sea of photographs. Every single one was a selfie of Natalie.

"Jesus!" breathed Sasha. "I mean, I know the girl thought she was hot, but this takes narcissism to a whole new level."

But as she leafed through the date-stamped pictures, Darla wasn't so sure. Usually people in selfies smiled at the camera, or tried to pout seductively. But Natalie didn't look happy in any of these photographs. She wasn't showing off how pretty she was, or what a good time she was having.

"I don't think Natalie wanted anyone to see these," Darla said. "So how did Leeroy get hold of them?"

There was only one answer to that question. He had to have been in her house. The more important question was: before or after Natalie had died? As they continued to sift through the pictures, Sasha gasped.

"What is it?" cried Darla.

Wordlessly Sasha handed her the photograph. It was dated the previous week, the day Natalie had died. She was standing in a bedroom, her face red and her long blond hair tied back into a ponytail. It looked as though she had been exercising. Behind her the door to her closet was ajar. A pale, indistinct face was peering out over Natalie's shoulder.

"That is messed up," Frank murmured. "She

197

caught her own killer on camera just before it happened."

"Can you see the face?" Sasha asked eagerly. "Is it Leeroy?"

Outside, an engine gunned in reply.

Frank leaped up, startled, spilling pictures of Natalie all across the floor. He ran over to the window and peered through the blinds.

"Not good," he said. "I repeat: *not* good."

Outside a swirling cloud of dust had got up, a red truck crunching to a halt outside the trailer. Leeroy Mills was home.

Chapter Fifteen

At the sight of the pick-up outside the trailer, Darla's blood froze. Sasha raced over to the window and swore loudly.

"What are we going to do?" she said.

"Find somewhere to hide and pray he doesn't find us?" Frank suggested.

Sasha gestured around the cramped trailer. "Where? We can't all fit under the bed, Frank!"

"The door's unlocked, anyway," said Darla. "He's going to know someone was here. We gotta go – now."

Leeroy jumped down from the truck, flicking a cigarette end into the dirt and grinding it beneath his heel. As Darla looked desperately around the trailer, her eyes settled on the bathroom door. She ran through into the tiny room and yanked the net drape aside, revealing a small window on a latch.

"C'mon!" she called out. "Through here!"

With Sasha still hovering by the door, transfixed by the sight of the approaching Leeroy, Frank slipped past Darla and climbed up on to the toilet seat. Skinny enough to wriggle through the window, he fell headfirst to the ground outside. Darla bundled Sasha into the bathroom, drawing the bolt across the door just as Leeroy entered the trailer. His footsteps were wary, alert to the presence of intruders. As Sasha struggled through the window, the toilet door rattled.

"Who's hiding in there?" a sly voice called out. "Don't be shy now – come on out and let Leeroy see you."

Darla glanced helplessly up at Sasha, willing her to hurry. Outside the trailer Frank reached up and grabbed Sasha's hands, pulling her clear from the window and sending her tumbling down on top of him. A loud bang made Darla cry out – Leeroy was charging the toilet door with his shoulder. Darla scrambled up towards the window and pushed herself through the narrow space. The door shuddered again, the bolt threatening to spring free. As Darla squirmed she felt something catch. She twisted round.

A belt loop of her jeans had snagged on the latch.

There was another bang behind her, even louder than before. The toilet door exploded open.

"Look out!" Sasha screamed.

Darla wrenched her jeans free of the latch and threw herself forwards, plummeting out of the window even as Leeroy dived for her with a snarl. She hit the ground hard, knocking the wind from her lungs. Leeroy's fists hammered angrily on the glass. Coughing, Darla let Frank pull her to her feet. Sasha had already sprinted away into the trees. As they stumbled after her Darla heard the trailer door fly open, and Leeroy's angry voice echoed around the undergrowth. Their only option was to head deeper into the woods. Darla focused on trying to keep up with Frank, who was zigzagging along the trails and hurdling tree roots. But her chest was hurting from where she had landed and it was hard to breathe. She wanted to call her friends back but was too scared Leeroy would hear her. Darla glanced fearfully over her shoulder.

And went sprawling to the ground.

Dazed, she lay flat on her back in a small clearing, a half-dug hole inches from her face. A spade was lying across the path where she had tripped over it. Heavy footsteps were stamping through the wood behind her – there was no time to run now. Forcing back a wave of panic, Darla crawled on her hands and knees over to a giant fern and hid behind it. She pulled her knees up to her chest, praying that she wouldn't be seen.

Ten seconds went by. Twenty.

Every muscle in Darla's body was tense and ready to spring. Voices in her head screamed at her to run. She forced herself to stay still.

Thirty seconds. A minute.

And then she knew he was there.

"C'mon out, li'l girl," a croaking voice called. "Leeroy's got himself this here rifle, and he's hunted bigger and meaner creatures than you. C'mon out now, before someone gets hurt."

Darla hugged herself into a tighter ball, willing herself into invisibility. Inches from her hiding place, a twig snapped. Leeroy was so close she could hear his shallow breaths.

Then, on the other side of the clearing, mocking laughter rang out. Leeroy whirled round, and the clearing rang to the sound of a gunshot. Birds erupted from the trees. Darla bit her lip to keep herself from screaming. In the aftermath of the shot there was silence, and then Leeroy's heavy tread stomped away through the undergrowth.

Darla let out a shuddering breath. She hadn't even realized she had been holding it. Cautiously she stood up, peering around the clearing. There was no sign of Leeroy – or anyone else, for that matter. She was sure it had been Frank who had laughed; Darla hoped that he was OK. What were they doing here, playing hide-and-seek in the woods with an armed madman? She cursed herself for agreeing to come down here.

There was no telling where her friends were now – all Darla could do was try to get out of the woods alive. She left the clearing with its half-dug hole behind her and tiptoed away through the trees, until her ears picked up the sound of running water. Presently Darla came out on the banks of the creek, her shoulders sagging with relief at the sight of the slow-moving water. The creek would lead her home to safety. As she picked a path along the bank Darla listened out for shouts and further gunshots but there was only birdsong and trickling water. Maybe Sasha and Frank had managed to double back to the pick-up and drive away. If Leeroy really was Natalie's killer, the thought of what he might do if he caught up with them was too terrible to contemplate.

The creek rounded a bend and Darla recognized the houses from her lane. She broke into a stumbling run, suddenly desperate to get home. As she crashed through the bushes she heard a voice call out.

"*Darla?* Is that you, honey?"

Annie was standing at the bottom of her yard, peering down towards the creek. It looked like she had been working on the House of Narcissus: she was wearing her heavy-duty gloves again, and her clothes were flecked with white paint.

"Goodness, you had me worried for a moment!" she said. "I heard all this noise and I wondered what was going on, thought there might be an intruder. What are you doing down there?"

"I... I was..."

Darla trailed off, aware that she was close to tears.

"I just had a call from the school," Annie told her gently. "I'm afraid there's been some more bad news. Have you heard?"

When Darla nodded, Annie came over and gave

her a big hug.

"What a terrible thing," she murmured. "Ryan was in my art class – such a charming boy. And TJ too. It's just a tragedy."

The artist led Darla past her house of mirrors and up on to the back porch, where she sat her down in a swing seat.

"Now, honey," she said gently. "Why don't you tell me what's going on?"

Darla's story came out in a hot tumble of words. Annie let her talk, watching her carefully and occasionally nodding. The Plain Girls website, the murders, Leeroy Mills ... everything that had happened since she came to Saffron Hills. Well, almost everything: Darla didn't say anything about the photograph of her mom, and she wasn't ready to share her visions with Annie just yet.

"That's quite a story!" said Annie, when she had finished. "I'm glad you're safe but you've got to promise me one thing – no more private detective work, OK? You could have got into all sorts of trouble in that trailer. What if this man had tried to hurt you? You leave people like Leeroy Mills to the police, you hear me?"

Darla nodded.

"I'm guessing you haven't told Hopper any of this."

"He wants me to stay out of it. We're just getting settled and … he worries."

Mostly that the police would end up discovering his criminal record and bring him in for questioning, but Darla didn't say that. Thinking about her daddy reminded her that she was already late – she got up from the swing seat.

"I gotta go," she told Annie. "Hopper will be wondering what's happened to me."

"Tell him you were here with me, and we lost track of time," said Annie with a smile. "I reckon he'll forgive you."

Darla nodded. The light was beginning to fade now, the last rays of the sun slicing in through the window of the House of Narcissus and bouncing off the mirrors, filling the little house with dazzling light.

"It's nearly finished," Annie told her, a note of satisfaction in her voice. "Just a couple more days, I reckon."

"It's looking neat," Darla said politely. "I was

kinda wondering, though... Out of everything you coulda built it out of – why mirrors?"

"Why do you think?" Annie shot back.

Darla shrugged. "I don't know. I'm not an artist."

"What do you see when you look in the mirror?"

Darla hesitated. That wasn't an easy question to answer. She saw a small room with a killer inside, surrounded by photographs of screaming faces. Horrifying glimpses of the future.

"Nothing I like," she said truthfully.

"I know that feeling," said Annie. "I was a teenager too, remember. And some girls at that age can be so pretty – almost like they're from another planet, like they're... I don't know..."

"Angels?" suggested Darla.

Annie laughed. "I guess that's one way of putting it," she said. "But you listen to me: they ain't got no wings on their back or halo on their head. They're flesh and blood, just like the rest of us."

"Then how come this town gets so excited over a beauty pageant?"

"That's a complicated question. Put it down to a little bit of misplaced civic pride and a whole lot of money. Over the years Miss Saffron has become

one of the most prestigious pageants in America —
all kinds of hair and beauty companies have got
sponsorship deals. If it turns out the pageant can't
go ahead because there's a killer on the loose, what
do you think they're going to do?"

"I guess they'll take their money somewhere else,"
Darla replied.

"Damn right they will. And they won't be back."

"But people are *dying*, Annie. There's no way they
can hold it, right?"

"Anywhere else, maybe so. But if I know Saffron
Hills, the pageant will happen all right." Annie
glanced over at the House of Narcissus, as the sun
dropped below the horizon and the light dimmed.
"No matter what the cost."

Chapter Sixteen

News of Ryan and TJ's deaths broke over Saffron Hills like a rain of cold ash. One brutal murder had been shocking enough, but now with two more teenagers dead — more rich, good-looking young people from the mansions in the hills — no one could hide from the truth any longer. There was a killer on the loose.

For the second time in a week, West Academy students filed into the gym to hear a special address from Principal Bell, his face graver than ever. It was clear, he told them, that someone very dangerous was targeting local teenagers. The police were pursuing lines of enquiry but in the meantime he warned everyone to take extra special care: not to go anywhere alone, to keep an eye out for strangers and to report anything suspicious to the authorities, no matter how small. Until the killer had been found, a town curfew of 10 p.m. would be in operation for all teenagers. The principal announced that a candlelight vigil for the three victims would be held outside the Presbyterian Church the next evening, led by Pastor James. The students listened in numb silence, but as Darla studied the pale faces around her she thought she could detect another emotion lurking beneath the shock and sadness: a guilty thrill of excitement, running through the bleachers like an electric current.

And she wasn't the only one.

"This school makes me want to puke," muttered Sasha, as they left the gym. "I mean a full-on *Exorcist*-style puke-fest." She pointed at a sobbing girl being comforted by her friends. "Look at Heather Brodie! Ryan and TJ didn't even know she existed, and now she's wailing like they were best friends."

Whatever she might have thought deep down, Darla wasn't in the mood to agree. "People have been *murdered*, Sasha, OK?" she snapped. "It's upsetting. Just because you don't care about anyone apart from yourself."

"Hey! What was that for?"

"Forget it."

Sasha caught her arm. "Forget what? Are you still

pissed about the trailer?"

"It was one thing you made us go down there, even though I said it was a bad idea," Darla said accusingly. "But you coulda at least called to check I made it home alive afterwards. Frank did."

"I know Frank did! Because then *he* told *me* you were OK." Sasha blew out her cheeks. "Jeez, I thought you'd be happy."

"Happy? Why?"

Sasha's voice dropped to a whisper. "Because now we know who the Angel Taker is! Frank phoned the cops anonymously last night to tell them about Leeroy. One look at his Creepy Trailer of Horrors, and he'll be headed straight for the nearest maximum security prison – and it'll all be thanks to us!"

Darla wished she could be so sure. Everything they had seen in the trailer in the woods – the weird shrine to Miss Saffron, the box of Natalie's selfies – pointed to Leeroy being the Angel Taker. And yet... Darla had been inside the killer's skin, and she had sensed a savage and fiendish intelligence that she wasn't sure Leeroy possessed. But how could she tell Sasha that, let alone the cops? They'd probably end up arresting her, for wasting their time.

"Maybe," she said.

"You know I'm right. And deep down half the people here will be sad when Leeroy's caught, because I'm telling you, secretly, they're loving every minute of it. Natalie and Ryan and TJ are dead and they're not. It's a buzz!"

"A buzz?" Darla echoed dubiously.

"Admit it," said Sasha. "What can make you feel more alive than to be surrounded by death? Killing is like the world's greatest extreme sport."

"Maybe someone should phone the cops and tell them about you," Darla said.

Sasha grinned wickedly. "I believe I would make an *exceptional* serial killer." Heather Brodie looked up, shocked. Sasha glared at her. "What? Don't make me add you to my list."

She made a stabbing motion with an imaginary knife.

"Ugh, God!" said a voice behind them. "You are *so* grotesque, Sasha."

Darla didn't need to turn round to recognize Gabrielle's voice. It felt like the Picture Perfects were constantly stalking them, just waiting for the right moment to pounce.

"Ryan's dead and you're making *jokes* about it?" said Carmen. "Even for you, that's pretty low."

"Carefully polishing that halo of yours, Carmen?" Sasha shot back. "You don't want the Angel Taker sizing *you* up for a new pair of wings."

Gabrielle stepped forwards and jabbed her finger into Sasha's chest.

"You think you're so smart and funny, don't you? Hear this, girl: you're just the same as this sicko murderer. Just another jealous, inadequate loser. Enjoy your fun while it lasts."

She made a sound of disgust and spun on her heel, stalking down the hall. Sasha smirked triumphantly but for once Darla could understand Gabrielle and Carmen being angry. Three of their best friends had been murdered, and Sasha was turning them into punchlines. Was she really that callous, or was it all part of her rebellious image? After their narrow escape from Leeroy's trailer, and the nightmarish chase through the woods down by the creek, Darla was beginning to doubt the wisdom of hanging out with Sasha and Frank. Annie was right: Saffron Hills was dangerous enough without inviting trouble by playing private detective.

The Angel Taker's shadow had fallen over the whole town, reaching all the way to their house by the creek. Darla was starting to worry about Hopper. He was preoccupied and restless, had barely even noticed that she had returned home late the previous day. Darla had seen this mood before – usually before Hopper went out on a drinking binge. At night she lay awake in bed, dreading the creak of the screen door and the Buick's engine revving into life. But the house stayed quiet, keeping its secrets close to its chest.

The next night, Hopper surprised Darla by taking her and Annie to the town's candlelit vigil. As far as Darla could tell, her daddy and the artist were just friends – which was unusual for Hopper, who only seemed capable of having one kind of relationship with women. Secretly Darla was delighted. She needed all the help she could get keeping him sober and on the straight and narrow.

They parked the Buick on the street and walked the short distance to the Presbyterian Church, where a large circle of people had gathered in front of the steps. Candles flickered in the breeze. Everywhere Darla looked she saw groups of West Academy students, their faces pale and drawn, but there was no sign of either Frank or Sasha. In a way, Darla was relieved. People had come here to share in their grief and sorrow, and the last thing she wanted was anyone whispering sarcastic one-liners into her ear.

She took a candle and stood at the back of the circle next to Annie. Pastor James was speaking at the top of the church steps. He was an imposing man, tall and bespectacled, and younger than Darla had guessed. His congregation stood in front of him, nodding in agreement with his rich baritone. Closing his eyes, the pastor led a prayer for the murdered teenagers, commending their souls to heaven. When the prayer reached its resolute "amen", Gabrielle Jones stepped forwards from the congregation. She was dressed in a roll-neck sweater and a long skirt, her skin glowing in the candlelight. Gabrielle began to sing – a gospel number, "Jesus Promised Me A Place Over There", which Darla recognized from a talent show she used to watch. Gabrielle had to fight to control the emotion in her voice, tears glistening on her cheeks as she sang. All around Darla people were snuffling and crying, clutching hold of one another.

Click.

Darla flinched as a bright light went off next to her. She whirled around, but it was only a little girl taking a picture of Gabrielle on her phone. The girl checked her screen and gave Darla a gappy smile. All around them, people were taking photographs of Gabrielle, training their cell phones and cameras on her as she sang. An icy shiver ran down Darla's spine. What if Leeroy was innocent, what if the Angel Taker was somewhere in this crowd, taking secret delight in the suffering they had caused? Or photographing the beautiful girl singing on the church steps?

Finally the last mournful note spiralled away into the night air, greeted by a hushed chorus of 'amens' from the crowd. Pastor James put a comforting arm around Gabrielle, who was openly crying now, and led her gently back to her parents. With the vigil coming to a close, and the curfew due to start before long, the crowds began to drift away. Hopper spotted his boss at the music store and went over to talk to him, while Annie had taken out her camera and was taking shots of the flowers people had left at the bottom of the church steps. Alone, Darla turned and looked through the crowd – and caught a glimpse of Luis Gonzalez.

The Realtor King of Saffron Hills was standing with his wife Celeste, whom Darla recognized from the photograph on Luis's desk in his office. A little boy was pulling at her sleeve, pointing excitedly at the brightly lit storefront across the street. Celeste laughed and nodded, kissing her husband on the cheek before leading the boy out of the church grounds. Seized by a sudden, reckless thought, Darla slipped through the crowd towards Luis.

"Mr Gonzalez?"

He blinked with surprise at the sight of her. "Hopper's girl? What are you doing here?"

"I need to talk to you."

"Hey listen," said Luis, holding up his hands, "if Hopper wants to talk to me about the lease, he can do it himself."

"It's not about the house," Darla told him. "It's about Sidney. My mom."

A shadow fell across Luis's face. "I'm sorry, I can't help you," he said, glancing over in the direction of the departing Celeste. "I didn't really know her. You should talk to Hopper."

Darla caught his arm as he tried to walk away. "You said you came to Saffron Hills because of something she said," she reminded him. "That's an awful long way, Mr Gonzalez. You must have known her a *little* bit."

"It was a long time ago," he insisted. "I don't remember much of it."

"Anything. Please."

Luis looked around helplessly. "What do you want me to say?" he said in a low voice. "A lot of things happened in New Mexico that shouldn't have. Me and Hopper were different people back then. We fell into business together, made a little money. Sidney used to stay in the trailer looking after you – you couldn't have been more than two or three. She was a nice lady, didn't complain, just went along with things. Most girls, they end up with someone like Hopper and they're going to be bitching and whining day and night, but Sidney wasn't like that."

"Did she talk about growing up – about Saffron Hills?"

"Not much," said Luis. "Coded hints, mostly."

"Hints about what?"

"That something bad had happened here. You gotta understand, Darla, back in those days pretty much everyone I met was running away from *something*. Sidney wasn't any different. She had demons, all right. I could see it in her eyes."

Demons. Darla shivered, trying to push the image of the half-opened bathroom door from her mind, Hopper screaming at her younger self to look away. "So why did you come here?"

Luis shrugged. "It sounded like a rich place, and I figured I could make some easy money. But when I got here I met Celeste and suddenly I found something I wanted more than money. So I went straight, worked two jobs whilst I studied for my realtor's license. Now I'm a husband and a father and an honest-to-goodness citizen."

There was pride in Luis's voice as he spoke.

"Did you ask if anyone knew my mom?" asked Darla.

"I kept my mouth shut," Luis replied firmly. "I left that part of my life behind me in New Mexico. At least, I thought I had. Then you and Hopper walked in through my door."

"What about Walter West?" said Darla, thinking back to the photograph of her mom. "Do you think she might have known him?"

Luis shrugged. "Who knows? I wasn't around back then, and people round here don't really like to talk about that guy. I did a bit of digging around Tall Pines a few years back – that mansion is the Holy Grail of South Carolina real estate. But the title deeds are a mess. When Allen and Madeline died they should have passed to Walter's sister, Amy—"

"There was a sister?"

"Sure, like I said, her name was Amy. She went to school in another county so she wasn't well known around here. When her parents died people tried to track her down but she'd moved out of the state. So the house just sits there, gathering dust and a bad reputation. It's a real shame, you know? I've seen the photos – it was a beautiful property." He glanced across the street, to where his wife and son were staring into the shop window. "Listen, I gotta go, Celeste and Rafael will be waiting for me. Don't tell Hopper we talked, OK?"

"I won't."

"I mean it, Darla!" Luis said urgently. "He's your father and I know he can be charming but Hopper's got a dark side and I don't want to make him mad. I saw some things in New Mexico, when he'd been drinking…"

He stopped abruptly, aware that he had said too much.

"I promise I won't say anything," Darla told him.

Luis nodded, and turned to walk away.

"Thank you," she added quickly, almost embarrassed. "For everything. It's because of you that we got to sleep with a roof over our head, and now Hopper's got a real job. Maybe one day he might become a honest-to-goodness citizen too."

A small smile of surprise flickered on the realtor's face. Then he was gone. Darla turned back to find Annie watching her from across the church lawn, a curious expression on her face.

"Darla? Darla!"

It was Hopper, hurrying over to her. "Where in

God's name did you go running off to?" he said crossly. "I was gonna introduce you to my boss, but I turned around and you'd gone."

"Sorry, Daddy," Darla replied. "I saw a friend from school."

"Sasha?"

"No, um, someone else. How was your boss?" Darla asked, quickly changing the subject.

"He had some news," said Hopper.

"Good news or bad?"

"I'm hopin' it's good news, if it means these killings will stop. The cops arrested Leeroy Mills this afternoon – they're questioning him over the murders."

Chapter Seventeen

It was Saturday afternoon. Darla wandered up and down the aisles of a deserted Criminal Records, leafing aimlessly through the stacks of vinyl. Occasionally she held one up for Sasha to inspect – and almost every time received a thumbs-down in reply. Since Darla had arrived at the record store only a handful of customers had shuffled through the door, almost all of them teenage boys. Judging by their furtive glances towards Sasha at the counter, they weren't there for the music. It was almost funny when one of them summoned the courage to buy something, red-faced and stuttering at Sasha before fleeing out of the store. Sasha – as usual – either didn't notice her admirers, or didn't care. No one so much as looked at Darla. She was utterly invisible.

She had only decided to come down to the mall at the last minute, when Hopper had pulled an extra shift at the music store. It felt as though the town had breathed a sigh of relief at the news of Leeroy Mills' arrest. He was a known troublemaker with a criminal record — it stood to reason that he was the Angel Taker. Darla only prayed they were right. As she'd walked through the mall towards Criminal Records, she had looked up to the spot where she had first seen Natalie McRae and her friends. They had looked so beautiful and haughty they had seemed almost untouchable, but now three of them were gone for ever. Their ghostly presence seemed to shimmer in the air where they had once stood.

At least Sasha had been pleased to see Darla, telling her with a groan that she was dying of boredom. Now Darla picked out a fresh record sleeve and held it up so her friend, who was sprawled lazily out across the counter, could see it. Sasha nodded approvingly.

"Sleater-Kinney? That is a *serious* record you are holding right there," she said. "Hey, if you like that, you should try X-Ray Spex. Poly Styrene is, like, the First Lady of punk. No, screw that, she's the *president* of punk."

Darla nodded dutifully. As hard as she was trying,

Sasha was never going to turn Darla into some great music expert. Slipping the Sleater-Kinney record back with the others, she glanced up at the clock.

"That's an hour since anyone came in," she said. "Is it always this quiet in here?"

"It is *always* this quiet in here," replied Sasha. "If it weren't for my dad, Danny would have had to close the store years ago."

"Danny?"

"The store owner – and the only other person in Saffron Hills with any taste in music. My dad writes him a cheque every now and again to keep this place open. I think it's the only reason he lets me work here. But c'mon, where else am I going to get a job?"

It was a good question. Darla couldn't imagine Sasha flipping burgers or waitressing or being a maid in a hotel. Then again, it was easier to be a rebel and do what you wanted if you had a rich daddy who was willing to foot the bill.

Sasha's phone buzzed on the counter. She checked the screen, sitting abruptly up.

"What is it?" asked Darla.

"Frank's sent me a link to some kind of blog. Said

225

I should check it out… Oh, you've *got* to be kidding me!"

Darla put down the record and came over to look at Sasha's phone. Beneath the headline 'SLAY CHEESE!' was a photograph of a page from a West Academy yearbook, splattered with lurid red streaks. Natalie, Ryan and TJ were all there. Over Sasha's shoulder, Darla read:

Twenty years after infamous son of Saffron Walter West killed a beauty queen and ended up swinging from a tree in his backyard, the town is wondering whether there's a new Angel Taker on the prowl. Three West Academy students – Natalie McRae, Ryan Cafferty and TJ Phillips – have been brutally murdered in the space of a week: stabbed, strangled and electrocuted. With beautiful people once again becoming an endangered species, you don't have to be Sherlock Holmes to work out that Carmen Russo and Gabrielle Jones might be the next names on the Angel Taker's hit list.

Any normal town would be in lockdown until the killer is caught, but then Saffron Hills is only slightly less crazy than our knife-wielding red-haloed friend. Word is that the powers that be are determined to

*protect their precious sponsorship money and make sure
that the Miss Saffron beauty pageant goes ahead next
week. At least there's a suspect in police custody, so
let's hope they've got the right guy — else the winner
might find themselves getting a victory slash instead of
a victory sash...*

Sasha groaned. "Really? I mean, isn't it bad
enough that some freak is going around killing
people without stuff like this? People are ghouls,
Darla. There's no other word for it."

Darla nodded in agreement. The blog was
drenched in sick glee that made it seem that whoever
had written it was actually *enjoying* what was
happening in Saffron Hills.

"Does it say who wrote it?" she said.

Sasha scrolled to the bottom of the page. "Doesn't
look like it."

"Maybe it's the killer," Darla suggested, "trying
to get more attention."

"Maybe. More likely it's someone from the West
Academy. A loser with questionable hygiene and no
friends who'll get a kick out of upsetting people."

"It might not work. People might not read it."

Sasha rolled her eyes. "Darla, *everyone* is going to read it."

They were interrupted by an unexpected sound: the bell above the door ringing. Someone had entered the store. Darla looked up to see Patti Haas peering uncertainly into the gloomy interior.

"Sasha, darling?" she called out. "Are you there?"

"Mom?" replied Sasha. "What are you doing here?"

Patti edged towards them along the aisles, carefully skirting around a patch of damp on the floor. "It's very dark in here," she complained. "I can barely see a thing."

"It's called mood lighting, Mom." The petulant tone of Sasha's voice made Darla smile – she sounded like a little girl. "I thought I told you not to come in here!"

"I know you did, dear," Patti replied vaguely. "But I was walking past and I thought it would be rude not to say hello. I don't know why you're so worried, anyway. I'm not going to start plastering baby photographs of you on the wall." She peered around at the peeling band posters. "Although anything would be an improvement on the current decor."

Darla tried to stifle a giggle, and failed. Sasha glared at her.

"Who's your new friend?" asked Patti.

"Her name's Darla, Mom," Sasha sighed. "You've met her before."

As Patti stared at Darla, her face suddenly broke into a smile. "Why yes, of course!" she said. "You came over to the house with Franklin. I'm glad to see you girls are sticking together. This is no time to be going about on your own."

"If you mean the killings, they arrested somebody," Sasha told her.

"So I heard," Patti said dubiously. "As if Leeroy Mills could be capable of all this... *evil*. Nothing changes in this town – the innocent get hurt, and the guilty get away with it. It was the same when I was your age."

"That guy is not innocent, Mom, take it from us."

"Who do you mean, 'the guilty'?" Darla asked suddenly. "Like Walter West?"

The change in Patti was instantaneous. Her eyes narrowing, she grabbed hold of Darla's arm. "What do you know about him?"

"N-nothing..." Darla stuttered. "I just..."

"You stay away from that man, you hear me? He's *evil*. I don't want him anywhere near my girl."

"Okay, Mom, okay!" said Sasha. "Walter West's dead, remember?"

Patti squeezed even tighter. "Crystal was a sweet, beautiful girl, and when they pulled her out of the creek her skull had been shattered," she told Darla fiercely. "You remember that."

"Mom, let go of her!"

Sasha pulled the shocked Darla away and marched Patti down the aisle towards the exit, firmly closing the door behind her.

"I'm really sorry about that," she told Darla, returning to sit on the counter. "Don't take it personally."

"It's my fault," said Darla. "I shouldn't have upset her."

Sasha picked at her black nail polish. "It's not you. Mom's on Xanax to stop her getting panic attacks. She used to get them a lot when I was younger. They're ... they're pretty scary."

Sasha studiously refused to look up as she spoke, concentrating on her nails. For the first time, Darla felt she was looking at how her friend truly felt – as though Sasha had unlocked a padlock like the one she kept on her bedroom door, and allowed Darla a glimpse inside. Aware of Darla's sympathetic gaze, Sasha looked up and smiled brightly. The door slammed shut again.

"You know what we need?" she said briskly. "Music. This *is* supposed to be a record store, after all."

She jumped down from counter and put on a record, cranking up the volume with a whoop and dancing along the aisles. Darla rubbed her sore arm, thinking about what Patti had said to her. Sasha's mom had been talking as though Walter West wasn't dead at all, even though the rest of the town seemed certain that he was. Could it really be down to her medication?

"Come and dance with me!" Sasha called out.

Darla shook her head. "I'm gonna go," she said. "Hopper will be home from work soon."

She hugged Sasha and left Criminal Records, leaving her friend defiantly dancing on her own. Stores in the mall were closing for the afternoon, the last remaining customers drifting away. Chairs were being put on tables in the café forecourt. The banner advertising the Miss Saffron pageant rippled forlornly above Darla's head. As she headed past the elevators Darla felt a hot itch on the back of her neck. Glancing towards the upper floor, she saw someone hurriedly draw back from the balustrade. She was being watched.

Trying to keep calm, Darla threaded a path through the café tables and slipped out of the mall through a side door. She found herself on a quiet street facing a small, smart building set back from the sidewalk – the Taylor gallery. Offering up a silent prayer of thanks, Darla hurried across the street and pushed through the glass door, a small bell tinkling above her head. There was no sign of Annie, though a half-drunk mug of coffee was cooling on the sales counter. Darla looked back through the glass door at the empty street. Whoever had been watching her must have got bored – if anyone *had* been watching her. It was getting harder and harder for Darla to be sure what she was seeing was real or not.

She turned and examined the silent gallery. Dividing walls ran at angles across the room, artfully chopping up the space and turning it into a maze of alcoves. As Darla wandered curiously through the gallery in search of Annie, at every corner she was confronted with a new piece of artwork. A shattered mirror, cracks in the glass spreading out like a jagged cobweb. A video running alongside the artwork showed Annie taking a giant hammer to the mirror, the footage playing over and over on a loop. A giant doll's house, that when Darla crouched down to look through a window she saw was in fact an empty shell. Over dinner, Annie had told Hopper that art was all about how people reacted to it – and it felt as though every piece in this gallery had been designed to unsettle and disturb.

In the final alcove there was a self-portrait of Annie sitting in an artist's studio, her intelligent hazel eyes examining Darla. Next to the self-portrait were four exact reproductions, each increasingly disfigured with black daubs of paint until Annie's face was completely obscured. Darla couldn't understand why Annie would go to so much trouble to paint such a beautiful picture only to deface it afterwards, like a child with a crayon. Maybe that was why Annie was the artist, and she wasn't.

As Darla stared at the paintings, the bell above

the gallery door rang out again.

"Annie?" Darla called out. "Is that you?"

No reply.

Darla peered around the dividing wall back towards the front of the gallery, but there was no one there. Maybe whoever it was had seen there was no one behind the counter and left. Or maybe whoever it was just didn't want Darla to see them.

"Hello?" she said. "Is anybody there?"

The lights went out, plunging the gallery into darkness.

Chapter Eighteen

Darla froze, waiting to hear someone's voice call out. But no sound disturbed the shadows. Lights went out all the time, she told herself, it didn't have to mean that something was wrong. So why was her heart racing in her chest? Darla slipped into the adjoining alcove only to be confronted by the mirror Annie had shattered. Tiny fragments of her own face stared back at her.

As Darla looked into the broken glass, she felt herself being swallowed up by a mind that wasn't her own. She was transported from one darkened room to another, where a girl with bright blond hair and a white tank top was slumped lifelessly in a chair. Her head was bowed, hiding her face. She let out a groan of pain, and Darla looked down and saw a knife in her own hand, blood on its blade...

A sudden sound wrenched her back to the present.

Footsteps, soft as a breath. There *was* someone in the gallery with Darla. And they were trying very hard not to be heard. Had the person watching her in the mall followed her here? What did they want with her?

"Annie," Darla whispered to herself. "Where are you?"

The footsteps were drawing nearer. Darla edged along the wall, drawing further back into the gallery. In the next alcove, the oversize doll's house sat in the middle of the room. Darla crept over to it and opened up the front, pulling her knees up to her chest and squashing herself inside. In the darkness it would be almost impossible to see her without looking closely through one of the windows. It would have to be enough.

Darla waited. Seconds stretched out into minutes. The gallery remained silent.

And then she heard a floorboard creak.

Peering out through the dollhouse window Darla could just make out a figure moving stealthily around the alcove, little more than a shadowy outline in the darkness. With careful, even steps they circled the dollhouse. A hunter's stealthy tread.

Darla couldn't bear to look — she closed her eyes and silently mouthed the Lord's Prayer to herself over and over.

"*OurFatherwhoartinHeavenhallowedbethyname…*"

The footsteps paused.

"*ThykingdomcomethywillbedoneonEarthasitisinHeaven …*"

Slow, shallow breaths.

"*Giveusthisdayourdailybread…*"

The intruder had to be standing inches away from her. Darla was a tight ball of terror.

"*Andforgiveusourtrespasses…*"

One footstep, and then another. Whoever it was, they were leaving the alcove. Had they seen her? The footsteps grew firmer even as they went away, before the bell above the gallery entrance rang out. Darla slumped her head against the side of the dollhouse.

"Hello? Is anybody there?"

Darla almost burst into tears at the sound of Annie's voice. Suddenly the gallery was flooded with warm light, and she could hear footsteps. Pushing open the dollhouse, Darla unfolded her cramped limbs and walked stiffly out of the alcove.

Annie was standing in the middle of the gallery, a paper bag in her hands.

"Darla, honey?" she said. "You look like you've seen a ghost! What's wrong?"

Darla's story came out in a rush, a nonsensical garble of words in her ears. When she told Annie about hiding in the dollhouse, the artist's eyes widened.

"They didn't hurt you, did they?"

"They didn't do anything, except kinda walk about. I don't know, maybe they were trying to scare me."

"That sounds horrible, hon, I'm so sorry I wasn't here. I was feeling kinda peckish and went out for a Danish – I was in such a hurry I didn't think to lock the door. Art thieves don't tend to be a problem in Saffron Hills."

Now that Annie was here, fear had eased its sweaty grip on Darla's heart. Together they searched the gallery from top to bottom, but there was no sign of any intruder. As they peered into one empty alcove after another, Darla began to feel a little foolish. Maybe she had imagined it, maybe her visions were getting more intense. And what about the girl in the white tank top? Her blond hair made Darla wonder whether it had been Carmen, only this girl hadn't had the Perfect's long, tumbling tresses. How could Darla warn someone they were in danger when she didn't know who they were?

"Well," said Annie, as they checked the final room, "whoever was here, they're gone now. But I'm thinking maybe we should go down to the police station and make a statement."

Darla shook her head quickly. Turning out the lights and walking around was creepy but not exactly illegal. And Hopper was already unhappy at the way she had been drawing attention to them both – what would he say about Darla going to the police about this? No, keeping quiet was the best thing.

"Are you sure, hon?" Annie said.

She nodded – and to her relief, the artist didn't try to change her mind. It was dark by the time Annie locked up the gallery and drove Darla back to the creek. When they pulled up outside her house, Darla paused as she unbuckled her seatbelt.

"Promise not to tell Hopper about today? I don't want him worrying."

Annie patted her hand. "You can trust me, honey."

Darla smiled gratefully and got out of the car. The lights were on in the front window of her house, strains of country music drifting out into the evening air. As Darla entered the hall, she heard Hopper's laughter coming from the back room. It sounded like he had company. When Darla walked into the back room and saw who it was, she blinked with surprise.

Sasha was sitting cross-legged in the middle of the carpet, vinyl records scattered around her: Johnny Cash, Merle Haggard, Patsy Cline – all of Hopper's favourites. Her dark hair had been dyed a shocking shade of red, and she had deliberately smudged her thick mascara to make it look as though she had been crying. But at that moment she was laughing at Hopper, who was crooning along with the record.

"Help, Darla!" wailed Sasha, her hands over her ears. "Make it stop!"

"What are you doing here?" said Darla.

Sasha held up a record – it was the Sleater-Kinney album Darla had picked up earlier. "I brought you a present," she said. "I got so bored I closed the store and went home to change and dye my hair and now I am officially ready to have fun. Hopper kindly said I could wait here with him until you got back. But it turns out it was just an evil trap to force me to listen to country music."

Hopper. So now they were on first-name terms. Great.

"You oughta be thanking me!" Hopper told Sasha indignantly. "I am introducing you to a whole new world here – a world of love and heartbreak and lap steel guitar. Forget about your hip-hop and your emo or whatever the hell it is you kids listen to these days. This right here is the real sound of the wrong side of the tracks."

"What, like Taylor Swift?" teased Sasha.

Hopper winced. "Ouch."

Darla couldn't believe it. Only a week ago Sasha had been insistent that her daddy was a sleaze, but after an hour of playing records together the two of them seemed to be as thick as thieves. She glared at Sasha but, as usual, her friend didn't seem to notice as she bounded to her feet and wrapped her arm around Darla.

"So now you've *finally* decided to turn up, do you

want to come out with me?"

"I don't know, Sasha," Darla said reluctantly. "It's been kinda a long day…"

"All the more reason to go and have some fun!" Sasha replied brightly.

"I was gonna stay in…"

"Aw c'mon now, darlin'," Hopper said encouragingly. "Your friend's come all the way here to see you, and you're going to turn her down?"

She couldn't believe her daddy was taking Sasha's side. Maybe if he had heard himself being called a sleaze he'd think differently, Darla thought to herself. After what had happened in the gallery the last thing she wanted was to go out with Sasha, but with a sinking heart Darla realized that she wasn't going to be able to resist her friend. When had she been able?

"OK," she said. "I'll come."

Sasha clapped her hands together with glee.

"And you're sure you girls will be safe, now?" said Hopper. "I know that Leeroy's behind bars, but the curfew's still in force."

"Scout's honour," Sasha replied dutifully. "We're going over to Frank's place to watch movies. He'll drive us there and back."

"Then you have my paternal blessing," Hopper told Darla. "Go and have fun, and leave this old man alone with his records."

She felt like screaming at the pair of them. Why had they chosen today to buddy up? Darla was dragged from her house before she could protest, Hopper's voice yodelling farewell as he turned up the volume on his record player. Sasha's eyes were shining and she was babbling with excitement.

"An entire *hour* of country music, Darla!" she gasped. "He just wouldn't stop playing it. Thank God you came home."

"I don't know about that," Darla muttered. "Seems to me you two were getting on just fine without me."

"Hey!" protested Sasha. "What does that mean?"

"Nothing."

"That did *not* mean nothing."

"Forget about it," Darla said stubbornly.

"Weren't you the one who told me to give your dad a chance? But now I get on with him, and that's a problem too? Jeez, Darla, make up your mind!"

Maybe Darla was being unfair. But something

about the sight of Sasha and Hopper joking around together made her uncomfortable. It wasn't that she didn't trust her daddy around her friends. But Sasha was no ordinary girl — for one thing she was strikingly beautiful, and for another she acted older than her age. It was a potentially dangerous combination.

They walked down the lane in silence, Sasha moodily thrusting her hands in her pockets.

"Wait," said Darla, looking up and down the empty road. "Where's Frank?"

Sasha shrugged. "How should I know? Alphabetizing his sock-drawer, probably."

"You told Hopper we were going to his place to watch movies!"

"Darla, of *course* I told Hopper we were going to his place to watch movies. How else were we going to get him to let you out?"

"So you lied to him?"

"It certainly looks that way."

"Sasha, what's going on?"

"Why are you always so suspicious? C'mon, it's Saturday night — don't you want to go out, just me and you?"

Darla stopped, her hands on her hips.

"No games, Sasha," she said firmly. "Tell me where we're going."

"To hear some music, OK?" said Sasha. "Some *real* music."

Chapter Nineteen

When they reached the end of the creek lane Sasha stood on the verge of the highway, scanning the darkness for cars. Darla, who was already getting an ominous feeling about the night ahead, watched her dubiously.

"What are you doing?" she said.

"We're going to need a ride," replied Sasha, holding out her thumb. "Look appealing."

"You want us to *hitch*?" hissed Darla. "Are you crazy? There's a serial killer on the loose!"

"Yeah, I think I heard something about that," Sasha said.

"It's not funny!"

"Do you see me laughing? But Leeroy Mills is locked up in a prison cell where he can't harm anyone and I think it's time we stopped hiding under the blankets, you know what I'm saying?"

"We don't know that Leeroy was the Angel Taker."

"Oh, come off it, Darla!" Sasha sounded exasperated. "You saw inside his trailer – that guy was off-the-charts creepy. Total psycho. Don't you remember him chasing us through the woods with a rifle? He could have killed Frank!"

"I'm not saying Leeroy's a good guy," Darla said weakly. "I'm just not sure he's the killer."

"OK, then, Sherlock Holmes, if the Angel Taker isn't Leeroy, who is?"

A car pulled over to the verge before Darla could reply. The window hummed down, revealing a bespectacled middle-aged man.

"Kinda risky to be hitching tonight, ain't it, girls?" he asked in a thick Southern accent. "There's a killer been running around these parts."

"We know," Sasha replied. "Our friend was supposed to be giving us a ride but her car broke down and now we're late and we haven't got money for a cab, so…" She trailed off hopefully.

"Where are you headed?" asked the man.

"You know Shooters?" said Sasha.

He nodded. "I've heard of it. Lucky for you, I'm heading that way. You'd better hop in."

Darla tried to pull Sasha back, but she was too

slow to prevent her friend diving gleefully into the backseat. Forget about the Angel Taker — at that moment Darla could have happily killed Sasha herself. But now her friend was alone in the back of a stranger's car, so Darla had no choice but to get in after her. The vehicle smelled of leather polish and car soap, like it had just been bought straight from the dealers. An old country song was playing on the radio. 'Stand By Your Man' by Tammy Wynette — Darla had lost count of the times she heard it growing up.

She dug her elbow into Sasha's ribs. "Shooters?" she hissed. "Have you gone crazy? I can't go to a bar — I haven't got any ID!"

Sasha laughed. "So? Neither have I. Relax, Darla!"

She leaned forwards and asked the driver to turn up the radio. When he obliged she began singing along with Tammy Wynette in an out-of-key voice, having apparently called a temporary ceasefire on her war against country music. At least the old man driving them seemed harmless enough, even if his scrupulously clean car made Darla feel a little uneasy. Was he just proud of it, or had he spent hours sponging the blood of his hitchhiking victims from the upholstery? Everywhere she looked these days, Darla saw potential murderers.

She stared out of the window at the dark creek as the car turned off the highway and rattled along a dirt track, tree branches scraping against the roof. Up ahead, the headlights picked out a building in the middle of a lonely patch of scrubland. The sign above the bar blared out the word 'Shooters' in violent green neon letters beside a blinking snake's head. Metal grilles covered the windows, and the ground was littered with broken bottles. Motorcycles were parked in a row outside, a couple of bikers staring suspiciously at the car as it approached. There was a queue huddled outside the entrance, where a huge, shaven-headed man in a leather jacket filled the doorway.

The driver eyed the bar dubiously. "You girls sure you want to get out here? This place looks kinda rough."

"It's cool," said Sasha. "Our boyfriends are waiting for us in the line."

"If you say so," he replied. "Have a good night,

249

y'all. Make sure you get home before the curfew."

"Thanks, we will!"

They got out of the car, which performed a crunching U-turn across the gravel and drove away into the night. Now that she had left his backseat Darla had convinced herself that the driver wasn't in fact a serial killer, and as his twinkling tail lights were swallowed up into the gloom she felt her last hopes disappearing with them. But there was no turning back now. Sasha grabbed Darla's hand and marched her towards Shooters, ignoring the waiting line and heading straight for the fearsome-looking bouncer at the door.

"Hey there, McGee," said Sasha, grinning.

He nodded back. "Hey, Sasha. Here for the bands?"

"I hear it's a killer line-up tonight."

McGee laughed roughly, a match striking across sandpaper. "You're talking to the wrong guy," he rasped. "They all sound terrible to me. Come on in."

"She's with me," said Sasha, casually jerking a thumb at Darla.

Darla tried not to flinch as McGee looked her

up and down. She didn't look eighteen, let alone twenty-one. But to her amazement, McGee merely shrugged.

"If you say so," he said. He stamped both of their hands with an inked design of a snake and ushered them inside.

It was dark within, bottles gleaming dirtily in the neon glare of the sign behind the bar. Burly men with long hair and bandanas hunched over their drinks. It was exactly the kind of place Hopper liked: a dingy dive, where the shadows would hide your wrinkles and the grey in your hair, and you could pretend you were ten years younger. Darla could picture him at one of the stools at the bar, spinning stories made of hot air for whichever pretty girl would listen to him.

"See?" Sasha said smugly. "I told you getting in wouldn't be a problem. My family and McGee go *way* back. My dad helped get him off a charge a few years ago – so every now and again McGee does the odd favour in return."

"What kind of charge?" Darla asked dubiously.

Sasha waved an airy hand. "I don't know, there was some kind of fight. McGee's not a bad guy."

"I'll take your word for it," said Darla.

They walked past the hulking bikers at the bar and headed deeper into Shooters, towards a staircase in the corner of the room. There was a door at the bottom of the rickety row of steps, with a homemade poster advertising a host of bands all 'Playing Tonite'. Loud music flooded out from the basement, the thrashing guitars and pounding drums making the door pulse like a beating heart. Sasha clapped her hands together with delight and threw open the door.

A wall of heat and noise hit Darla, making her take a step back. The basement of Shooters was a cramped room with low ceilings and a bar running the length of one wall. A three-piece punk band was playing on a stage in the corner of the room, a small crowd spraying beer everywhere as they pogoed up and down in front of them. The air was heavy with sweat and serrated guitar chords. Sasha's cheeks flushed with excitement and her eyes shone as she slipped through the audience.

"Isn't this *great*?" she shouted.

Darla nodded enthusiastically, not quite sure what to say. As Sasha queued for drinks at the bar

Darla stood near the booths at the back of the room, watching the band play. The guitarist was a whirlwind of manic, angular energy, jamming out chords as he snarled into the microphone, whilst the dark-haired bassist kept his head down as he played, totally absorbed in the music. Their song came to a sudden, savage end, and the crowd whistled and roared their approval. Sasha reappeared, pressing a plastic glass of Coke into Darla's hand. When Darla took a sip, she could taste the strong kick of rum. She glanced at Sasha but didn't say anything. After another short number the band's set came to an end and the crowd headed to the bar: girls with skinheads and boys wearing thick black eyeliner, old men in leather jackets running with sweat. Darla didn't see a single face she recognized.

"Does nobody else from school come here?" she asked Sasha.

"You're kidding me, right?" laughed Sasha. "This scene is *way* too raw for the hills. It's way too raw for South Carolina, full stop. People come hundreds of miles just to see these bands play."

She drained her drink and went back to the bar to get two more, even though Darla had barely started hers. And when Sasha returned, she had company: the guitarist and bassist from the band they had just been watching, their sleeveless T-shirts stained with sweat and beer.

"This is Evan and Jaime," Sasha told Darla. "I was just telling them how awesome they were sounding tonight."

"You were really good," Darla said politely.

Evan, the singer and guitarist, barely glanced at her. But tousle-haired Jaime smiled.

"Thanks," he said.

"The next band's about to come on," Evan told Sasha. "You want to get a good spot by the stage?"

Sasha looked at Darla, who meaningfully widened her eyes to say, *Don't you dare!*

"I would be... delighted!" Sasha said brightly. She linked arms with Evan and headed over to the stage, looking back at Darla and saying as she went, "Don't do anything I wouldn't do!"

Darla felt her cheeks burn with embarrassment. For the second time that night, she contemplated killing her friend. This was just so typical of Sasha, so typically selfish. Darla took an awkward sip of her drink, waiting for Jaime to take pity on her and leave her alone. But, to her surprise, he showed no sign of moving.

"So you liked our set?" he said.

"I guess!" Darla replied. "I only caught the last couple of songs – we only just got here."

"That's cool," Jaime said. "We're called 'Where's Walter?' You know, after the guy who killed that beauty queen years ago."

"Walter West?" said Darla.

"He's supposed to be dead but there's this urban legend that he's still out there somewhere." Jaime shifted uncomfortably. "Personally I think the name sucks, but it was Evan's idea and it's kinda his band. So please don't tell him that."

Darla laughed. "I won't."

"I'm from Arizona," Jaime told her. "All this Saffron Hills local mystery crap doesn't mean anything to me."

"I'm not from here either," Darla told him.

"Really? Where you from?"

Darla laughed. "Everywhere."

"Cool."

She caught sight of a flash of red hair amongst the crowd by the stage – Sasha, leaping up and down with Evan. Darla giggled. She seemed to have finished her first drink and had started on her second. Maybe it was the alcohol or maybe it was Jaime, but a strange thing was happening: Darla was starting to enjoy herself. Jaime seemed to like the fact that she wasn't from Saffron Hills, and didn't seem to care that she didn't know any of the bands he talked about. They sat in one of the alcoves at the back of the basement and chatted, shouting to make themselves heard above the music. Every time Darla finished her drink, a fresh one seemed to appear in front of her as if by magic. She stopped worrying about alcoholic parents and dead teenagers and serial killers. She laughed and made jokes. Occasionally Sasha would appear, drenched in sweat, whooping and kissing Darla on the cheek and taking selfies of them together before Evan dragged her back into the crowd. Even the music seemed to improve.

As the last band of the evening took to the stage, Darla was suddenly aware of Jaime's arm around her shoulder. She nestled against his chest, her heart thudding. She had never dreamed the night could have ended this way. It felt as though her head was spinning, that she was faint. And not totally in a good way.

"Hey, are you OK?" Jaime asked.

"I'm fine," Darla replied woozily. "I just need to go the bathroom. Wait a minute, I'll be back."

She left the booth and pushed her way through the flailing audience gathered around the stage. All of a sudden the basement was too hot and too crowded – Darla felt like she couldn't breathe. As she struggled towards the bathroom she accidentally elbowed a girl, who turned around and shoved her back. Darla mumbled an apology and reeled away, gasping with relief when she stumbled through the door into the ladies' room.

The bathroom was small and dirty. Paper towels were strewn over the floor, the walls a black scrawl of graffiti. This close to the stage, the entire room shook to the sound of the band – Darla could barely hear herself think. She went over to the basin and splashed handfuls of cold water in her face, trying to ignore her churning stomach. She had drunk too much. If she threw up, she would just die of embarrassment. Her heart sinking, Darla realized she was going to have to call Hopper for a ride home. She would never see Jaime again – of course. Nothing like that ever worked out for her.

Darla took a clean paper towel from the dispenser and dried her face. She looked up into the mirror, and screamed.

The bathroom wasn't empty any more. A man was standing right behind her.

It was Leeroy Mills.

Chapter Twenty

Up to now, Darla had only caught glimpses of Leeroy through car and trailer windows. Close up, he was bigger than she had realized, wiry rather than skinny. He was wearing jeans and a black cowboy shirt with roses sewn into the collar and cuffs, a bolo tie around his neck. The harsh bathroom light didn't do Leeroy any favours, showing up his bad skin and thinning hair. His eyes were vague and unfocused. Darla knew that look well – Hopper used to get it too, when he had been drinking.

Leeroy didn't move or speak. He just stared at her. Darla looked over his shoulder, praying that someone would walk in and save her. But the door remained resolutely closed.

"I think you're in the wrong room," she said, shouting above the music.

He shook his head. "Nah, I don't think so."

"What do you want?"

Leeroy scratched his stubbled cheek. "I seen you," he said. "Around the way. In the car with your daddy. Outside those big ol' mansions up in the hills." He smiled. "Leeroy don't forget a face, li'l girl."

"So?"

"I *also* seen you creeping around my trailer with those friends of yours. Got out there pretty damned quick, didn't you? Like itty bitty mice, scuttling away when they see a pussy cat."

"You should be in jail," Darla told him. "I know the cops arrested you."

"The cops had to let Leeroy go. Because he didn't do nothin'."

He took a step towards her, enveloping Darla in a sour cloud of whiskey and cigarettes. She edged backwards, feeling herself bump up against the basin.

"P-please don't hurt me," she stammered.

Leeory feigned an innocent look. "Whaddya mean by that? Leeroy don't hurt anyone – not least, no one who don't deserve it," he said. "Do you deserve to get hurt, li'l girl?"

Darla shook her head quickly.

"Well now, there you go," he said. "No need to be scared. We can have ourselves a li'l talk. Tell Leeroy what you were doing going through his things, looking at his photographs."

"They weren't your photographs!" Darla shot back. "They were Natalie's — you stole them!"

Leeroy shrugged. "She didn't need them no more. I weren't doing no harm."

"So you were in her house the night she died."

"Now maybe I was, and maybe I wasn't. But Leeroy didn't touch a hair on her pretty little head. I was trying to protect her."

Darla laughed incredulously. "I don't believe you."

"That's the thing, you see — no one listens to Leeroy. I told them years ago that Walter West weren't dead, that he was still out there, but they were too busy trying to hush everything up. But I knew he'd come back eventually. And now the pretty ones are dying again." Darla shuddered as Leeroy took a strand of her hair in his fingers and toyed with it. "This ain't no time to be pretty, l'il girl."

"Help!" screamed Darla, but her cry didn't stand

a chance against the music in the next room. Leeroy pressed a nicotine-stained finger against his lips.

"Hush now," he said. "Ain't no need to holler."

The door banged open, and Sasha marched inside the bathroom. At the sight of Leeroy, she fumbled in the pocket of her denim jacket. He pushed Darla out of the way and lunged towards her, only for Sasha to produce a slim canister and spray it in his face. Leeroy howled with pain, clutching his eyes as he staggered into the hand dryer.

"You little bitch!" he spat. "I'm gonna git you!"

"Screw you, asshole!" Sasha screamed back. "Stay away from her or I'll kill you!"

Leeroy made a blind swipe at her but Sasha easily ducked out of the way. Grabbing hold of Darla, she pulled her away from the basin and dragged her out of the bathroom. The door slammed shut behind them, cutting off Leeroy's cries. In shock, Darla stared numbly at a sea of strange faces as Sasha elbowed her way through the crowd and out of the basement. Upstairs they stumbled through the bar and out into the night air, where Darla dropped to her hands and knees in the dirty earth. She was retching violently, her whole body shaking.

"What's going on, Sasha?" a voice rasped — McGee, the bouncer.

"Some slimeball just attacked my friend in the bathroom," Sasha told him angrily. "I pepper-sprayed him but he's still down there."

McGee's face darkened. "You know the guy?"

"His name's Leeroy Mills," Sasha told him. "Look for a guy with a black cowboy shirt and burning eyes."

"You girls need to get out of here," McGee said. "We never spoke, OK?"

He jerked his head at a couple of bikers and the three men disappeared inside the bar, the front door banging ominously shut behind them. Sasha took out her phone and dialled a number, stroking Darla's hair with her other hand.

"Frank?" she said. "Yes, I know what time it is! Can you come to Shooters and pick us up? It's an emergency. Yes, I'm fine, but Darla... Look, just come quickly, OK?"

Darla had stopped retching, her mouth swimming with the stinging aftertaste of bile. She pulled herself into a sitting position and put her head in her hands, letting out heaving sobs of shock.

"I did it again, didn't I?" she said miserably. "I ruined another night!"

"Hey, hey!" Sasha told her, putting Darla's face between her hands. "It wasn't your fault."

"I'm sorry!"

"Shh!" Sasha wrapped her up in a tight embrace. "It's OK now. Frank's going to come and take you home, and McGee will take care of Leeroy Mills. He won't ever bother you again, don't you worry about that."

Darla wasn't sure how long they waited outside the bar – it only felt like a couple of minutes before a pair of headlights appeared in the night and the pick-up pulled up beside them. Frank peered out of the driver's window, concern in his eyes.

"What the hell happened?" he asked. "What are you doing here?"

"No time to explain," snapped Sasha. "Just get us out of here."

She helped Darla up into the backseat and followed her inside the vehicle, hugging her and whispering shushing noises into her ear. As Frank hurriedly drove the pick-up away from Shooters, Darla thought she saw a group of men carry a prone figure out of the door. She turned away, not wanting to see any more.

Darla had thought that she couldn't have felt any worse than she had when she had been scrabbling around in the dirt outside Shooters. But that was before the hangover hit. She woke up with a groan, her mouth parched and a searing pain inside her skull. Her memories of the night were shattered fragments, like broken bottles: talking with Jaime, his arm around her; Leeroy Mills' sudden appearance; McGee striding back into the bar. She barely remembered anything of the journey back – just a pensive silence, Frank's anxious glance into the rearview mirror. But the worst thing was the sight of the men bundling Leeroy out of Shooters. Leeroy might be weird and threatening but Darla didn't want anyone getting beaten up in her name. At the time she had been too shocked to stop Sasha and McGee, but now she felt a horrible, lurching responsibility. What if they had really hurt him? Darla had the feeling that there wasn't much McGee wouldn't do for the Haas family, especially their beautiful teenage daughter.

She wanted to go back to sleep and try to forget everything that had happened, but she was thirsty and her head was hurting too much. Reluctantly Darla climbed out of bed and went into the kitchen – where she found Hopper waiting for her. He was sitting at the table, angrily drumming his fingers.

"Nice of you to join us," he said. "I was wondering if you were going to spend the whole day in bed."

Darla said nothing. Opening the fridge, she drank orange juice straight from the carton.

"Guessing you've a real thirst on you this morning," said Hopper. "Headache too, no doubt."

"You're a real detective, aren't you?" Darla muttered.

"I heard you come crashing in last night – not that you would have realized, you were so outta it."

"You're going to tell *me* off for having a hangover, Daddy?"

"You're damn right I am, Darla!" Hopper shouted. "You're sixteen years old! What the hell were you thinking?"

"It wasn't my idea, remember? You wanted me to go out with Sasha."

"You said you were going to a friend's house to watch movies! Not get wasted on booze!"

"You don't know Sasha," Darla said stubbornly. "She *always* wants to drink."

"Where were you?"

"It doesn't matter."

"I'll be the judge of that, young lady."

They glared at each other across the table. Finally Hopper sighed, and wearily rubbed his face.

"I was worried, darlin'," he said finally. "Can't you see that? There's someone dangerous out there. I don't want to lock you up in the house, you gotta spend time with your friends. But going out and getting drunk like that, you can't take care of yourself at all. You're my daughter, Darla, you're everything to me. If I lost you too, I wouldn't be able to live with myself."

Darla could cope with her daddy getting mad at her and shouting, but this she hadn't been expecting. She went over to where Hopper was sitting and put her arms around him, resting her head upon his shoulder.

"I'm sorry."

"Me too," he whispered back. "For everything."

There were tears in both their eyes now. Hopper coughed and got up to close the fridge door. When he turned back to her, his stern expression had returned.

"So how *are* you feeling there, missy?"

"Put it this way," Darla groaned, "I don't think you have to worry about me drinking again."

"Glad to hear it." Hopper pointed a finger at her. "But that don't make it all right, you hear me? Consider yourself grounded for the rest of the week. And you can tell Sasha from me that Happy Hour is over."

Darla rubbed her aching temples. "Are we done now? I *really* need to go back to bed."

"Yeah, we're done," said Hopper. "Go on, scat."

He opened a newspaper and began to read. In one way it seemed grossly unfair to Darla that he could punish *her* for going out drinking. All those years of lies and broken promises, angry men hammering at their door, the moonlight flights to safety … and yet because of that, part of Darla almost liked the fact that Hopper was angry. He was behaving like a normal daddy should. Even as she trudged back to her bedroom and pulled the blankets over her head, Darla could feel a tiny seed of happiness taking root in the depths of her soul.

Chapter Twenty-One

Carmen Russo sat in the front seat of her Cadillac in the family driveway, examining her resigned reflection in the rearview mirror. Ryan's parents had finally returned from Africa, and his funeral was taking place that morning. She didn't want to go. Funerals were just so ... *depressing*. Wasn't it bad enough that three of her friends had been murdered? Wasn't she going through enough, without having to sit there and watch a bunch of losers wail and cry like they were Perfect too? Thank God TJ's family had had a private service, sparing her that one at least. It had taken Carmen hours to work out her outfit, and apply her make-up so it was *just so*. It was the first thing she did every morning, putting on her face so the world could see her. Her daddy had taught her the importance of that; he had made millions teaching women across the country the same thing. Carmen could almost hear his voice telling her to sit up straight and smile.

She wondered whether the boys' murders meant they would call off Miss Saffron. Secretly Carmen was hoping that the pageant would still go ahead. Before everyone had just assumed that Natalie was going to win it because her mom was a big deal up at the country club. Now she was gone, maybe it might be a fair contest. And who would be a more fitting winner than one of Natalie's best friends?

Sunlight was shining in through the passenger window, framing Carmen's face perfectly. Brushing the hair out of her eyes, she held her phone above her head and tilted her chin up. She carefully arranged her face into a sorrowful expression – people had to see how sad she was feeling.

Click.

Carmen lowered her phone and inspected the photograph. Her mouth curved into a small, satisfied smile.

Perfect.

Hidden away behind high stone walls and forbidding iron gates, Saffron Hills' Azalea Cemetery was a solemn, beautiful secret. Rows of stark white crosses marked the approach to elaborate tombs adorned with carved angels; stone tears running down stone faces. A series of pathways ran between the graves, offering mourners glimpses of the epitaphs etched into the headstones. At the height of summer the flowerbeds would have exploded with colour but now everything was tinged with solemn hues, from the oak trees covered in wispy fringes of Spanish moss to the fading camellias and the azaleas that had given the cemetery its name. The graveyard's still heart was a small ornamental lake – a large spoonbill perched on a low-hanging branch over the water, peering into the depths.

Inside the Azalea's crowded chapel Darla sweltered beneath her black cardigan, white blouse and thick black woolen skirt. She didn't have much clothing to wear that was appropriate for a funeral, and it wasn't as though there was money for new clothes. Beside her Frank surreptitiously checked his phone whilst Sasha stared dead ahead, quiet for once. Judging by the packed rows inside the chapel, most of the school had turned out to pay their respects. The building echoed to the sound of muffled sobs.

Ryan's handsome face stared out from a blown-up photograph at the front of the chapel, his mouth twitching with some unspoken amusement. His parents stood in the front row, the disbelief still visible on their drawn faces.

Word of Leeroy's release had spread quickly around Saffron Hills, shattering the fragile cocoon of relief that had enveloped the town upon word of his arrest. The Angel Taker was still out there. As she looked around the chapel Darla felt a complex mixture of fear, anger and frustration. What was the use of her visions if she couldn't stop the murders before they happened? Why hadn't people listened to her when she tried to warn them? At the front of the chapel, Ryan's crooked smile almost seemed to be mocking Darla.

Frank covered his mouth with his hand, coughing back laughter. Darla elbowed him in the ribs.

"What is wrong with you?" she hissed.

"My bad," he said apologetically. "I couldn't resist checking."

He showed his phone to Darla, who looked at it reluctantly. Frank had visited Carmen's Instagram profile, where she had posted fresh photographs of herself on her way to Ryan's funeral. She was sat in the front seat of her car, wearing another expensive black dress and pushing her sunglasses up on her head to reveal her red-rimmed eyes. Beneath the photo she had written the hashtags: '#tears' '#restinpeace' '#beautiful' '#anotherfriendgone'.

"She can't help herself, can she?" said Frank.

There was a ripple of noise around them – Darla looked up and saw Gabrielle walking slowly down the chapel aisle, a picture of elegance in a plain black dress and veil, her hair pinned up beneath a hat.

"*Though I walk through the shadow of the valley of death...*" Frank murmured.

"What is Gabrielle *doing* here?" Darla whispered. "Doesn't she know how much danger she's in?"

"Her mom and dad were going to send her to Cleveland, but last night Gabrielle stood up in Pastor James's church and said she was staying put – something about being safe in the Lord's hands. Her parents are crazy worried but they go *way* back with the Pastor and don't want to lose face. I'm telling you, give it a week and it'll only be me, you and Gabrielle left at school."

Frank seemed to find this idea more amusing than Darla did. She didn't find anything funny right now. What was more surprising, neither did Sasha. As the service began Darla was sure she caught her friend brushing a tear away from her eye. Maybe Ryan's murder had affected her more than she was willing to admit. In a strange way, Darla hoped so. She knew that Sasha and Frank loved to compete in saying outrageous things, but sometimes there was a callous edge to their jokes that made her wonder if they really cared about anything. Sasha sensed Darla looking at her, and shot her a fierce glare. If she was upset, she was never going to admit it.

Ryan's family had invited Pastor James to speak, and the congregation fell silent when he stepped forwards and cleared his throat. But as the pastor's sonorous tones echoed around the chapel, Darla had the uneasy sense that something was wrong. She turned and looked through the window, only to see her ghostly reflection in the glass. Instantly Darla tried to look away, but it was too late... Already she could feel herself being swallowed up by a mind that wasn't her own.

The Angel Taker was sat at a laptop in their dark room, scrolling down through a page filled with photographs. There were hundreds of pictures, all taken by Carmen Russo of herself – pouting into her bathroom mirror, lying out on the beach in her swimsuit, pretending to yawn at the back of the classroom. In one of the photographs, Carmen was leaning against the hood of her white Cadillac. The Angel Taker reached out and touched the screen, stroking a gloved finger down her cheek…

Darla put her head in her hands, fighting back a wave of dizziness. Frank gave her a concerned look

"You OK?" he whispered.

"Where's Carmen?" Darla hissed back.

Frank looked around the congregation, which was rapt in Pastor James's address. "Can't see her. Probably lost track of time taking photographs of herself. Why?"

"I saw something…" Darla said hesitantly. "I think she's in trouble."

A man in the pew behind them shushed her.

"I gotta go," Darla muttered.

"Now?" said Frank.

Around her people were turning and staring disapprovingly, but Darla didn't care. Pushing her way past a surprised Sasha, she ran down the aisle and out of the chapel, the heavy oaken doors booming shut behind her.

Solemn strains of organ music were wafting out over the graveyard as Carmen hurriedly parked her car in the lane leading up to the chapel. She was *seriously* late. It wasn't her fault, the traffic had been snarled up on the strip. But that wasn't going to stop Gabrielle lecturing her, Carmen knew. Gabrielle seemed to think that she was better than everyone else just because she sang at church, but Carmen knew she wasn't quite as pure as she made out. For one thing, she had a very un-Christian crush on Pastor James. Since Ryan and TJ's murders Gabrielle had been acting distant with Carmen – she could pretend all she liked it was down to grief, but Carmen was sure it was because Gabrielle knew she was the only serious competition left at Miss Saffron.

Carmen went to open the car door – and stopped herself. She took a deep breath. There was no point spending all that time choosing her outfit and getting her make-up perfect if she rushed into the chapel looking like Natalie after one of her psycho jogging sessions. Pulling out her mirror, Carmen carefully reapplied her lip gloss. Could you be fashionably late for a funeral?

There was a sharp rap on the window. Carmen jumped, dropping her lip gloss. It rolled under her seat, and she swore as she scrabbled around for it on the floor of the car. Her fingers closed around the thin cylinder; she straightened up, and looked angrily out through the window. Someone was standing beside her car. Probably another do-gooder wanting to know why she was late. Carmen opened the automatic window.

"What?" she snapped.

A hand reached in through the window and latched around Carmen's neck, trapping her scream in her throat.

Darla ran through the gravestones, taking deep gulps of air. She knew that she had caused a scene back at the funeral but she couldn't worry about that now. The Angel Taker had Carmen Russo in their sights, and Darla had to find her before the killer did.

The Azalea Cemetery was deserted. As Darla ran up a slight incline she fell under the shadow of a giant oak, gooseflesh breaking out across her skin. When she came out in front of a large marble tomb, complete with praying angels on either side, she drew to a halt.

The West family grave was an ornate building draped in Spanish moss, twice the size of any other tomb in the cemetery. An inscription read: 'Here lies Allan West, the Father of Saffron Hills, beside his loving wife Madeline.' Walter's grave was next to his parents' tomb, a plain stone oblong on a raised plinth. As Darla examined the grave, she saw that a bunch of white lilies had been laid on the earth by the plinth. She knelt down by the grave, tracing a finger across a delicate white petal. They were fresh — someone had left them here recently. But who? Walter's family were all dead, apart from his missing sister. Who would want to pay their respects to a known killer?

As Darla straightened up, a gleam caught her eye.

Carmen's white Cadillac was parked in the lane behind Walter's tomb. She picked her way down the slope towards it, a knot of dread tightening in her stomach. The car's windows were shaded, but she could see the outline of someone sitting in the backseat.

Slowly, almost as though in a dream, Darla walked over and opened the rear door. A wave of revulsion washed over her.

Carmen was dead, her eyes bulging with nameless horror and her body carefully arranged on the back seat. Her throat had been slit and her hair had been savagely hacked off, tufts of beautiful blond hair strewn all over the leather seats, which were caked with blood. Something was jutting out of her mouth. Almost against her will, Darla looked closer and realized that it was Carmen's phone. The Angel Taker had tried to make her eat it.

Darla took a step back, and fainted clean away.

Chapter Twenty-Two

It was different this time. After Natalie's death, Darla remembered how kind and gentle everyone had been with her. But when the police took her from the cemetery to the station their faces were stony, hard edges in their voices when they questioned her. And when Hopper picked her up afterwards he seemed angry too, speeding home and slamming saucepans around the kitchen as he made dinner.

"What's wrong, Daddy?" asked Darla. "You seem kinda mad with me."

"I'm sorry, darlin'," said Hopper, slumping into a chair. "I just wish it had been someone else's kid who kept finding dead bodies. I came back early from my lunch break today and saw the store manager talking with the police. I ducked outta sight and waited until they had gone before going back. The store manager didn't say nothin' about it, but I could swear he was acting funny with me the rest of the day."

"You were probably just imagining it," Darla said, trying to sound reassuring. "Maybe his car was broken into or his neighbours got robbed or something like that."

"Maybe – or maybe the police were asking questions about me, trying to see if I fit the bill for this Angel Taker."

"But that's crazy!" said Darla. "You haven't done anything!"

"Not here," Hopper said meaningfully.

He was in a dark mood for the rest of the evening, and no matter how hard Darla tried she couldn't shake him out of it. In the middle of the night, a nightmare jolted her awake – she sat bolt upright in bed, her skin damp with freezing sweat and the taste of terror in her mouth. Darla didn't sleep another wink, and when she met Hopper in the kitchen the next morning there were dark circles beneath his eyes too.

With another student murdered, Darla had assumed that the West Academy would be closed. But to her dismay she saw that there were students milling about the school entrance as the Buick pulled up outside. Two stern-faced policemen were standing guard at the front door, scanning the crowds through their sunglasses. Frank and Sasha were sitting at the bottom of the steps, deep in conversation. At the sight of Darla they broke off and waved her over. She hurried across the lot, painfully aware of the wary looks the other students were giving her.

"You're brave," said Frank. "Didn't think you'd come to school today."

"I wasn't sure it would be open."

"There was an emergency meeting of the school board last night," Sasha told her. "They voted to keep the school open, but only with added protection. Hence the Donut Patrol by the door." She looked up at Darla, shielding her eyes from the sun. "How are you doing?"

"I don't how to begin to answer that," Darla replied wearily.

"Frank said you saw the Angel Taker again in the chapel. You know, before Carmen…"

Darla nodded.

"You ever wonder why you're getting these visions?"

"Only every minute of the day," she said. "I don't

know, maybe I'm just as crazy as the Angel Taker. These damned visions make me feel like … like I'm some kinda accomplice or something. But what am I supposed to do, spend the rest of my life hiding from my own reflection?"

"The visions will stop when they catch the killer," Sasha told her.

"*If* they catch them," Frank added, pushing his glasses up the bridge of his nose.

"Hey, what kind of talk is that?" said Sasha. "You know, Franklin, you are developing a seriously uncool attitude."

"My apologies," he said sarcastically. "You just can't get the hired help these days, can you?"

"Aw, don't worry," Sasha grinned. "You'll always be my accomplice."

She reached out to ruffle his hair but he irritably knocked her hand away. In recent days Darla thought she could detect a hairline fracture in Frank and Sasha's relationship. They had seemed inseparable when she had first met them, mischievous co-conspirators. But, to her surprise, Sasha seemed increasingly interested in hanging out with her – and both Darla and Frank knew it.

Great. Something else she could feel guilty about.

"Listen — there's something you need to see," Sasha told her.

Darla's heart sank. "What is it now?" she said.

Frank handed her his phone. "Another blog was posted this morning," he told her. "Look."

HELL'S ANGEL STRIKES AGAIN!

Another day in Saffron Hills, another brutal murder. This time the victim was walking make-up doll Carmen Russo, who had failed to show at the funeral for fellow Angel Taker victim Ryan Cafferty. Only minutes before her untimely death, Carmen had posted a delectable selfie of herself so the world could see how upset she was. Which is just the kind of thing that gets the Angel Taker's attention.

Life is getting pretty dangerous in this quiet little corner of South Carolina. So here are some Top Tips to help you stay alive:

1.   If your name is Gabrielle Jones, you might want to think about going on vacation about now.

2.   Right now PRETTY = DEAD. It's time to put

285

away the make-up and go au naturel, ladies. (Same goes for anyone wearing guyliner.)

3.   *Anyone contemplating entering any local BEAUTY PAGEANTS might want to have a re-think.*

4.   *Avoid DARLA O'NEILL at all costs. That girl is a murder magnet. Seeing as Saffron Hills' finest law enforcement officers are struggling for leads, maybe they should ask Darla for help. She seems to know where all the bodies are buried...*

"I don't believe it!" Darla groaned. "Hopper's going to freak when he hears about this!"

"Like it's your fault!" Sasha said sympathetically. "Whoever's writing this blog is a complete asshole."

"An asshole who *everyone* in Saffron Hills is reading and talking about," Frank pointed out.

Sasha turned on him. "Oh really. And that makes it OK, does it?"

The homeroom bell burst into life before Frank could reply. There was nothing for it but to go inside. As she passed through the entrance Darla shrank back under the gaze of the police. Was she being paranoid, or were they looking straight at her? They might have been placed here to protect

286

the students, but the presence of armed men only made Darla feel more edgy. Even school wasn't safe now. The corridors seemed emptier than usual – a host of concerned parents had withdrawn their children from school. For those who remained, there was an eerie carnival atmosphere in the halls and classrooms: whoops and screams, screeches of laughter and nervous cries.

As she looked around the nervous throngs by the lockers, Darla realized that something else had changed. The cheerleaders had taken off their make-up and had dressed down in jeans, T-shirts and sneakers. Even Gabrielle looked less glamorous than usual, her hair tied back into a brisk ponytail and her nails unvarnished.

"I don't believe it," said Sasha, with a disbelieving laugh.

"What is it?" asked Darla.

"They're trying to make themselves look less attractive. They think if they don't put make-up on that's going to protect them from the Angel Taker."

"You shouldn't call him that," Darla told her. "It makes it sound like some kinda horror film. It's not, it's real."

"Who says it's a he?" Sasha replied archly.

The fact that half of the girls in the school were trying to look as plain as possible only made Sasha stand out even more. Darla loved Sasha's fashion sense, but she couldn't help worrying that the anonymous blogger was right – this wasn't the time to be standing out from the crowd.

As they filed towards homeroom a jock in a West Academy football shirt jumped out at Gabrielle, wrapping his arm around her and taking a camera selfie of the pair of them.

"Slay Cheese!" he cackled.

Gabrielle screamed, pushing the boy away and hurrying down the corridor. The jock roared with laughter, high-fiving his friends and showing them the selfie on his phone.

Sasha shook her head. "This place," she muttered.

The rumours began in the canteen, hushed whispers beneath the clatter of lunch trays. Darla was sitting apart from the others at the end of one of the tables, picking at her food while Sasha bit into an apple. Frank appeared without warning, leaping into the chair beside Darla.

"Breaking news from the beauty pageant world," he reported. "Gabrielle's pulled out from Miss Saffron."

Sasha chewed slowly on her apple. "Big deal."

"She was the hot favourite to win it! Apparently Gabrielle says she's too upset because of all the murders, but if you ask me she's just scared of being victim Numero Cinco."

"So what if she is?" Darla replied. "It's just a beauty pageant. It's not worth dying over."

"I guess," Frank said carelessly. "But without Gabrielle the field's going to be wide open. Anyone could win it!"

"You enter it, then," Sasha told him moodily. "You're the only one who cares."

"Am I really the only one who gets this?" Frank said, his blue eyes twinkling with amusement. "They're holding a beauty pageant in the middle of a killing spree! It's *hilarious*."

Darla wasn't sure she saw the joke, and for once Sasha wasn't laughing either.

"The sooner this whole thing is over the better," she declared. "This is getting beyond ghoulish.

What if this asshole blogger is right? Is everyone in the audience going to sit there and watch while the Angel Taker chops up the contestants?"

"At least come with me while I see the final line-up," said Frank. He clutched Darla's arm theatrically. "It's not safe to be alone right now."

Sasha tossed away her apple core and stood up, brushing her hands. "Come on, then. Before we have to get back to class."

They left the canteen and headed past the lockers to the West Academy noticeboard, where the Miss Saffron entrant sheet had been hanging for weeks. A giggling crowd had gathered around it. Darla and Sasha followed Frank as he burrowed through the throng until they were close enough to study the piece of paper. There were five names on the list, beneath Gabrielle's crossed-out signature. But Darla only had eyes for the last name on the list, signed in red pen.

Her own.

She stared at the sign-up sheet in horror.

"No way!" said Frank, bursting out laughing. "Why didn't you tell me you were going to sign up?"

"I didn't!" Darla replied. "That's not my signature.

I don't want to be in Miss Saffron!"

"Well, it looks like someone didn't get the memo," said Frank.

"It's just a stupid joke," Sasha told her. She scrabbled around inside her bag and pulled out an eyeliner pencil. "Just cross your name out."

Darla took the pencil and pushed to the front of the crowd. But as she stared at the imposter's signature, the bloody, almost mocking scrawl of her name, Darla paused. So someone thought it would be funny to play a joke on her – another excuse to laugh at the Plain Girl in the class, the murder magnet.

"Darla?"

She looked up to find Sasha looking curiously at her.

"You *are* going to withdraw, aren't you?"

Chapter Twenty-Three

One day a year, the electronic gates of the Saffron Hills Country Club slid open to allow non-members a precious glimpse inside its walls. Cars were guided through the grounds to a hall at the rear of the club, barely a stone's throw from the woods that enveloped the crumbling remains of Tall Pines. In this hall, the identity of Miss Saffron would be decided. As she waited backstage in the wings, nervously adjusting the gown she had borrowed from Sasha, her feet rubbing in unfamiliar shoes, Darla felt a sudden wave of terror wash over her. She was breathing in panicky gulps and she was desperate to pee. What had she been thinking? Why on earth hadn't she withdrawn?

At the time, Darla had simply been too mad to give the crowd around the sign-up sheet the satisfaction of seeing her cross her name out. But her anger ran deeper than that. The pageant seemed to embody the town's obsession with wealth and good looks, the privilege of beauty. As long as there were people in Saffron Hills, there would always be a Miss Saffron – no matter what the cost. Darla didn't want to win the competition, and she knew that she didn't stand a chance anyway. But she was getting sick of being pushed around, and being made to feel ashamed or scared. It was time to make a stand.

With just two days before the pageant was due to take place, Darla had spent Saturday evening at Sasha's house trying on clothes. She didn't own anything glitzy enough for a beauty pageant, while Sasha had a wardrobe filled with dresses with the price tags still attached – gifts from the elderly ranks of the Haas family, who were still clinging on to the futile hope that their granddaughter might dress in a more ladylike fashion. Given that Sasha was several inches taller than Darla, it was a struggle to find anything that fitted. But just when Darla had been ready to give up, Sasha had dug out a smaller dress from the back of her wardrobe: a crimson taffeta ballgown with a bow at the back.

"For junior prom," Sasha explained. "But I think it might just do the trick."

Darla held up the dress in front of the mirror, dubiously eyeing her reflection. "You think?"

"Sure! You'll knock 'em dead."

Frank winced. "Probably not the best choice of words, given the circumstances. You don't want to be talking about people dying when there's a good chance someone's going to try to kill Darla."

He ducked as Sasha kicked a shoe at him, narrowly missing his head as it thumped into the wall.

"Hey!" he said. "That coulda hurt!"

"Would have served you right for being such an asshole," Sasha told him.

"Don't worry about the Angel Taker, Frank," Darla said. "He only cares about beautiful-looking people, and I sure as hell ain't one of them."

"Ignore him, Darla," Sasha said firmly. "You're going to look great."

Darla gave her friend a suspicious look. "You seem kinda keen all of a sudden. I thought you hated these pageants."

"I do. But you're not ... you know, the pageant type."

"Ohhhhh, I get it," Darla drawled. "It's OK for

me to enter it, because I ain't pretty?"

"I didn't meant it like that!" Sasha said, exasperated. "I just meant it was nice you're not some airheaded bimbo, that's all. Do you want the dress or not?"

Darla nodded. "Sure," she said quietly. She couldn't help noticing that Sasha hadn't tried to tell her she *was* pretty.

Now, as the other contestants gathered around her, checking their make-up in their compacts, Darla could almost have laughed at the absurdity of it. Did she want to be beautiful and in mortal danger, or plain and safe? The hall was electric with nervous anticipation. The ghoulish publicity swirling around the competition seemed to have only swelled the crowd, and there was standing room only at the back of auditorium. Security was tight. Police lined the hall, checking the ID of everyone who came in. The judges were sitting at a table in front of the stage: Miss Saffron 1977, a middle-aged woman in a crisp blue suit; the owner of a boutique in the mall; and the president of the country club.

Darla scanned the faces in the audience, wondering whether a killer might be training their camera lens upon her. Her palms were damp with sweat and her stomach was queasy. At least neither Hopper nor Annie were in the crowd – she didn't want either of them to find out what she had done. The one friendly face Darla could pick out was Sasha, sitting at the end of a row halfway back in the hall. She leaned her head back against the chair and blew a large bubble from her gum, visibly bored. For all his apparent enthusiasm for the pageant, Frank was nowhere to be seen. He had bailed on Sasha at the last minute, forcing her to call a cab to take her and Darla up to the country club.

A waft of aftershave announced the presence in the wings of the pageant emcee, a middle-aged man with thick, wavy hair and a fixed smile. After checking his teeth in a handheld mirror, he picked up a microphone, swept past the girls and bounded out on to the stage.

"How y'all doing, folks?" he said in a smooth voice. "This is Ron Frazier, your drive-time host from your favourite local station, Radio KWPR. Welcome to the annual Miss Saffron beauty pageant – where the most beautiful roses in South Carolina bloom. Due to certain unforeseen events this year's contest will be slightly shorter than usual, but rest assured the competition is as fierce as ever. Contestants will be judged in four categories: Attire, Poise, Speech-Making and Stage Presence. Whoever gains the highest overall score will be crowned Miss Saffron. So without further ado, let's bring on our contestants!"

Polite applause greeted the five girls as they trooped out on to the stage, taking their places on marks drawn on the stage floor. It wasn't really the line-up that the crowd had been hoping for – a couple of the girls were pretty, one could play the flute and another was apparently destined for Harvard, but none of them had the dazzling glamour of the Picture Perfect girls. Ron seemed taken aback by the lukewarm reception, hurriedly shuffling his cue cards. "Now, please give a warm hand to our first contestant … Miss Darla O'Neill!"

The spotlight zeroed in on Darla, blinding her view of the audience. Her name was greeted with stony silence, punctuated by a lone shout of support – Sasha, she guessed. As she stepped towards the microphone stand at the front of the stage, Darla flinched at the sound of a camera flash going off somewhere in the audience. It wasn't the Angel Taker, she told herself firmly, he didn't care about people like her. She cleared her throat, the sound echoing out through the microphone.

"I'm not sure what y'all want me to say," she said. "I know that I'm no one's idea of a beauty queen, and if it weren't for all the terrible things that have been happening round here I wouldn't be on this stage. Someone else signed me up for this – I don't know why, maybe they thought it would be funny – because this is a beauty pageant and I'm sure as hell no beauty. I got freckles all over my face and my ears are too big, I'm as plain as you like. And I guess that's why I didn't cross my name off the list, and that's why I got up on this stage – because there are other Plain Girls out there just like me, and they won't be Miss Saffron either. But it doesn't mean we shouldn't try. Thank you all very much."

Darla shuffled away from the microphone. The shocked silence was broken by a grinning Sasha, who started clapping loudly. As the punk got to her feet other girls started to join in, applause catching and rippling out across the auditorium like bushfire. Suddenly half the hall was standing up, cheering and whooping. Sasha stuck her fingers in her mouth and whistled her approval. Darla went bright red, and looked down at her feet.

"Ladies and... Ladies and gentlemen!" Ron called out making calming gestures with his hands. Reluctantly the noise abated. "Thank you very much for that ... spirited speech, Darla," he said. He consulted his cue cards. "Now, next on stage we have—"

He was interrupted by a disturbance in the wings, raised voices filtering through on to the stage. An anxious murmur ran through the crowd. The emcee glanced backstage. Suddenly Gabrielle strode out from the wings, her long dark hair falling in graceful waves around her beautiful face, her flawless skin gleaming in the spotlight. She was wearing a Saffron Tigers football jacket over the top of a yellow cheerleaders' outfit, white sneakers on her feet. Don smiled with relief. Applause rang out once more across the hall, and Gabrielle waved at the audience.

"Good afternoon, y'all," she said into Don's microphone. "I apologize for being late... I nearly didn't come at all. But I have something important to say, and I was hoping I could get the opportunity to do so."

Don glanced over to the judges, who nodded as one.

"Be my guest," he told Gabrielle, handing her his microphone. She walked to the front of the stage and looked out over the audience.

"My name is Gabrielle Jones," she said. "Those of you who know me will know that I've lost some friends recently..." Her voice faltered. She paused, blinking back tears. "They were kind, beautiful people who deserved long and happy lives but that was taken away from them. And it made me scared – too scared to come up here. It made me wish I went to another school, lived in another state where maybe I'd be safer. But I realized today that if you live in fear it doesn't matter whether you die or not, because that's when killers and terrorists win. I'm not a cheerleader, and I'm not a football player, but I chose to wear these clothes to show that my school spirit burns deeper and brighter than ever before, and no one can terrorize me into hiding or staying silent. My name is Gabrielle Jones, and I am *proud* to be a member of the West Academy student body, and I am *proud* to be a citizen of the beautiful town of Saffron Hills!"

The hall erupted with applause, twice as loud as the ovation that had greeted Darla. This time Ron made no effort to quieten it, joining in with the clapping as Gabrielle sashayed back to the others. In the crowd, Sasha sat on her hands, an eyebrow raised ironically in a way that said to Darla, 'What can you do?' As the judges huddled together, nodding and frantically scribbling on their notepaper, it was obvious to everyone that the competition was effectively over. Darla barely remembered the other contestants' speeches — most of them looked beaten before they even opened their mouths.

When the speeches were over, the judges took less than five minutes to come to their decision. Ron beamed as he opened the winning envelope and read out Gabrielle's name. Her hands flew to her mouth — if she was surprised, she was the only person in the hall. She bounded forwards to accept her bouquet of flowers, waving graciously at the audience as the 'Miss Saffron 2015' sash was slipped over her and a sparkling tiara placed on top of her head. Gabrielle looked every inch a queen, thought

Darla. She might not have liked Gabrielle but she could see how much this meant to her, and to her surprise Darla found it impossible to begrudge the new Miss Saffron her victory.

The beaten contestants were ushered off the stage, leaving Gabrielle to soak up the applause. Darla let out a sigh of relief as she headed into the shadow of the wings. She hadn't won, but she had survived.

"You. Were. *Incredible!*" screamed Sasha, bounding over to her and giving her a fierce hug. "Seriously, I've never been so proud."

"I didn't really do anything," said Darla. "It wasn't like I won."

Sasha laughed. "Of course you didn't win, Darla – you went up there and showed everyone what a shallow joke this all is. That makes you my queen any day."

She took a badge with the slogan 'President Evil' off her bag and pinned it to Darla's taffeta ballgown.

"I now declare you the inaugural Miss Sasha," she said. "How do you feel?"

"Gosh, I guess I'm just overwhelmed," giggled Darla, impersonating a breathless pageant queen. "This is all too much! I'd like to thank my daddy,

Hopper, and all the people who voted for me!"

As the girls fell about laughing, Darla saw Gabrielle walk through the crowd, stopping to pose for photographs with the judges and members of the audience. She looked so confident and glamorous that it seemed almost ludicrous to think that she might have been in danger.

"You know, it was pretty brave of her to to show," said Darla. "I don't think I woulda, in her place."

"Have you seen the amount of cops that are around here?" Sasha replied. "Half the audience were wearing ear-pieces – this is probably the safest place in America right now."

"I guess you're right," said Darla. She pulled at her gown's neckline. "I gotta change out of this dress."

Sasha accompanied her to the changing room backstage, a cramped space strewn with contestants' clothes. As Darla slipped back into jeans and a T-shirt, Sasha amused herself by tottering around the room on a pair of high heels, blowing kisses at an imaginary crowd. Darla picked up a handheld mirror so she could wipe off her make-up. But when she looked into the glass she didn't see her own face looking back. She had been dragged back to the Angel Taker's dark room, forced to look through eyes that weren't her own. Gloved hands were carefully hanging a framed photograph upon the wall. It was a long-lens shot of a lone figure walking up the entrance steps into the West Academy, a stack of books under their arm. The subject was too far away for Darla to make out their face, but with a sickening lurch she recognized the only vehicle parked in the school lot.

"Darla?"

She looked up to find Sasha staring at her intently. "You've seen something, haven't you?"

It was all Darla could to do to nod.

"The Angel Taker? Are they going after Gabrielle?"

She shook her head.

"Darla, who did you see?"

Chapter Twenty-Four

Frank sat alone at the computer, the only live machine in a row of dead screens. The tap of his fingers upon the keyboard echoed around the empty library. None of the other students were allowed inside the West Academy over the weekend but Frank had been given a special passkey from Principal Bell, who knew that Frank's family didn't have the money for a computer and was a soft touch when it came to students asking to do a project for extra credit. And anyway, people trusted Franklin K Matthews. He was a good guy.

Frank paused, and read over his sentence again.

So the good ol' town of Saffron Hills won't let the bodies piling up in the morgue get in the way of its precious beauty pageant. And with murder magnet Darla O'Neill taking to the stage, you can bet your bottom dollar that the killings will continue.

He chewed on his lip uneasily. In hindsight, signing Darla up for the pageant had been a mistake, an impulsive joke that hadn't proved to be funny. But Frank had never for a second thought Darla would actually *enter* the stupid thing. For all her quiet, mousy exterior there was a stubborn core to her that surprised Frank. In a way, she was a photo negative of Sasha, whose brashness masked a fragile heart.

Not that Sasha was acting particularly fragile today. Her angry texts had been swarming over Frank's phone like a horde of buzzing wasps all afternoon, forcing him to turn it off. He had decided to swerve the pageant at the last minute, figuring that he would rather spend time working on a new blog post. And if the Angel Taker did decide to make a guest appearance at the country club, Frank wanted to make sure that he was nowhere near them.

A muffled thump made him pause, mid-sentence. Frank swivelled round in his chair, only to find himself staring at a still wall of books. Other people might have found the deserted halls and classrooms creepy, but he delighted in having the school to himself. There were no spoiled rich kids to look down their noses at him, as though Frank was some kind of sub-species just because he had been born in the wrong part of Saffron Hills. With their designer clothes and expensive cars and skiing vacations, the Perfects had convinced themselves that money made you a better person.

Talk about karma coming to bite you on the ass.

Frank had started the blog on a whim, killing time on a bored Saturday afternoon. He had never anticipated that so many people would read it, or the thrill he would get every time he pressed 'POST'. His last entry had received 2,000 views, and he had overheard people talking about it at the mall and in the halls at school, sending a shiver of satisfaction down his spine. It wasn't as though he actually *wanted* anyone to die. Darla wasn't the only one who had seen what the Angel Taker had done to Natalie Parker, and as much as Frank tried to banish the image of her corpse from his mind, it still haunted him. But if the town could pretend nothing was wrong, pressing on with their ridiculous pageant, he didn't see why he couldn't write about it. Everything he said was true, after all.

He sat back in his chair, lacing his fingers together

behind his head. The clock at the top left of the screen read 16:05 – the pageant should have ended by now. Frank wondered how Darla had got on. He liked the fact that she wasn't rich or stuck-up, and he probably had more in common with her than anyone else at the West Academy, even Sasha. But the hard truth was, ever since Darla had showed up in Saffron Hills with her messed-up life and her 'visions', she had got in the way of the thing that Frank cared about the most – his relationship with Sasha.

They had been friends since third grade: Sasha had seen Ryan trying to take Frank's milk money and come over and smacked him across the head until he ran away. At the time Frank had been amazed that this rich, confident girl could care about someone like him, but little did he know that he had also fallen into a trap. From that moment on, he was doomed to become Sasha's sidekick, driving her around like a chauffeur and doing her homework and listening to her complain about her problems as though she was the one who had it rough... It made Frank angry just to think about it. And now it seemed like he wasn't even fit to be her friend –

it was Darla who was going to bars with her and spending time with her. And it was because of Darla that Sasha acted so disapprovingly about the Angel Taker blog – if it had just been the two of them, she would have found it just as funny as he did, Frank was sure of it.

The cursor blinked insistently on the screen, urging Frank to continue his sentence. He hurriedly finished his blog and posted it online, before logging out and switching off the computer. When he turned on his phone it immediately began to buzz with alerts: ten texts and three missed calls from Sasha. Frank rolled his eyes. That girl was so high maintenance, she didn't even know. He scrolled through his texts.

Where are you?

Jerk. You could have texted.

Sasha's texts got progressively ruder until Frank reached the ones at the top of the list, and the tone abruptly changed.

The Angel Taker's watching you.

Frank smiled thinly. This was so typical of Sasha, he thought to himself. She was mad because he hadn't given her a ride to the pageant, so now she was trying to get her own back by creeping him out. How stupid did she think he was? As he picked up his bag, Frank noticed a book lying on the desk next to him. He picked it up and checked the library code on the spine. Unlike some people he could mention, Frank liked to leave things neat and tidy. He walked away from the computer banks and wandered into the dingy aisles of bookshelves, the soles of his shoes scratching on the coarse green carpet.

He was slipping the book back into its correct space on the shelf when his phone buzzed again. Sighing, he pulled it out of his pocket and checked the new text.

SCHOOL NOT SAFE, GET OUT OF THERE!

Frank frowned. He hadn't told anyone that he was coming to school, so how did they know?

Unless Darla had seen something. He still wasn't sure he believed her stories about her visions, but even Frank had to admit that the girl had a knack for stumbling across the Angel Taker's victims. And hadn't he thought he'd heard something earlier? Doubt stroked its icy fingers down Frank's neck as he looked around the aisles. Maybe it would be best if he went outside and phoned Sasha, just to check that she was trying to play with him.

Click.

The noise came from behind the shelf in front of him. Frank slowly pulled a book off the shelf, revealing a smooth camera lens behind it. His mouth went dry.

Click.

Darla chased after Sasha as the punk sprinted out through the auditorium fire exit into the lot behind the country club. A grey SUV carrying a large family was pulling out of its space – Sasha ran alongside and banged on the window.

"Wait up!" she shouted. "I need a ride!"

The driver of the SUV took one look at Sasha's

face and hurriedly accelerated, leaving her trailing in the vehicle's wake.

"Asshole!"

The sound of someone giggling made Darla turn round. Heather Brodie, the girl who had sobbed at the news of Ryan and TJ's murders, was chatting into her cell phone as she opened the door of a soft-top convertible.

"Hey, Heather!" Darla waved. "Over here!"

Engrossed in her conversation, Heather didn't hear Darla as she got behind the wheel. But Sasha did. She strode over to the convertible and grabbed the door.

"Brodie, get out of the freaking car!"

Heather shrieked as Sasha dragged her out of the front seat, leaving her in a heap on the tarmac. Sasha slid behind the wheel and turned the key in the ignition.

"Get in, Darla!" she shouted.

Heather was lying on the ground crying, but there was nothing Darla could do to help her now. They had to save Frank. She ran to the passenger seat and jumped in, barely sitting down before Sasha slammed her foot on the accelerator and the convertible roared out of the lot and along the driveway. The automated gates opened just in time to let them through.

The wind tugged at Darla's hair as the convertible hurtled around the tight corners of the hills. Sasha drove with grim fury, quickly catching up with the grey SUV. Darla flinched as Sasha overtook it on the bend, veering back to the right-hand lane just before a car came in the opposite direction. A discordant chorus of car horns rang out. Sasha beeped back, and tossed her phone into Darla's lap.

"Try Frank's cell," she ordered. "See if you can warn him."

Darla scrolled through Sasha's phonebook for Frank's number, but when she called it his phone cut to voicemail.

"He's not picking up," she said.

Sasha punched the car horn in frustration. "This doesn't make any sense!" she shouted. "The Angel Taker only goes after the beautiful people. What would they want with *Frank*?"

"Frank *is* beautiful!" Darla told her. "You just didn't see it!" In desperation she tapped out a couple of texts to Frank, hoping that he would read them. At the intersection at the bottom of the hill Sasha hit a hard left, screeching into the road that led up to the West Academy. The convertible hit a pothole, rattling Darla's teeth in her head. They pulled up outside the school to find it was deserted – there were no police officers standing guard on a Sunday. The parking spaces were empty save for one: a black pick-up truck. More than ever, Darla had wanted her vision to be wrong. But Frank was here, all right.

Sasha jammed on the brakes, bringing the convertible to a shuddering halt beside the pick-up truck.

"No sign of Frank," she said as she climbed out, shielding her eyes against the late-afternoon sun. "Any idea where he might have been going?"

"He was carrying books," Darla said uncertainly. "The library?"

Sasha nodded, and they ran up the steps and through the front entrance, which Darla noted with a chill had been left ajar. The sound of their footfalls echoed around the empty halls as they sprinted through the West Academy. At the sight of the library at the end of the corridor they slowed, sharing the unspoken fear of what might lie on the other side.

The library door swung open at Darla's touch. Someone had been here recently – the lights had been switched on, shining down over the bookshelves and blank computer screens. But the chairs were empty, and there was no sign of anyone.

"Frank?" Sasha called out uncertainly. "Are you in here?"

Silence.

As Darla crept through the bookshelves, ahead of her she saw that the lights were out in a solitary aisle, shrouding it in darkness. A pair of glasses lay on the floor, their frames twisted and their lenses smashed. It looked like they had been ground beneath someone's heel. Paling, Sasha reached down and took Darla's hand in her own hot palm. Darla had never seen her friend looked frightened before. They edged forwards together and peered around the corner.

There, in the funereal gloom, they found Frank. He lay sprawled across the floor, surrounded by a pile of books with the pages torn from their bindings. There was a gaping wound in his chest where he had been stabbed, his bright blue eyes wide open and frozen in horror. But the Angel Taker hadn't been satisfied with that – Frank's face and hands were covered in countless thin red scars, covering his flesh like vicious veins. Paper cuts.

Darla stared at the body, numb with disbelief. Beside her Sasha was screaming but no sound was coming out from her mouth. She clutched at Darla and slid to the floor, tears streaming down her face as she wept in her arms.

If Darla thought the horror had ended that day, she was wrong. As she walked down the lane towards her house, she saw flashing lights ahead of her. A ring of police cars was parked around her house. Darla raced down the lane, praying that she was mistaken. But as she reached the wire fence she saw her daddy being wrestled out of the front door by two police officers. Hopper's hands were cuffed behind his back, and his shirt was torn.

"Get your hands off me!" he snarled. "I ain't done nothing!"

"Daddy!" screamed Darla. She tried to run towards him, only for a cop to pull her away.

"You need to step back, ma'am," he said.

"But that's my daddy! Where are you taking him?"

"He's going down to the station to answer some questions."

"Questions? About what — the murders?"

The cop said nothing.

"But that's crazy!" cried Darla. "He ain't no killer!"

"Then he's got nothing to worry about," the policeman replied impassively.

At the sight of Darla, Hopper abruptly stopped fighting. "Don't you worry now, darlin'!" he called out. "This is just one big ol' misunderstanding. We're going to sort this out at the station and I'll be back before you know it."

He tried to tell her that he loved her, but his words were cut off as he was bundled into the back of a squad car.

"You let go of him, you hear?" Darla shouted. "You got no right — he didn't do anything!"

The policeman said nothing, keeping firm hold of

her arm. Through the back windshield of the squad car, Darla caught a glimpse of her daddy's face as he twisted in the seat. Hopper looked small, scared – she had never seen him look that way before, and the sight chilled her to the bone.

Then the squad car pulled away, and he was gone.

Chapter Twenty-Five

Almost from the moment she had arrived in Saffron Hills, it felt as though Darla had been buffeted by one shock after another – from her violent visions to the discovery of Natalie's dead body and the brutal murders of the other Perfects. Through all of it, Darla had managed to keep it together. But Frank's death and the sight of Hopper being led away in handcuffs had brutally snapped something inside of her. Overwhelmed, her mind and body had just shut down.

As the police continued to pore over their things in the house, Darla dimly remembered Annie breaking through the cordon. The next thing Darla knew, she was being ushered away to the safety of the artist's house. In a numb daze, she said nothing. In the front room Annie turned on the TV and hurriedly closed the drapes in order to hide the patrol cars still parked in the lane. Someone had said something about the police searching their house and yard. *For what?* thought Darla. *Weapons? Bloodstained clothes? More dead bodies?*

It couldn't be true. The cops were just doing what Hopper had always feared they would – rounding up local people with criminal records in the hope that one of them would turn out to be the Angel Taker. Darla's daddy might have done a lot of things wrong in his life, but he was no killer. He had no reason to harm the Perfects, let alone Frank. The thought was just ridiculous.

And yet. As Darla sat on Annie's couch, gazing vacantly at the TV, she was aware of a tiny sliver of doubt, like a splinter digging painfully into her heart. She remembered Luis's fear about Hopper finding out they had talked; his assertion that her daddy had a 'dark side'. Darla knew that returning to Saffron Hills had brought back some painful memories of Sidney and her suicide – what if these had affected Hopper more than she had realized, and he was lashing out in the most violent way imaginable? Maybe that might explain her visions: – warnings from her own subconscious that she was in danger.

Darla hated herself for even thinking these thoughts. But just when it seemed that their lives might be turning around, things had fallen apart worse than ever. This time, there didn't seem to be any way to put the pieces back together.

Annie called her through into the kitchen where she was zapping TV dinners in the microwave. Darla could see that Annie had been just as shocked by Hopper's arrest as she was – even if she was trying to hide it. The artist fluttered around the kitchen taking out plates and cutlery, talking gaily as if it was a normal day and nothing bad had happened.

"You just wait, this will all be over before you know it," she said. "Hopper will be home and everyone will know he had nothing to do with it. Innocent until proven guilty, that's how we do things in this country."

She tipped the steaming food from their plastic trays on to plates and served them up. Darla barely tasted hers – didn't even look down to see what it was. She sat in silence as Annie chattered desperately. Finally Annie gave up, pushing her plate to one side.

"Yeah, you're right," she said wearily. "There

isn't any sense in pretending. This is bad. I'm so sorry, hon."

Darla shrugged. "It's not your fault," she said. "Hopper spent a long time doing things he shouldn't have. It was always going to catch up with him some day."

"That doesn't mean he should be charged for something he didn't do, though." Darla was suddenly aware that Annie was watching her closely. "You don't think he actually did it, do you, Darla?"

"Of course I don't," she replied, but the words sounded hollow even to her.

They watched TV for another hour or so before Darla went to bed early. She followed Annie up the stairs to the guest room, which was filled with a jumble of cardboard boxes, teetering stacks of books and a single bed with a metal frame.

"Sorry about the mess," Annie said. "Six months home, and I still haven't finished unpacking."

Darla didn't care about the boxes. She didn't care about anything. Annie offered to lend her a T-shirt to sleep in but Darla climbed into bed fully clothed and pulled the blankets up around her head. Wishing her a faltering good night, Annie flicked off the light and left her alone.

It was a long, wakeful night. Darla couldn't have fallen asleep if she tried. Every time she closed her eyes, she saw Hopper being led away in handcuffs. She imagined him alone in a prison cell, waiting to be dragged back under the harsh lights of the interrogation room. It didn't matter whether he was guilty or not – the image still left her feeling desolate.

The next thing Darla knew, her room was growing light and there was a hesitant tap at her door. Annie appeared, carrying a steaming cup of coffee.

"Morning," she said. "Better get up now. I'm teaching a class today, and at this rate we're both going to be late."

"I'm not going to school," Darla said flatly. "I don't want to."

"Of course you don't, hon," Annie replied, taking a seat on the edge of her bed. "But Hopper wouldn't want you missing any more school because of him. And I don't want him thinking that I couldn't take care of you while he was away. So can you be brave for me – for both of us – today?"

Darla sat up in bed, reluctantly accepting the

coffee mug. Annie smiled.

"Good girl," she said. "I'll drive you."

Even on her happiest days, Darla often dreaded going to school. But that morning was different – she was almost too distracted to care. She got into the shower and washed herself, only to put yesterday's dirty clothes back on afterwards. Annie suggested returning to the house to pick up some things, but Darla shook her head. She wouldn't go back home until Hopper could. Annie might have wanted to argue but they were running late as it was, so they had no choice but to go down to the car. Annie drove slowly and carefully over to the West Academy, pulling up outside the entrance.

Darla had been praying that Sasha would be waiting for her outside school, but this time the steps outside the front entrance were empty. Darla had to pass through the stony gaze of the cops at the door alone. She could almost feel the collective intake of breath as she walked past the lines of the students by the lockers. Darla hugged her textbooks tightly to her chest, wishing that she could shrink and shrink and shrink until she was so small that nobody could see her. But when she reached her locker, Darla realized that there was going to be no hiding place that day.

Across her locker, someone had scrawled 'Killer Bitch' in thick black marker pen.

As the rest of the students in the corridor fell silent, Darla whirled round and eyed them coldly.

"Who did this?" she demanded.

Everyone stared. No one spoke.

"*Someone* must have done this." Darla's voice echoed defiantly around the corridor. "Where are they? If they're brave enough to write this, aren't they brave enough to say it to my face?"

The uncomfortable silence was broken by Darla's contemptuous laugh.

"Of course not," she said. "You ain't nothin' more than cowards, the lot of you."

It was as though she had been branded. Everywhere she went, people saw a Killer Bitch. Boys barged past her in the hall, so hard they nearly knocked her to the floor. Girls whispered to each other, abruptly falling silent when she looked over. Secret notes flew around her classes in a paper blizzard. Even the teachers seemed to treat her coldly. It looked like everyone in Saffron Hills had made up their mind that Hopper was the Angel Taker, and in their eyes that made her guilty, too.

During recess Darla went searching for Sasha. Eventually she found her in the gymnasium, sitting alone on the top bleacher. As Darla crossed the floor and climbed up the steps towards her, she saw Sasha take a sip from her hip flask.

"You're going to get into trouble if anyone sees you doing that, you know," she said softly.

Sasha ignored her. She had been crying, Darla could see now, her eyes red-rimmed and glistening.

"Is it true what they're saying?" said Sasha. "The cops arrested Hopper?"

Darla nodded.

"They think he's the Angel Taker? They think he killed Frank?" Sasha snorted humourlessly, and took another swig from her hip flask. "I'll say one thing for this town – it is just *full* of surprises. Do you know the cops found out what Frank was doing here? He was writing his latest blog post, about the Angel Taker."

"It was Frank who had been writing all that stuff – about me?" Darla said, bewildered. "Why?"

Sasha shrugged. "I don't know. Turns out that even after ten years of friendship I didn't know

Franklin K Matthew as well as I thought I did. You can ask him yourself if you want. Oh that's right, you can't. He's dead."

A heavy silence hung in the air. Recognizing Sasha's tone from the time they had argued at Tall Pines, Darla stayed quiet. The last thing she wanted to do now was fight.

"These visions of yours, these broadcasts from Psycho Radio," Sasha said. "You ever think to yourself, why me?"

"All the time," said Darla. "I never asked for this."

"No, of course not," Sasha said quickly. She took another swig. "But there's gotta be something wrong with you, right? I mean, it's not *normal*."

"I guess," said Darla.

"It's kinda funny, when you think about it," Sasha continued bitterly. "You see everything the killer sees, apart from who they really are. Not so much as a glimpse. Couldn't you get them to look in the mirror, or something? Five people have been killed, Darla."

"It's not my fault Frank died, you know," Darla told her. "You're not the only who's upset."

Sasha slipped her hip flask back into her jacket.

"Ignore me," she said, getting to her feet. "Frank always said I was a mean drunk."

She put on a pair of sunglasses and began to walk unsteadily down through the bleachers.

"Where are you going?" Darla called out.

"Anywhere that isn't here," Sasha called back, without turning around.

The rest of the day couldn't go quickly enough for Darla. She was relieved when the final bell went, and she could walk past the policemen guarding the school entrance and see Annie's car waiting for her outside. They drove back to Annie's house, where she went straight into the kitchen and put the kettle on. Darla sat at the table, staring out of the window at the house of mirrors in the backyard.

"I would ask you how you're doing," Annie said sympathetically. "But I'm thinking that'd be a dumb question."

As they shared an awkward silence, Darla heard a car pull up outside the house. There was a rap on the front door. She followed Annie through into the corridor and peered at the familiar silhouette outlined in the screen door, her heart leaping with relief.

"Daddy!" cried Darla. When Annie opened the door she ran over and flung her arms around him, squeezing him tightly.

"Hey there, darlin'," Hopper said back. "I'm sorry I gave you such a fright."

His eyes were tired and his cheeks covered in stubble – he looked like he'd been on a three-day drinking spree. But Darla didn't care.

"I'm so happy you're back!" she exclaimed.

"Not half as happy as I am, believe me," Hopper replied wearily. "They were riding me pretty hard down at the station. Killing a bunch of kids – how could they think I could do that?"

"But they released you, so they know you're innocent, right?" Darla said eagerly. "They're going to leave us alone now?"

"I can't promise that, but they've let me out for now." Hopper paused awkwardly. "See, the reason they let me out was because something happened while they were questioning me. It's the new Miss Saffron, some girl called Gabrielle? She's gone missing."

After all that had happened, maybe Darla shouldn't have been surprised. But it didn't tally with the vision she had seen in the broken mirror in Annie's gallery. The girl in the chair had had blond hair, and she hadn't looked anything like Gabrielle. Every other vision had come true – could it really be that this one had been wrong?

"*Another* girl?" Annie shook her head. "I'm not sure how much more this town can take."

"I don't know about you, I'm not sure how much *I* can take," Hopper replied ruefully. "We're going to head on home now. Thank you for taking care of Darla, you're a real friend."

"It was nothing," she smiled. "The least I could do."

"Just let me get my bag," Darla said.

She ran upstairs and into the jumbled guest room. In her haste to grab her bag, she swung it round and knocked a pile of books to the floor. Muttering under her breath, Darla went to pick them up. She stopped. At the bottom of the heap was an old West Academy Yearbook, 1995. The year that Walter West had killed Miss Saffron. Darla picked up the book and stared at the front cover.

"Did you get lost up there?" Hopper called out from the bottom of the stairs. "C'mon, girl!"

Maybe it was Hopper's impatience that did it, or maybe some deeper curiosity. But Darla didn't even think about it — slipping the yearbook into her bag, she hurried downstairs.

Chapter Twenty-Six

As things turned out, Darla didn't get the chance to look at the yearbook that night. She was so pleased to have Hopper home that she stayed up with him watching TV before her exhaustion caught up with her, and she passed out on the sofa. The next day Darla went to school to find that the halls of the West Academy were deserted. With the news of Gabrielle's disappearance, only a handful of students had shown up. Looking around, Darla wasn't surprised to see that Sasha wasn't one of them. The students sat together in a single classroom, reading and talking to each other. They were let out of school early, and Darla returned home to find Hopper still sitting in a dressing gown, morosely picking at an acoustic guitar in the living room. He grunted at Darla when she came in.

"No work today, Daddy?" she asked.

"Boss gave me the week off," Hopper replied.

"Doesn't want a murder suspect trying to sell his guitars. Can't say I blame him, neither."

"They'll find the real killer soon," Darla told him. "Then things will go back to normal."

"And what is normal, when it's at home?" Hopper said, scratching his stubbled cheek. "Me and you having to leave town again? Me going back to grafting?"

Darla folded her arms. "So you're just going to give up now?"

"What do you want me to do?"

"You could take a shower, for a start. Day's nearly over."

Hopper stared at her coldly. Putting down his guitar, he trudged upstairs into the bathroom. Darla waited until she heard the shower running before going to her bedroom and closing the door. Diving on to her bed, she took the yearbook out from her bag. It was filled with the usual kind of school photographs: the teaching faculty, the gym team in their spangly uniforms, the rangy basketball squad. A full spread was devoted to the Saffron Tigers football team, who had made it to the state semifinals that year. Over the page, Darla was greeted by a photo of a pretty girl with tight blond curls sitting on a carnival float, waving to a crowd. It was Miss Saffron, 1995. Her full name was printed neatly below the photograph: Crystal Mills. Darla sat up. No wonder Leeroy had so many photos of Crystal scattered throughout his trailer – he wasn't a stalker, he was family.

She flicked on through the yearbook with rising excitement, searching for Walter West. But when she ran her finger down the page of Walter's class, Darla saw that his photograph had covered in white-out fluid, obliterating him completely. Had Annie done that? As Darla searched through the rest of the yearbook, she realized that Walter wasn't the only missing face. It might have been her yearbook, but there was no sign of Annie Taylor anywhere.

The front door slammed – startled, Darla slipped the yearbook under her mattress. She rushed out of her room and ran downstairs. Hopper was striding moodily down the path towards the Buick, muttering to himself under his breath.

"Hey, wait!" cried Darla. "Where are you going?"

"Out," Hopper said tersely.

"Weren't you going to say goodbye?"

"Wasn't planning on it, no."

"Didn't you think I'd worry?"

"I don't want to hear it, Darla," he told her, climbing into the front seat of the Buick. "Not now."

"Are you coming back?"

"I guess."

"When?"

"Later." He slammed the car door shut and turned the engine on, drowning out Darla's protests. She banged on the window, only for the Buick to leap away from the curb and fly off down the lane.

"Damn it!" swore Darla, kicking a stone after the disappearing car. She ran back inside the house, took Hopper's leather jacket from the back of his kitchen chair and put it on, taking comfort from its reassuring weight and familiar smell. Slipping her keys into a pocket, she went back outside.

Darla knew what she was doing was dangerous, maybe even downright crazy. But she was running out of time and options. The Angel Taker was doing more than taking lives – he was tearing people and relationships apart. As Darla headed out she briefly thought about calling Sasha, then decided against it. The person she was going to see wouldn't want to see Sasha. They wouldn't want to see Darla either, but she didn't have any choice. She had to speak with them.

Night was falling by the time Darla had located the dirt track leading down towards Leeroy Mills' trailer, trees rustling forlornly in the lengthening shadows. With every step that brought her closer to her destination, she felt a growing unease at her decision to come alone. The lights were on in Leeroy's trailer, his pick-up parked out front. As Darla headed across the waste ground the trailer door banged open, spilling a rectangle of dirty light on to the earth. Leeroy's silhouette filled the doorway. He had a rifle locked and loaded, and was training it out over the waste ground.

"Who's there?" he spat. "Don't think Leeroy can't hear you creeping about. He's got a big ol' rifle here, and he knows how to use it."

Darla took a deep breath and stepped out from behind the pick-up, holding her hands in the air. As Leeroy peered out into the darkness towards her, she gasped. His face was puffy with purple bruises, his left leg in a plaster cast.

"You!" he snarled. "I oughta put a bullet in your skull! Thanks to you, I got the living hell beaten out of me."

"I know," said Darla. "I'm sorry, I shouldn't have let it happen. I was scared. You scared me."

"Sorry don't help Leeroy's bones knit back together," he said ominously. "Sorry don't make the pain go away. Why are you here?"

"I wanted to talk to you," Darla called out. "About Crystal."

Leeroy flinched, like he had been slapped. "You don't know nuthin' about her," he said gruffly. "No one does."

"I know about people dying," Darla told him. "I know how it feels when someone you love dies and don't ever come back. Nothing can make that pain go away neither. I'd rather have broken bones."

Leeroy glanced around the surrounding trees and lowered his rifle. "Come in if you want."

Darla hesitated. Reluctantly she stepped up into the trailer, re-immersing herself in the stale smell of tobacco and body odour. Leeroy had put down his rifle and was staring at the small shrine of photographs of Crystal Mills.

"That's your sister, isn't it?" Darla said gently.

Leeroy nodded.

"She's very pretty."

"Most beautiful girl in the county," he replied. "Like a flower growing in the weeds. We came from a bad home – pappy drank, and our momma was too busy trying to avoid gittin' hit to look out for us. But Crystal was pure sunshine. I remember the day she won Miss Saffron, the smile on her face when they put that sash over her. Seeing her so happy, it was the best day of my life. Then one day she went up into the hills, and she never came back."

"To Tall Pines," Darla said.

"Crystal told me it weren't nothin' to worry about, Walter West just wanted to take some pretty photos of her. Said she was gonna need pretty photos if she was gonna become a model like she wanted." Leeroy's voice was hoarse. "When she went missing I told the cops that something bad had happened to her up at Tall Pines but they didn't want to know, kept telling me that she'd prob'ly just run away. It weren't till they pulled Crystal's body from the creek that they dared ring Allan West's doorbell. No wonder Walter went round killin' people – he thought he could do anything and get away with it. And he was right, too. I *tried* to tell people. I went to Walter's funeral and hollered that it was all a lie. But his family had damned near built the whole town! You think anyone was going to listen to Leeroy? I got hustled away and the next night a couple of guys jumped me in a bar, and when the dust settled it was good ol' Leeroy who ended up doing time over it. The Wests did everything they could to shut me up. By the time I got outta jail, no one cared about the truth."

"What truth, Leeroy?" Darla said urgently. "What were the Wests lying about?"

He stood by the window and looked out into the night, running a hand through his thinning hair.

"Walter didn't hang hisself," he said quietly. "He didn't regret what he'd done, he didn't care. But Allan West couldn't have his son in jail, so he made up a story about a suicide and smuggled the boy outta town. You listen to Leeroy, l'il girl – Walter West is still alive. He's been away for a while, but he's home now."

"That's why you were outside Natalie's house," breathed Darla. "And Ryan's party. You were trying to stop him!"

"I've been hunting in these woods twenty years now," Leeroy said, gazing out into the darkness. "I could feel it when he came back, like an alligator slipping into the creek. I swore that he wasn't going to hurt any more kids. But Walter's *real* smart. He outfoxed me, twice. Then people started talking about ol' Leeroy, as though it was *my* fault these kids were dying." He eyed Darla. "Guess I've got you to thank for that."

"Don't blame me!" she shot back. "Maybe if you hadn't taken Natalie's photographs people wouldn't have suspected you."

"That a fact?" Leeroy said slyly. "So why did they take your pappy in, then? Whose photographs did he take, l'il girl?"

Darla shook her head. "Maybe I should go," she said.

"Maybe you should," he replied. "Leeroy's done talking. Go on now, git."

Leeroy flung open his trailer door and pushed her out, slamming it behind her. As relieved as she was to have escaped the trailer, Darla couldn't shake the nagging suspicion that something was wrong here. Leeroy had seen her coming too quickly, his gun had been too readily to hand. He was on edge about something. Maybe it was the beating he had received outside Shooters, or the fear that his suspicions about Walter West were true, and the killer might come to try to silence him. Or maybe it was something else making him watch the trees so carefully. Darla thought back to the previous time she had come here – breaking inside the trailer, Leeroy's unexpected return, the headlong flight through the trees, the half-dug hole in the clearing...

The breath caught in Darla's throat. When she reached the trail leading back towards the road she headed in the opposite direction, plunging deeper into the darkness. She slipped into the trees, skirting around the back of the trailer. Through the windows she could see Leeroy pacing angrily up and down, taking swigs from a whiskey bottle. Darla ducked down as he strode to the kitchen window and stared out into the night.

Finally Leeroy turned away. Darla crept deeper into the wood, wincing at the leaves crunching and

341

twigs snapping underfoot. Last time she had been running blind, terrified that Leeroy might catch up with her. It was hard, in the darkness, to try to retrace her steps. As threatening shadows crowded in around her. Darla found herself wishing that she had brought a flashlight, or swallowed her pride and called Sasha. This was no time to be alone.

And then, suddenly, she came out into a small clearing. As she peered around, Darla recognized the giant fern she had cowered behind as Leeroy had called out to her. But there was no sign of a hole any more, only a thick carpet of bracken covering the ground. Darla knelt down and brushed a handful to one side, revealing a layer of wooden boards beneath. Moving quickly now, she scraped the rest of the bracken away and began lifting up the wooden boards, her fingernails digging into the cool dirt. Piece by piece, she uncovered a hole in the heart of the clearing. She had been right after all – Leeroy *had* been up to something. But as she moved the boards to one side, Darla's eyes couldn't penetrate the inky well below her. Had Leeroy gone to all this trouble over an empty hole? Or had he just not had chance to fill it yet?

At that moment the moon came out from behind a cloud, casting its milky eye over the clearing. With a start, Darla realized that the pit wasn't empty after all. Someone was sitting at the bottom of it.

It was Gabrielle.

She was huddled beneath a dirty blanket, her hands tied in front of her and a gag in her mouth. Her clothes were torn and covered in soil. Gabrielle shrank back as the final board was removed, emitting a terrified squeak – but at the sight of Darla, her eyes widened hopefully. She began to make urgent noises through her gag. Darla put her fingers over her lips.

"Hush now!" she whispered, as loud as she dared. "Don't let him hear you. I'm going to get you out!"

Easier said than done – the pit was pretty deep. In the moonlight, Darla spotted the handle of Leeroy's shovel poking out from beneath a bush. She ran over and picked it up, taking hold of each end and lowering it horizontally into the pit as Gabrielle climbed unsteadily to her feet. A tall girl, reaching up she could grab hold of the spade with her bound hands. Darla gritted her teeth and pulled up the spade as Gabrielle used her feet against the side of the pit to scramble out. Somehow she managed to clamber free from the pit, gasping with relief as Darla removed the gag from her mouth.

"H-help me!" she moaned, as Darla untied her hands. "Be-before he…"

A light shone in Gabrielle's eyes, cutting her off. She clutched at Darla as Leeroy limped into the clearing. He was carrying a bucket in one hand and a flashlight in the other.

"Now what do we have here?" he said, a smile playing on his lips. "See what happens when you go around meddling?" he told Darla. "We had ourselves a nice ol' chat but you couldn't stop poking around Leeroy's business, could you? And now we got ourselves a serious problem."

"S-stay away from us!" sobbed Gabrielle. "P-please!"

Leeroy shook his head sadly. "We talked about this, Gabrielle. It ain't safe for you out there right now. There's some crazy lunatic trying to hurt pretty girls just like you. But don't worry, you got yourself a guardian angel. Leeroy's gonna take real good care of you – however long it takes."

Gabrielle moaned with fear.

"Stop threatening her, creep!" Darla shouted.

The flashlight shone in her eyes, temporarily blinding her. She heard a snarl as Leeroy lunged towards her, hands outstretched. Darla didn't have time to think. She picked up the shovel and swung it at Leeroy as he charged at her. The blade connected with the side of his skull with a horrible sound of iron on bone; Leeroy didn't even cry out as he collapsed to the ground. His limbs twitched, and then he fell perfectly, terribly, still.

Chapter Twenty-Seven

"You killed him!" screamed Gabrielle.

Darla dropped the shovel. She felt dizzy, her stomach heaving as though she was going to be sick. The blood on Leeroy's temple glistened in the moonlight. Had she really killed someone? Darla wanted to run, but she wasn't sure she could leave the clearing without knowing whether or not Leeroy was dead. His eyes were closed, his chest still. She edged forwards and crouched down beside him.

"Are you *crazy*?" Gabrielle said frantically. "What the hell are you doing?"

Darla ignored her. She leaned closer to Leeroy, until her ear was nearly touching his mouth, and felt his stale liquor breath upon her cheek. She closed her eyes with relief.

"Is he…?" Gabrielle trailed off.

Darla shook her head. "Alive and kicking," she reported. "But I don't want him running away when he wakes up." She hooked her hands underneath Leeroy's arm and lifted him. "Here, help me with him."

Gabrielle stared at her. "You've got to be kidding me."

"Just do it!" Darla shouted, exasperated.

Gabrielle hurried over and picked up Leeroy's feet, suppressing a shudder at the touch of him. Together they carried the body to the edge of the dark hole and let go, sending Leeroy sprawling to the bottom of the pit. He stirred, letting out a groan of pain.

"That should do it," Darla said, brushing her hands together. "The police can take it from here."

She turned to walk away but Gabrielle had stayed where she was, her face hardening as she gazed into the pit.

"Do you like it down there, huh?" she called down to Leeroy. "How about I cover *you* up and leave you here? Hey? See how *you* like it."

She kicked the ground, sending a shower of dirt down over Leeroy's prone form. Darla gently took Gabrielle's trembling arm and led her away from the hole.

"C'mon," she said softly. "Let's get outta here."

She led Gabrielle back through the trees, coming out by the waste ground in front of Leeroy's trailer. Seeing the shaft of light shining out through the open trailer door, Gabrielle started to hyperventilate. She stumbled, wincing as her bare feet stepped on a sharp stone. Darla helped her across the ground to the track leading back towards the highway. The moon had sunk behind a cloud. When they reached the top of the trail, Darla saw a pair of headlights approaching from the direction of Saffron Hills. She ran into their path, waving her arms. The car slowed, and Pastor James warily rolled down his window.

"What are you girls doing...?" He trailed off, his eyes widening as he peered into the darkness behind Darla. "Gabrielle? Lord have mercy, is that you? Are you all right?"

Gabrielle nodded.

"The whole town's been looking for you, child, we've been so worried! Quickly, get in."

Darla helped the shaking Gabrielle into the back seat of the car, and Pastor James quickly drove off.

"It's OK," Darla said reassuringly, as the track to

Leeroy's trailer disappeared in the rearview mirror. "You're safe now."

"I thought ... he was going to keep me locked up ... forever," said Gabrielle, in shocked bursts. "Was that him ... the Angel Taker?"

Darla shook her head. "I don't think so."

"For real?" Gabrielle laughed shrilly. "How many psychos are there in this town?"

Darla didn't know what to tell her. There was no doubt that Leeroy was crazy and dangerous, but she still believed that – in his own twisted mind – he thought he was trying to protect Gabrielle. The Angel Taker was cold and calculating; they didn't kidnap teenagers, they only cared about killing. No, Darla was sure that Leeroy had been right: Walter West had been in hiding but he was back now, somewhere out there in the darkness. Watching. Waiting.

Gabrielle wrapped her arms around herself, still shivering violently. Darla took off Hopper's leather jacket to drape over her shoulders, and saw something fall out of the pocket on to the seat. It was a book of matches with a logo of a snake's head on it. Darla thoughtfully turned the matches over in

349

her fingers. She looked out of the window and saw the creek running alongside the road.

"Can you let me out here, please?" she called out.

"You can't!" Gabrielle said frantically. "It's not safe!"

"You can say that again," the Pastor added from the front seat.

"It's all right," Darla said reassuringly. "My daddy's seeing some friends just down the way." She took Gabrielle's hand in hers and gave it a squeeze. "You're going to be fine, I promise. You need to go to the hospital and let them check you out. Tell the police about Leeroy. When he wakes up, he's probably going to try to make a run for it."

If he wakes up, a spiteful voice added in Darla's head. She tried to ignore it. Gabrielle nodded, and gave Darla a grateful smile.

When Pastor James pulled his car over to the roadside Darla got out, watching the red tail lights disappear into the night. The temperature had dropped, and there was a cold wind that sent waves of gooseflesh crawling up Darla's bare arms. She was regretting leaving Hopper's leather jacket with Gabrielle. But this was no time to be feeling cold, or tired, or scared – she had to find her daddy. And since Hopper had driven off with a squeal of tyres without any clue as to where he was headed, technically he could have been anywhere in Saffron Hills. On the other hand, he was angry and depressed, feeling wounded and sorry for himself.

Of course there was only one place where Hopper could be.

There were no bands playing in the basement of Shooters that night, no queues waiting outside the door. But Hopper's battered Buick was there, parked beside the row of motorcycles. As Darla approached, a raccoon scampered across the gravel and disappeared into the reeds down by the creek. McGee was leaning against the doorway, cleaning his fingernails with a toothpick. He didn't even bother to look up as Darla marched to the entrance, just stretched a bear-like arm across her path.

"Hold up there, missy," he rasped. "Where do you think you're going?"

"Inside," Darla replied obstinately.

McGee smiled. "That a fact? I'm gonna need to see some ID."

"I didn't need any when I came here with Sasha."

"Who?"

"Don't pretend you don't know her," said Darla. "Sasha Haas, the girl with the high-powered lawyer daddy who got you off a charge? Tall, nose piercing, likes to drink? You let us both in the other night."

The bouncer shrugged. "Don't know her, don't recognize you. Take my advice, missy – turn around and go home. This place ain't for you."

Darla clenched her fists into a ball "Now you listen to me, McGee, and you listen good," she hissed. "My daddy's in this bar, fresh out of the police station, probably fall-down drunk, and I need to take him home before he gets into more trouble than he's already in. I'm not going to drink, I'm not going to stay a second longer than it takes to get him out of here. You let me in, or I'll go straight to the cops and tell them what happened last time I came here – and how Leeroy Mills ended up looking like he got run over by a truck."

McGee let out a bark of surprised laughter. "You got balls, missy, I'll give you that."

"My *name* is Darla," she said firmly. "May I pass, please?"

He scratched the back of his neck, and then jerked his head inside. "You've got five minutes," he warned. "And if I come in and find you doing shots at the bar, you'll get the same treatment Leeroy got. Fair warning."

Darla nodded, and sidestepped the bouncer through the doorway. Inside Shooters, a sullen silence reigned. The bar was half-empty, all but a couple of stools at the bar left vacant. Yet the atmosphere was tense, soured by unfriendly gazes and dark mutterings. The barman, a tall red-haired man with a beard reaching down to his waist, watched Darla as she peered through the gloom for Hopper. Two men broke off their game of pool, openly staring at her.

Darla forced herself to keep walking. A row of booths ran along one side of the wall – in one a couple were pointing fingers and arguing, in the next a guy was slumped alone in his seat, his head drooping on to his chest. She found Hopper in the last booth. He was in the middle of a story, waving his arms and swigging from a beer bottle as he spoke. There was a cluster of empty shot glasses on the table in front of him, the wood sticky with spilled alcohol. He wasn't alone: a girl in an off-the-shoulder pink T-shirt with a bright blond bob was sitting with her back to Darla, her laughter echoing around the bar. The same haircut Darla had seen in her vision of the girl in the dark room.

Hopper looked up and saw Darla, his bottle freezing in mid-air. The girl twisted round on her stool.

"*Darla?*" said Sasha. "How the hell did you get in?"

Darla gasped and took a step backwards. It felt as though she had been punched in the stomach.

"What are you doing?" she asked in a small voice.

"Nothin' to fret about," Hopper said quickly. "Just havin' a coupla drinks is all."

"Together? Just the two of you?" Darla laughed nervously. "Is this a date or something?"

"Of course not!"

"She's seventeen," said Darla. "And my best friend."

Hopper took a swig of beer, slamming the empty bottle down on to the table. "You know what, darlin'?" he said. "I've had a pretty rough coupla days. I don't know if you heard, but I got arrested on suspicion of being a psychopath who goes around butchering kids. So I went to the mall to buy me some records, and Sasha here saw how miserable I was looking and suggested we go out and have some drinks, try to have a little fun. Yeah, I said OK. I said fine. I said great. You tell me, Darla, what terrible crime am I committing here?"

Darla stared at Sasha in disbelief. "This was your idea?"

She held up her hands in mock surrender. "Guilty, your honour."

"It's not funny."

Sasha rolled her eyes. "It's just a drink, Darla. Jesus, you're such a buzz killer."

"It's not *just* a drink, Sasha. Hopper's an alcoholic. How could you?"

"I thought it might cheer him up!"

"You could go drinking with any guy in Saffron Hills you want, and you choose my alcoholic daddy? What kind of friend are you? You think you're some kind of rebel but you're not – you're just a rich, spoiled bitch who uses everyone she meets."

"Tell it to someone who cares," Sasha replied.

Darla was so angry her whole body was shaking. "You better watch your step," she warned.

Sasha stared at her. "Or what?"

A large shadow loomed behind Darla, a meaty hand clamping down upon her shoulder.

"Your five minutes are up, missy," said McGee. "Time to leave."

"Get your hands off me!" Darla shouted, twisting out of the bouncer's grip. She took a final pained look at Hopper and Sasha, turned and ran out of the bar.

Chapter Twenty-Eight

Darla went slipping and stumbling through the darkness, hot tears of anger on her cheeks. She ran down to the creek, following its winding path through the trees. Back at the bar, she heard someone call out her name: had Hopper gone after her? Darla didn't stop to find out. He could go to hell, as far as she was concerned.

How could he? After all they had been through! It wasn't that he had gone back on his word and started drinking again, although that was bad enough. But to take her best friend to the bar with him? The last time Darla had seen Hopper and Sasha together, something about the way they had been goofing around had made her uncomfortable. Was there something going on between them? Would they really do that to her? Could they really be so selfish?

Darla ran until her legs felt weak and her breaths stung her chest. Finally she stopped, leaning against a tree trunk by the creek. No one was calling out her name now. No one was here at all. The water flowed like black syrup in the moonlight. There was a soft splash in the darkness — Darla looked down to see an otter slipping into the creek. She envied the silent speed with which it swam away. Had her mom felt like this, she wondered, the night she had decided to leave Saffron Hills and never come back?

"Hello, Darla."

Darla spun round. A woman in a thin black cardigan was standing in the rushes by the water's edge, gazing out over the creek. As Darla peered closer, her eyes widened.

"Mrs Haas?" she said. "What are you doing here?"

For a long time Patti didn't answer.

"I grew up around here, you know," she said finally. "Down by the water. It might not seem like I've moved very far, but the hills might be on the other side of the earth as far as us Creekers are concerned. I was sixteen the first time I ever went up to one of the mansions. To give Walter West his biology assignment."

The creek seemed to freeze at the mention of

the Angel Taker's name, the night air taking on a keener edge.

"You knew Walter?" gasped Darla.

"We were in a couple of classes together, but we weren't friends," Patti replied. "I had the same impression of Walter that everyone else did: a nice boy, courteous, a bit old-fashioned, even. Of course I knew that he was rich, but when I walked around his house and saw all the beautiful things that were in every room, it clean took my breath away. Then Walter asked if I wanted to see his photographs."

"In the basement?"

Patti looked at her sharply. "You know about those? My daughter took you there, no doubt. I told Sasha to stay away from that house, but she wouldn't listen to me. When does she? Part of me wishes that someone had put a torch to Tall Pines years ago. Maybe I should have done it. Tell me, were there still pictures on the wall, the landscapes?"

Darla nodded.

"I remember looking at those. They were so beautiful ... and Walter seemed so gentle... I never thought... " Patti pulled her cardigan tightly around herself. "He was taking photographs of me. I didn't think anything of it at the time. And then he told me to open his album. There were pictures inside. Of Crystal Mills, the girl who had gone missing. She was dead. Walter was still taking pictures, I think he wanted to see my reaction. Then suddenly he was holding a knife. I grabbed something to try to fight him off, but it was just animal instinct. Deep down, I knew that I was going to die." She paused. "And then the door at the top of the stairs opened, and Walter's sister appeared."

Amy West. In all that had happened, Darla had almost forgotten about her.

"At the time I didn't know it was her," Patti continued. "Amy went to another school, and it wasn't like I was going to bump into her at the country club. She was just a stranger, but I've never been so relieved to see anyone in all my life. Walter froze: I could see his brain ticking over, trying to work out if he could explain what was going on but I was screaming and he was holding a knife, and well…"

"So what did Amy do?"

"Nothing, at first. She didn't even look surprised – almost like she'd known all along. The two of them just stood and stared at each other. I wasn't even thinking, I just picked up a lighting stand and hit Walter with it, as hard as I could. I caught him in the head, and he fell. There was a lot of blood."

Looking at Patti, it was hard to imagine her violently striking anyone, let alone a cold-blooded killer, but Darla thought back to her confrontation with Leeroy by the pit, and how easy it had been to strike him in the heat of the moment. An inch to the left or the right, a softer piece of temple – who knew how close she had come to killing him?

"I screamed again," Patti continued. "Actually, I'm not sure I had stopped screaming. But Amy was so *calm*. She just walked over and hugged me and told me everything would be all right, she would take care of it. I ran from that basement faster than I had ever moved before, never looked back once, never told a soul what had happened. Maybe if I had, things would be different now."

"You shouldn't blame yourself," Darla said fiercely. "Walter was the killer, not you. You were just defending yourself."

Patti gave her an anguished look. "But that's just it, don't you see?" she said, her voice echoing around the creek. "At the time I was sure I had killed him, yet then word got out that Walter had hanged himself. For weeks I waited for the police to come and question me, barely slept a wink the whole time. But eventually I figured the Wests just wanted the whole thing wrapped up as quickly as possible – Walter was dead, what was the use in bringing another victim into it? Then one day, years later, I received a letter. From Amy. I hadn't seen her since that day in the basement. She'd gone to all kinds of trouble to find me. I guess there were some things she had to get off her chest.

"It turned out I had bashed Walter pretty good, but all I'd done was knock him out. When Allan West came home Amy told him what had happened. But even after everything, her father couldn't bring himself to turn his son in. Instead he gave him a bundle of cash and helped him get across the Mexican border. When Crystal's body was found in the creek, Allan said that Walter had hanged himself. He was so powerful in this town, he could do whatever he wanted – if that meant persuading the police to call off the investigation, or carrying out a staged funeral, then so be it. At the time I remember Crystal's brother causing a ruckus at Walter's funeral, but Leeroy had such a bad reputation no one paid him any mind. All the while, according to Amy, Walter carried on down into South America. That was the last she heard about him. She didn't really want to know, she felt so guilty. Like it was *her* fault for what her brother had done."

"And now Walter's come back," Darla said solemnly.

Patti nodded, tears glimmering in her eyes. "Why else are young, beautiful people dying? If only I'd have said something at the time, Walter wouldn't have felt it was safe to come back. But you have to understand, I thought I had killed someone, and then I started getting phone calls from lawyers threatening to take me to court if I said anything about Walter West — for defamation of character, attempted murder, you name it. In the end it was Sasha's father who stepped in to help me, that's how I met him. I was so scared I didn't know what to do with myself, and the doctor prescribed me some pills. But now people are being killed again and all these old memories are coming back. So I thought

I'd come down to the creek; I used to come here all the time, when I was a little girl. Before…"

"But if Walter's returned, how come nobody's seen him?"

"It's been twenty years," replied Patti. "A lot can happen in that time. Who knows what he looks like now?"

"Maybe you oughta try writing to Amy," Darla suggested. "Walter's a killer but she's still his sister – maybe she's heard from him."

Patti shook her head. "She said in her letter that she moved around a lot, and not to bother trying to keep in touch. Amy was in Arizona at the time, I think… no wait, I remember now, it was New Mexico. She said she had married a musician and they'd had a little girl together."

Darla's mouth went dry. She stared at Patti. "Amy, you mean – Amy West?"

"Yes, but she'd changed her name by then. To Sidney, if I remember rightly. Darla, are you all right?"

It couldn't be true. And yet… Suddenly Sidney's flight from Saffron Hills made perfect sense. No wonder she had left with the first charming man who'd taken a shine to her. It explained her quiet acceptance of the tough life that followed – and the guilt that had found its end in a trailer bathtub.

For a time neither of them spoke, both staring out over the creek. Then Patti shivered. "I've been daydreaming down here long enough," she said. "Sasha's father is away on business again, and I don't want her coming home to an empty house. Do you need a ride home, Darla?"

"Thanks, I'm OK," Darla told her. "I live just down by the creek."

Sasha's mom surprised her by reaching out and squeezing Darla, quickly and fiercely, before disappearing into the night. Darla stayed by the water's edge for a while longer, trying to come to terms with what she had just learned. Her mom was a West, which made Darla one too. It also meant that her uncle was a brutal killer. Could that explain the visions she had seen? Slowly Darla continued on down the creek, aware that she was nearing the lane leading home. When she passed Annie's house she saw that the windows were dark, the wind chimes playing a lonely lullaby in the breeze. She heard a voice calling out into the night, and the breath caught in her throat. But then Darla relaxed – it was the same cry for help she had heard the first time she had entered Annie's yard. She crept through the bushes and stopped, entranced by the scene before her. The House of Narcissus had finally been finished. A ring of candles had been lit inside the small house, their orange flames dancing in their own reflections. The effect was strange and beautiful at the same time, and for the first time Darla sensed she understood why Annie had built it.

All the time you've spent looking through the killer's eyes, Sasha had said scornfully in the bleachers, *and you never even got a glimpse of them*. At the time Darla had thought her friend was just being spiteful, but as she stared at the House of Narcissus she began to wonder whether Sasha had been right. Could Darla have done more? Instead of trying to hide from her visions, should she have been trying to experience more of them – to spend more time inside the Angel Taker's head, to try to learn anything that might reveal their identity? Maybe if she had tried, Frank would still be alive.

An eerie calmness washed over Darla. She walked slowly across the yard and through the entrance into the House of Narcissus. A hundred haunted faces stared back at her, a soft voice continuing to call "Echo" through the speakers. Darla forced herself to keep looking, to stare deeper and deeper into her own reflection. It felt as though the building began to tremble, and then suddenly Darla was plunged into an icy well of nameless, unspeakable rage. A flurry of images assailed her: she was grabbing Crystal by the hair and throwing her across the studio; she was slyly circling Patti, a knife in her hand; she was slitting and cutting and slicing through Perfect flesh; she was dragging Frank's bloodied carcass across the floor. And then suddenly Darla was somewhere else, stalking through a deserted corridor towards a doorway edged with red light. It looked like the entrance to hell itself. Darla pushed open the door, and felt her face being bathed in red light as she stared down a narrow flight of stairs.

Her dizzying vision ended with a jolt, and Darla went stumbling out of the House of Narcissus as though the building had spat her out. But she knew exactly what she had to do. Leaving the house of mirrors and its chorus of echoes behind her, she ran through the thick shadows of the creek lane back to her house and unlocked the front door. Hopper still hadn't come home – probably still drowning his sorrows in Shooters. Darla went over to the fridge and freed the piece of paper with Annie's cell number from the magnet. She went over to the house phone and dialled the number, praying that the artist would pick up.

"Hello?"

"Annie?" said Darla. "Where are you? I need your help."

Chapter Twenty-Nine

It was blacker than a snake's mouth beyond the gates of Tall Pines, the driveway a cracked tarmac tongue. Trees swayed woozily in the wind. Darla peered through the windshield of Annie's car into the darkness, searching in vain for a glimpse of the West mansion.

"I'm not sure about this, hon."

Annie had been working late at the gallery when Darla had called, and had driven straight over. Darla had been expecting her to have all sorts of questions, especially when she had told her she needed a ride up into the hills. Annie had taken one look at her face and simply nodded. But now her tone was dubious.

"I'll be OK," Darla told her.

"I don't think you should be creeping round houses in the middle of the night – it's not safe. Maybe we should call Hopper."

"No." Darla's voice was quiet but firm. "Wherever he is, he don't want to be bothered."

"Then why don't you tell me what all this is about?"

Darla hesitated. She didn't want to lie to Annie but she knew that if she told the artist the truth – that the Angel Taker was lurking somewhere inside Tall Pines – Annie would try to stop her from going inside. And Darla had to go inside. She had to end this now.

"Darla?"

She slipped off her seatbelt and opened the car door before the artist could stop her.

"Hey, wait!" Annie called out. "Where are you going, hon?"

Darla didn't look back, sprinting away from the car and through the gates into Tall Pines. The breeze funnelled through the trees, rustling leaves and prickling the bare flesh on her arms. She followed the sinuous path of the driveway as it snaked to the left, Tall Pines slowly rising up out of the darkness in front of her. The night had masked the mansion's rotten and rusted façade, and suddenly Darla could imagine how Patti Haas must have felt when she walked up the driveway twenty years earlier, carrying Walter West's assignment in her schoolbag. Now, as Darla melted into Tall Pines' imposing silhouette, she spotted a car parked under the trees. She slowed, her heart thundering in her chest.

It was Hopper's Buick.

Darla hurried over to the car and peered in through the window. The seats were empty, the keys still in the ignition. Why had her daddy left the bar and driven all the way here? As far as Darla knew, Hopper hadn't even heard about Tall Pines. She felt sick with unease.

Footsteps. Darla looked up, startled, to see Annie marching down the driveway towards her.

"What on earth do you think you're playing at, running off like that?" she scolded. "I was—"

She stopped at the sight of the Buick.

"That's Hopper's car," said Annie. "Darla, what in hell's going on here?"

"I don't know," Darla said apprehensively. "But I think Hopper and the Angel Taker are inside Tall Pines."

"I think we'd better call the cops."

"There's no time!" Darla pleaded with her. "It's

my daddy, Annie. If he's in trouble I have to help him."

A determined look settled on Annie's face. "Then I guess we'd better go in together," she said.

Darla hurried up the crumbling verandah steps before Annie could change her mind. Tall Pines swallowed her up with a cold gust of air. The corridors and rooms were pitch-black, the air thick with mould. Darla went noiselessly along, her eyes straining for any sign of movement ahead of her. A creature scuttled across her path, and she had to bite back a scream. She was suddenly incredibly grateful that Annie was with her, a pensive, reassuring presence at her side.

Soft light was spilling out through the doorway at the end of the corridor. Darla peered around the corner. She stared into the dining room where she had sat with Frank and Sasha the day of Natalie's funeral. Someone had been hard at work here. A single place had been set at the head of the table, a bone china plate accompanied by silver cutlery and an empty crystal wineglass. Candles flickered and wavered, picking out an old-fashioned camera and a photograph album placed carefully on the mahogany surface.

"Looks like someone was expecting dinner tonight," Annie murmured. When she came to the place setting she reached out for the photograph album.

"Wait!" hissed Darla. "Don't—"

Too late. Annie opened the album.

"Oh my Lord," she whispered.

Slowly she turned one page after another. All the killer's victims were there, their final moments captured in black-and-white photographs: Natalie, Ryan, TJ, Carmen... and last and most horribly of all, Frank, sprawled out across the library floor, his hands held up to the camera in a futile defensive gesture. Darla wished that Annie would close the album but the artist seemed lost in the photographs, lingering on each page.

"This is... I don't know what to say," she murmured. "Horrible. And kinda mesmerizing at the same time."

"Annie, put it back!" pleaded Darla.

She turned to go, only for the artist to call her back.

"What is it?"

Annie looked from the album. "There's another photo here."

She passed the album to Darla. As she stared at the new photograph, Darla went cold. It was a lurching close-up of Sasha Haas's face as she screamed into the lens. Darla slammed the album shut.

Click.

She looked up, startled. Annie had picked up the camera and was training the lens upon her.

"That's perfect, honey," the artist said. "Hold that thought."

Darla stared at her. "What are you doing?"

"What does it look like? I'm taking your photograph."

"Why?"

"I'm an artist, aren't I?"

"Annie, now really isn't the time."

"I disagree, hon. I believe now is *precisely* the time."

Click.

Darla backed away slowly. "I mean it, Annie," she said. "You're scaring me."

The artist put the camera down, a smile playing on her lips. "There's nothing to be scared of, Darla."

"What about the Angel Taker?"

"They're not going to want you, are they now hon? With your plain little freckle face and scrawny body. What kind of angel would you make?"

Darla tried to run, but Annie's hand darted out like a snake and fastened around her wrist. Grabbing a fistful of her hair with her other hand, Annie marched the squirming Darla out of the dining room and along the corridor.

"Let go!" cried Darla. "You're hurting me!"

She winced as Annie tightened her grip. The artist was surprisingly strong, and Darla had a sudden flashback to their first meeting, and the ease with which she had hauled the heavy mirror for her House of Narcissus. As they approached the basement door beneath the stairs, Darla saw a faint red glow shining out from behind it. She tried to fight but Annie was too strong. The artist pushed Darla through the door, sending her stumbling down the narrow steps.

Straight into a nightmare.

The basement had been turned into the dark room of her visions, red light bulbs bathing the room in crimson. Photographs floated in shallow trays of developing fluid on the desk. The beautiful landscapes had been taken down from the walls, replaced by portraits of blue-tinged corpses. A space had been cleared in the middle of the room, where Sasha was tied up in a chair. Her head was bowed, her peroxide fringe hanging down over her face. Glistening red marks punctured her white tank top. She was sitting horribly still.

When Darla tried to run to her friend, Annie viciously pulled her back.

"Ah ah," she tutted. "Don't touch the exhibits."

"Why are you doing this?" Darla sobbed. "I thought you were my friend!"

"I'm disappointed in you, Darla," Annie replied. "Didn't I tell you that I was working on a new artwork? But it wasn't in my backyard. Saffron Hills is my canvas, and I've been painting red all over it."

"It was you who left the lilies on Walter's grave, wasn't it?"

Annie smiled.

"But it don't make no sense — I know he didn't hang himself, it was all a cover-up so he could go to South America. It's Walter who's been killing everyone — *he's* the Angel Taker!"

Annie gazed at her steadily. "Walter West died

in Brazil fifteen years ago," she said. "I killed him."

Darla's throat was so dry it was hard to swallow. "What?"

"You see, Walter couldn't stand being away from Saffron Hills. This town is just filled with angels and pretty young things, and Walter loved pretty things. But he knew that he couldn't come back any more, not after what happened with Crystal and Patti. Not after he had been … interrupted. So when he arrived in Brazil he let someone turn their knife on *him*. A surgeon, who cut and sliced Walter everywhere, until he was a completely different person." Annie smiled. "A whole new woman, in fact."

The floor seemed to tilt and shake beneath Darla. She was dizzy with disbelief.

"You're Walter West?" she said faintly.

"My *name* is Annie Taylor," she shot back, through clenched teeth. "I told you, there is no Walter West any more. I killed him. I scribbled him out. I erased his every last trace."

Like the self-portraits in the gallery, and the whited-out photograph of Walter in the yearbook. Darla could never have believed it was possible.

It wasn't just that Annie had once been a man – although that was shocking enough. It was that the kindly artist, the woman who had talked to Darla and hugged and comforted her like no one had since her mom had died, had been a cold-blooded killer.

Was *still* a cold-blooded killer, Darla reminded herself.

"It's fitting, don't you think?" said Annie. "I turned myself into an angel of my very own – an angel of death. With my hunting knife and my camera I killed time and time again, first in Brazil and then in New York. I made albums filled with the most beautiful photographs. Only then did I feel ready to come home. I took a job at the school so I could select my angels. Everything was set. And then you washed up into town."

"You knew about Hopper and me from the start, didn't you?"

"Of course I did," Annie replied contemptuously. "My sister could call herself any name she liked, but she was still a West. My father had private detectives combing the state for her within hours of her leaving Saffron Hills. He knew all about Hopper the musician and his little Darla. And then there you were, in my backyard. I saw how far my sister had fallen – a drunken loser for a husband, and a helpless mouse for a child – no wonder she killed herself. It was so typical of Amy, she was always so weak."

"Don't talk about my mom like that," said Darla. "You don't know anything."

"I almost killed you on a point of principle. I had the chance in the gallery – do you really think I couldn't see you hiding in the dollhouse? But I realized that you and your father could help me take Sasha, my final angel."

Darla glanced over at her wounded friend.

"Isn't she perfect?" breathed Annie. "A beautiful fallen angel. I've been following her for days. I was watching outside Shooters when you made your dramatic exit – I waited a while and called Hopper, telling him you'd had an accident at Tall Pines. He couldn't drive here fast enough, he even brought Sasha with him. The concern on their faces was truly touching to see, Darla. Hopper was so worried he didn't see it coming – I hit him over the head with a tyre iron, right there in the driveway."

Darla's hands flew to her mouth.

"Don't worry, he's still alive," Annie told her. "I wouldn't kill Hopper, he's far too important for that. He's locked in the trunk of his car, out cold. Sasha put up more of a fight, but she soon calmed down once I brought her down here and went to work with my knife. And then you called me! It seemed too good to be true. When I'm finished with you and Sasha I'll make sure that the police find Hopper somewhere nice and close by – unconscious, stinking of alcohol and holding my knife. My artwork will be complete."

"Artwork?" Darla's incredulous voice echoed around the basement. "You're not an artist, you're just a sick maniac."

Annie smiled thinly. "I wouldn't expect you to understand. What would you know about art and beauty?" She slid a serrated hunting knife out from her belt. "Ready for your close-up?"

Darla ducked just in time, as a blade sliced through the air where her neck had been a second earlier. She twisted out of Annie's grip, stumbling into the desk where she had discovered the photo of her mom. As the artist lunged snarling towards her, Darla picked up a camera off the desk and set it off in Annie's face, the dazzling flash stopping her in her tracks. Darla rolled away from the desk, the knife biting into the wooden surface a moment later. Annie was after her in seconds, a thin smile spreading across her lips as her silver blade darted through the air. In the centre of the studio Sasha didn't stir, her head lolling forwards on to her chest.

Looking frantically around for a weapon, Darla scrambled over to the wall, where a heavy tripod was leaning against the brickwork. She picked it up and swung it at Annie, missing her head but knocking the knife from her hands. Annie screeched with rage and dived at Darla, her nails outstretched. Moving on instinct, Darla grabbed the developing tray from the desk and flung the contents in Annie's face. The woman shrieked as the caustic fluid stung her eyes.

"You're no West," she spat, wiping her face on her sleeve. Her eyes were bloodshot. "You're nothing, a cheap piece of trailer trash."

She strode over to Darla and wrenched the tripod from her hands, pushing her backwards. Before Darla could raise her hands to protect herself, a heavy blow caught her on the side of the head and she went reeling to the hard basement floor. She felt the cold kiss of the flagstones against her skin, and wondered whether she was about to die.

Click. Click. Click.

Darla felt the camera's merciless gaze upon her as Annie photographed her. The artist wasn't hurrying now. Groggily Darla pushed herself up on to her hands and knees and starting crawling away, trying to ignore the mocking laughter that greeted her attempts to escape. On the floor beneath the desk, something metal was shining in the red light. It was the hunting knife. Darla reached out desperately, and felt her hand close around the knife hilt. As Annie saw what was happening, she let out a scream and charged, the camera still in her hand. Darla rolled to her feet.

"Smile!" she cried.

Raising the knife into the air, she buried it in Annie's chest.

A jet of hot blood squirted out over her, splattering her face and hair. Annie dropped her camera, blinking with surprise at the sight of the knife jutting out of her chest. She took a faltering step backwards and coughed, blood spilling down her chin.

"You—!"

Darla stared at her defiantly. Annie collapsed to the floor, her limbs twitching violently before falling still.

Darla took a deep, steadying breath. Her head was still swimming, and there were black spots exploding before her eyes. She stumbled over to where Sasha was seated and untied her, catching Sasha as she slumped forwards into her arms. Pressing her ear to her friend's mouth, Darla thought she could detect a faint wisp of breath.

"You stay with me now, OK?" Darla pleaded, brushing Sasha's fringe out of her face with bloodstained fingers. "Don't you go anywhere, you hear me?"

Chapter Thirty

Summer's last heartbeats had stilled, the warmth faded from its breath. Crickets fell silent; birds lifted from the trees and headed south in formation. The drowsy, muggy heat that had hung over Saffron Hills from the cemetery to the creek had melted. The sky turned grey. Leaves tumbled from the trees, covering the town in a crackling carpet.

Darla watched from the passenger seat of the Buick as small children played in the street, squealing as they dumped handfuls of leaves over one another's heads. In a few weeks it would be Halloween, and Saffron Hills would be filled with young people in costumes running around trying to scare each other. Darla guessed that there would be at least one person who would run around with a camera pretending to be the Angel Taker, trying to frighten their friends by taking photographs of them. It was amazing how quickly people moved on. Darla only wished she could too.

Three weeks had passed since the night in the basement beneath Tall Pines. But it some ways it felt like Darla was still there, trapped in those terrible minutes as she held Sasha's bloodied body, staring at the knife that she had plunged into Annie's body jutting out of the artist's chest. It had taken Darla a long time to pluck up the courage to take Annie's cell phone from her pocket and dial for an ambulance. Eventually – she had no idea after how long – Darla heard footsteps and began screaming for help. Soon the basement was flooded with paramedics.

In the driver's seat, Hopper twiddled impatiently with the Buick's radio. They had spent a lot of time in silence these last few weeks – Darla sensed Hopper was still searching for the right words to say. She knew that he felt guilty that he had been out cold in the trunk of his car while Darla had been fighting for her life. Even if he had tried to talk to her, she wasn't sure what she could say back. So much was a blur – especially afterwards. She barely remembered the interviews with the police. They were gentle with her, could see what she had been through. Darla had killed someone. The weight of that horrible truth sat in her chest like a cold lump of iron. It didn't matter that Annie was a psychotic murderer who would have killed Sasha and Darla and more if she hadn't been stopped. Darla had taken a life.

Hopper switched off the radio, seemingly sensing Darla's darkening mood. He cleared his throat.

"Listen, darlin'," he said. "I know we haven't talked properly since the night you girls got attacked, and … well, I've been doing a lot of thinking. I wanted to say I'm sorry, Darla, truly I am. I really let you down – drinking again, taking Sasha to that bar. You know nothing happened between us, right? I sure as hell ain't perfect, but I would never do anything like that."

"I know," Darla said quietly.

"I was upset because of gettin' arrested, but there ain't no excusing my behaviour. That night you needed your daddy more than ever and I wasn't there to protect you. And I'm going to have to live with that for the rest of my life. You're the most important thing in my world, Darla, and I need to start acting like it." He coughed. "That's why I went to a meeting last night."

"Meeting?"

Hopper shifted uncomfortably. "You know, AA."

Darla couldn't believe her ears. Anytime anyone had mentioned Alcoholics Anonymous in the past, her father had laughed them off. "Really?"

"I gotta admit, it was awkward as hell at first — all these strangers staring at me, waiting for me to tell them all my problems. I kept checking out the exits, wondering if I could make a run for it. But I stayed. And I'm gonna keep going back, too."

"That's great, Daddy," said Darla. "I'm proud of you."

"I ain't done nothing yet," Hopper said firmly. "And I'm making no promises this time, you've heard them all before — too many times. I just can't believe I was so stupid about Annie. I shoulda known she was too good to be true."

"It wasn't just you," Darla said. "I wanted to believe she was for real too."

"I used to think there wasn't a lie or a scam I couldn't spot from twenty paces. Now it turns out I can't even see a serial killer when they're standing right in front of me. Seems like nothing's what I thought it was. Annie used to be Walter, Sidney used to be Amy. What is it about us and that damned West family?"

"Mom wasn't Amy with us," said Darla. "She was Sidney O'Neill. She was one of us, not the other way around."

"Maybe you're right, darlin'. You're wiser than I am, at any rate." Hopper glanced over at her. "How are you doing?"

"I'm OK."

"Because it's fine if you're not, you hear me?" he said quickly. "I know that ever since Mom died you've had a rough ol' time of it, and I didn't want to know because I was being so goddamn selfish. But you can talk to me."

"I know, Daddy. I'm OK, honestly."

Hopper didn't look convinced, but he nodded anyway. He took the next turning off the highway, following the signs for the Madeline West Memorial Hospital. Annie might be dead but as long as they stayed in this town there were always going to be reminders of the West family – *their* family, as strange as it felt to think it.

The hospital was the size of a mall, built from pinkish stone and with a grand portico entrance.

In front of it a fountain sat in the middle of a picturesque lake, sending water cascading into the air. Anywhere else, Darla would have expected to see a throng of reporters pressing around the entrance, a hailstorm of questions and microphones, but the parking lot was quiet. The unmasking of the Angel Taker had barely made the papers, and even the police weren't hurrying to announce that a killer had been stopped. Saffron Hills would always be a town that knew how to look after its secrets.

Darla and Hopper walked through the automatic doors and went past the waiting room to the reception desk.

"Good afternoon, darlin'," said Hopper, treating the pretty nurse behind the desk to a dazzling smile. "My daughter's here to visit a friend of hers, Sasha Haas?"

"I'm afraid Sasha's visitors are limited to family at the moment," the nurse told him.

"Then it's a good job they're cousins, isn't it?" Hopper replied.

The nurse raised an eyebrow. "Cousins."

"Distant cousins," Hopper clarified. "But very much family. Shared blood, if you will."

Hesitating, the nurse looked over at Darla, who adopted an innocent expression.

"Third floor," the nurse said eventually. "Room 305."

Hopper grinned. "Thank you, darlin'. You're a ray of sunshine on a dark and cold day."

The nurse quickly turned back to her monitor, trying to hide the fact she was blushing. Rolling her eyes, Darla turned towards the elevators.

"Are you going to come up too?" she asked Hopper.

"Maybe later," he said. "You go see your friend. Tell her get well soon from me."

As Darla waited for the elevator to open, she looked back and saw Hopper leaning against the counter, still chatting to the pretty nurse. The nurse burst out laughing, and Hopper gave Darla a helpless look across the reception. Darla shook her head, but she was smiling. Her daddy was never going to change *entirely* – but for the first time in her life, she thought that maybe he could change just enough to make things OK.

Darla rode the elevator up to the third floor, and wandered the gleaming corridors in search of room

305. Sasha had a corner room to herself, looking out over the rolling landscape of Saffron Hills. She was sitting up in bed, gazing out of the window. Her face was pale and her dark roots were showing through her dyed blond hair. She glanced up nervously at the sound of someone entering the room, her eyes widening with surprise at the sight of Darla.

"Hey, you!" she said weakly. "What are you doing here?"

"What do you think? Coming to see you."

"I wasn't sure you'd ever want to see my face again. Couldn't blame you if you didn't."

"How are you feeling?"

"Not too bad, considering. But then I am on an *insane* amount of morphine."

Darla pulled a chair up to Sasha's bedside and took a seat. There was an awkward silence.

"Listen," Sasha said eventually, "about what happened in Shooters..."

"It don't matter."

"No, Darla, it does. I can't believe I was such a bitch. You were right all along, you know? I use people and it isn't fair. I owe you my life, for Chrissakes!" She paused. "Why are you smiling?"

"Everyone's saying sorry to me today," Darla told her. "It's kinda fun."

"You sure earned it. If it weren't for you I'd be another photograph in the Angel Taker's album." Sasha's face brightened. "Hey, you know who else came to visit me? Miss Saffron herself, Gabrielle Jones! Said she wanted to see how I was doing. I think her brush with death might have done her some good. She seemed ... I don't know ... human."

"I heard that Leeroy is gonna be charged with kidnapping," said Darla.

"Couldn't happen to a nicer guy." Sasha replied. She fidgeted with her hospital gown. "You're here to say goodbye, aren't you?" she said gloomily. "I knew you wouldn't stay after what happened. Frank is gone, and now you're leaving me too."

"Actually, I think we might be sticking around."

Sasha pushed herself up on her elbows. "Really?"

Darla nodded.

"This is *exceptional* news, Darla! We can hang out together, it'll be so much fun. I could take you to the band night at Shooters again – Jaime and Evan might be playing!"

"I don't know, Sasha," Darla said reluctantly,

"I'm not sure Hopper's going to let me—"

"It's *music*, Darla! We don't have to drink!"

"Just do me a favour, OK? Lose the blond look."

Sasha gave her a mock salute. "Aye aye, Captain O'Neill." She winced, holding her side. "Ow! I think I just opened a stitch."

"Should I get a nurse?"

"No, I'll be all right." Sasha reached out and took Darla's hand. "I'm really glad you came to see me."

Darla smiled. "Me too."

They talked for an hour or so, as the sky darkened in the windows. As hard as Sasha tried to put a brave face on things, Darla could see how much pain she was in. There was no telling how long it would take her scar tissue to heal. But if anyone could come back fighting, Darla thought to herself, it was the irrepressible Sasha Haas. She was a force of nature.

When a doctor came into the room to examine Sasha, Darla said goodbye to her friend. She walked along a deserted corridor, absorbed her own thoughts, and called up the elevator. It arrived with a loud *ping*, the doors opening to reveal an empty life. She walked inside and pressed the button for the ground floor.

The doors closed, and as Darla stared into the

polished silver surface she saw her faint reflection staring back at her. The elevator seemed to shiver, and the lights above her head flickered. Darla stepped back with a cry of dread. The Angel Taker was dead, there couldn't be any more visions. It was over!

The lights steadied. As Darla's heart beat against her ribs, she realized she was looking at nothing more than her own face – imperfect and plain, but nothing to be frightened of. There were no horrors lurking in this mirror.

The elevator continued smoothly down to the ground floor, the doors pinging open. Darla smiled.

You'll be sleeping with
the lights on for weeks after
reading a Red Eye.

If you sleep at all...

Turn the page to
discover more stories in this
bloodcurdling series.

Dare you collect them all?

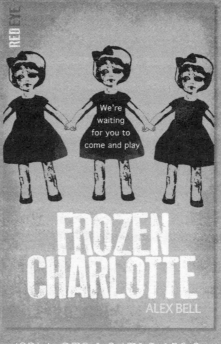

We're waiting for you to come and play

ISBN: 978-1-84715-453-8
EISBN: 978-1-84715-504-7

Frozen Charlotte

Alex Bell

Following the sudden death of her best friend, Sophie
hopes that spending the summer with family on a
remote Scottish island will be just what she needs. But
the old schoolhouse, with its tragic history, is anything
but an escape. History is about to repeat itself.
And Sophie is in terrible danger…

The nightmare begins when you're awake

SLEEPLESS
LOU MORGAN

ISBN: 978-1-84715-455-2

EISBN: 978-1-84715-573-3

Sleepless
Lou Morgan

The pressure of exams leads Izzy and
her friends to take a new study drug they find online.
But one by one they succumb to hallucinations,
nightmares and psychosis. The only way to
survive is to stay awake…

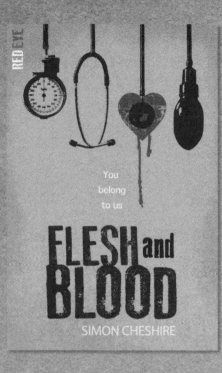

You belong to us

FLESH and BLOOD

SIMON CHESHIRE

ISBN: 978-1-84715-456-9

EISBN: 978-1-84715-574-0

Flesh and Blood

Simon Cheshire

When Sam hears screams coming from a nearby house, he sets out to investigate. But the secrets hidden behind the locked doors of Bierce Priory are worse than he could ever have imagined. Uncovering the horror is one thing, escaping is another.

eBook available

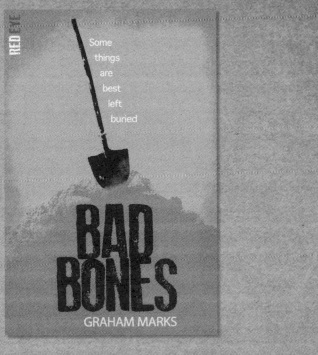

Some
things
are
best
left
buried

BAD
BONES

GRAHAM MARKS

ISBN: 978-1-84715-454-5

EISBN: 978-1-84715-505-4

Bad Bones

Graham Marks

Gabe makes a discovery that could be the answer to all his problems. But taking the Aztec gold disturbs the spirit of an evil Spanish priest hell-bent on revenge. Can Gabe escape the demon he's unleashed?

eBook available

Hunt or be hunted

SAVAGE ISLAND
BRYONY PEARCE

ISBN: 978-1-84715-827-7

EISBN: 978-1-84715-871-0

Savage Island
Bryony Pearce

A one million pound prize. Each. That's enough to get five friends entering a geocaching competition. But stranded on a remote island off the Scottish coast, they soon realize this is no ordinary challenge.

The other teams are determined to win too. Even if it means getting rid of the opposition. Permanently.

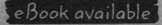

eBook available